Praise for James Ward and *SAFE TO SAY - A Novel of Corporate America*

"A well-paced, convincing novel about the decline of corporate America during the 1980s era of deregulation."

"The backstories are strikingly real and humorous, reminiscent of characters and situations portrayed on television series such as The Office and 30 Rock."

"Smart dialogue, concise description, a little romance and humor, creating a highly readable story that has a lot to say about the modern-day workplace."

"Delivers valuable insight for employers and workers from the boardroom to the copy room."

"Sharp storytelling and crisp prose keep the pages turning."

Kirkus Reviews

EVERY COMMANDMENT
BUT THE FIFTH

A novel of sin and sanity

by

JAMES WARD

Resilience Press

ISBN-10: 0-9975467-0-0
ISBN-13: 978-0-9975467-0-5

Cover design by MK McClintock,
        Self-Publishing Services LLC
Edited by Clare Wood, Self-Publishing Services LLC
Formatted by Self-Publishing Services LLC
(www.Self-Publishing-Service.com)

I know well what I am fleeing from
but not what I am in search of.

~ Michel de Montaigne

For Charles and Marian

Acknowledgement

I would like to thank my wife, Barbara, for her
constant love and support.

I

1

Stewart made his way through the woods and toward Scrapville. It was early Saturday evening but already dark along the trail where the thickly leafed oak and maple trees screened the remaining sunlight. An afternoon rain had turned the zigzag path into a slippery slide of wet rocks, roots, and leaves, and he stepped carefully, deliberately placing one foot in front of the other, a man heedful not to hurt himself.

Bloodthirsty mosquitoes pursued him the entire way. He fought them one-handed. In his other hand, he held a white paper bag close to his chest, careful to keep it upright and level. The bag held two cartons. The larger one had a silver-colored insulated top and held spaghetti and two meatballs; the smaller one was made of Styrofoam and held a lettuce and tomato salad with creamy Italian dressing. Wrapped separately in tinfoil were three slices of Italian bread. The food's warmth radiated through the bottom of the bag, and the anticipation of spaghetti and meatballs in tomato sauce with a hint of garlic made his mouth water.

Out of convenience, habit, and financial necessity, he usually had his evening meal at the nearby strip-mall's fast-food joint, a dingy McDonald's knock-off with the unimaginative name of Burger-Land. When he needed a change or could dig an unexpired coupon from one of the mall's garbage cans, he would trade up to Kentucky Fried Chicken, preferably the three-piece meal with two breasts and a wing, extra crispy instead of original with sides of mashed potatoes and whole kernel corn. He had difficulty digesting the corn, but he liked it and had become a reluctant advocate of living for the moment.

The extravagance of $12.75 spent at Frank's Ristorante for a spaghetti dinner was for more than nourishment or novelty. It was a Saturday evening reward for another week survived.

He always ordered his spaghetti to take out. The Ristorante's manager, a neatly dressed, patrician-looking man with olive skin and close-cropped white hair as thick as the bristles on a scrub brush, didn't want someone of such dispossessed looks seated in his nice place. Good for the manager and the social automatons who frequented Frank's. He preferred eating alone, if not sitting on a pumpkin at Walden Pond like Thoreau, whom he considered a kindred spirit, then on a plastic milk crate in a little tent in the woods with the wick from his kerosene lantern high enough so he could see his food but not high enough to encourage company. A few minutes of alimentary satisfaction was something everyone should be able to enjoy in peace, even the world's self-appointed ascetics and outcasts.

The woods grew thicker, and the mosquitoes buzzed around his ears. How could a creature of so little substance make so much noise? They sounded like dive-bombers terrorizing the innocents in a World War II documentary.

At least the mosquitoes were physical enemies, and against them he had a slapper's chance. Against his inner pursuers, he was defenseless. Tormenting anxieties trolled through his mind: the dangers, real and imagined, from his new circumstances and his new neighbors; the indignities of working another eight-hour shift as a retail store flunky; the insecurities of a formless future.

He would sneak into the far side of camp to avoid the other residents who, like their ancient ancestors, socialized around what seemed to be a perpetual fire. He would escape into the solitude and protection of his tent. He liked some kind of wall around him, even if it were just a polyester tent or a fabric-sided cubicle like the one he had occupied in his old office job.

The trail diverted around the trunk of a big tree and then narrowed and pitched downward. His stomach cramped. It was as if something sharp was stuck inside him and trying to get out. He had to stop and bend over. He had been entitled to Frank's men's room, but he remembered another time when some raggedy *misérable* used the bathroom, and the manager made a production of spraying the whole area with a can of Lysol Disinfectant and Deodorant, until the place smelled as if someone had shit in a citrus orchard. The manager followed up by waving a newspaper around as if chasing away plague vapors, all to the guffaws of the staff and respectable clientele. He couldn't live with that kind of humiliation.

He should have stopped at Burger-Land's bathroom. He should have made a prophylactic visit. He suffered from chronic GI problems and except for a copse of berry bushes, which were located in the dense woods fifty feet behind his tent and were probably poisonous and would lead to a tormenting rash, there would be no facilities for the rest of the night. His self-critical mind reminded him again that he must eat slowly and not gulp his food, as was his habit, lest his innards revolt.

With that unpleasant thought, he lost his focus for just a second and, still new to the trail, tripped over an exposed root. His right arm thrown out like a tightrope walker's, he regained his balance but juggled his package. The paper bag, wet on the bottom from leaking tomato sauce, broke open. The insulated carton and the Styrofoam box slid to the ground and spilled their treasure.

It took him a moment to accept what had happened; he was numb from far greater losses, but when he saw the pasta and salad mixed among the leaves and the red tomato sauce soaking into the mud, he knelt right there, raised his face to the heavens, and asked, "So that's how you want it, with no mercy?" He didn't expect an answer and got none, just a message in the form of a lightly browned meatball coming to rest on a thick tree root and miraculously balancing there, just to torture him.

A gray squirrel came halfway down a tree and stopped and beat its tail, sensing opportunity in another's misery, as wild things must. The rodent stared at him, its shiny black eyes alert and expectant. Stewart stood and gave the meatball a kick, catching it with the toe of his sneaker and aiming it at the squirrel but sending it deeper into the woods.

The foil-protected bread was all he salvaged. With it, he made his way toward his tent.

2

The boys weren't around. There was no racket and no campfire. Maybe they were off on some group debauchery, and he wasn't invited. He had only been in the woods two weeks and was still an outsider and planned to remain so.

He stopped in front of his tent, slid out of his backpack, and ducked inside. Despite the humid heat, he closed the flap and zipped the screen. Privacy trumped comfort.

He hung his white shirt and blue vest from an ingenious little clip that affixed to the tent's sidewall. He kept his sleeping bag stowed off the ground, on top of his plastic cooler, to prevent unwanted bedfellows. What vermin inhabited these woods he didn't know, but he had once seen a movie where a man pulled a boot on and got stung by a scorpion. That had happened in the California desert, but the image stuck in his head.

His fellow Scrapville residents, afflicted with chronic boredom and always in search of entertainment, had taken note of his squeamishness about things that crawled or slithered and went out of their way to tell him stories of all manner of indigenous and deadly creatures. Who knew that such dangerous things lived in northern New Jersey?

He yanked off the black sneakers and then the black pants that made up the bottom half of his store uniform. Mud coated the knees of his pants, and he squeezed and rubbed it out the best he could and hung up the pants and set the sneakers on the cooler. He spread out the sleeping bag and crawled in.

The tinfoil had done its job, and the bread was still dry and warm. He ate the bread, first separating and chewing the hard brown crust and then closing his eyes and letting the doughy insides dissolve in his mouth, for dessert. He folded the tinfoil into a small square and saved it for future use. There was nothing like desperation to breed a conservationist.

All he desired at that moment was sleep. He assumed the fetal position, but sleep wouldn't come, and like water seeking its lowest level, his mind went where it always did when left to wander, to his life's devolution.

His decline had been so rapid that each day required a new sounding. Two years ago, he was a financial analyst earning north of $200,000 and enjoying perquisites and benefits that required an annual catalog to enumerate. Now he was an associate at a locally owned big-box, Walmart wannabe store, where "associate" meant a combination stock boy, sales clerk, janitor, and people-greeter. For those multidimensional skills he earned $8.75 an hour. Two years ago, he lived in a two-story white Colonial with royal blue shutters on the end of a quiet suburban cul-de-sac with doctors, lawyers, and fellow Wall-Streeters for neighbors. Now he lived in a two-man tent pitched in the woods behind a lonesome railroad line and a dingy strip mall with degenerates for his neighbors.

Two years ago, he salved his conscience by nestling at night, spoon-style, with a healing wife. Now he played solitaire with his worries.

Stop!

He was a ruminator. That's what the lady psychologist said, the woman he had seen three times at his wife's urging back when he still had his benefits. What to do about his self-destructive brooding? *Notice, stop, and divert.* That's what she prescribed–notice when he obsessed over things and then stop and divert his mind in some other positive direction.

He reached under his pillow and found his MP3 player and earbuds. The player was a technological leftover from his past, part of the debris floating among the wreckage of his life. It had the same songs on it that were there two years ago, and he didn't care which one started. He just needed something to distract him.

The player wouldn't come to life. He needed to charge it at work, where he would hide it under the Sporting Goods counter because everything that wasn't nailed down got stolen. Tonight, he would have to use his imagination to distract himself.

Despite his best efforts to think about the favorite parts of his favorite books, he was soon back to musing over his misfortune and how all of it was self-inflicted. He asked himself the familiar question–how could he have been so unhappy, with a good job, a nice house, and a loving wife? He knew the answer. Because Milton was right. *The mind is its own place and in itself can make a heaven of hell, a hell of heaven.* His mind was a hell-maker.

Eventually, an overwhelming fatigue set in, and he began to slip toward unconsciousness. He stretched his legs to the end of the sleeping bag and turned a half turn. A cold tingling sensation ran over his calf. He thought he was cramping again but came fully awake when the tingle became the shivery touch of something foreign and alive crawling up his leg. He jerked up to a sitting position and pulled himself out of the sleeping bag.

He slapped at his leg, but nothing was there. He picked the bag up by the bottom and shook it. Nothing. He started to blame his imagination, but when he shook the bag harder, something did fall out. It was a small snake that immediately curled into a defensive circle. The sight of it made him shiver.

The snake had green and yellow stripes. He thought it was a garter snake or what his father called a *garden* snake. His father's critical voice came to him: "It's more scared of you than you are of it."

He backed to the front of the tent and unzipped the screen and opened the flap, thinking the snake wanted out as badly as he wanted it out. But the snake stayed still. He circled behind it and clapped his hands. The snake curled tighter.

The snake's head wasn't much bigger than a pencil eraser. It must have been a baby. He found his umbrella, held it out at arm's length, and gently poked at the snake. He didn't want to hurt it. The snake was as much a victim as he was. He tried lifting it with the tip of his umbrella, planning to carry it to the front and set it outside. He couldn't balance the uncooperative snake on the umbrella's tip.

What he did next was so strange that later he would wonder if he dreamt it. He put his hand out, palm up, inviting the snake to come to him. The snake did.

Maybe it was the warmth of his hand that attracted it, but the little reptile crawled onto his palm and coiled there as if ready for a nap. It felt improbably light, and it was cool and dry to the touch, not slimy as he had expected. He studied the snake more carefully, the vivid green and yellow stripes that were so perfectly delineated and the checkerboard pattern of dark spots between the stripes. It was a beautiful creature. Any artist would have been proud to create it. He carried it to the front of the tent and gently set it outside. He felt guilty for its getting involved in his mess.

On his hands and knees, he checked the tent. There were no holes in the floor. No way for a snake to get in. It was the Scrapville boys who did it. He was sure of that, and he knew why. The boys had to make his life more miserable than it already was because they wanted his life to be more miserable than their miserable lives.

With a jug of water and his antibacterial hand soap, he scrubbed his calves and his hands. He patted himself dry with paper towels and turned the sleeping bag inside out and beat it with his hand, like someone cleaning a rug. Then he sat and put his head in his hands and fought back tears. It was only a childish prank by childlike men, but he knew the boys were capable of far worse. How was it that he was here in such a place and subject to the whims of such men? He had tried that case over and over, and the ultimate verdict was always the same and rendered consistent with the evidence: It was all his own doing, the product of years of decadent thought finally degenerating into action.

In his former life, he had felt so desperately out of place that one day he just quit. He packed his essentials and a loaded Visa CheckCard and wandered away, leaving behind his wife and his job and the night class in existential literature that he taught at a community college to try and keep in touch with his truer self. Since then, his was a story of decline. When he manned the store's key-making station, he would stare at the rack of key blanks and wonder what had gone so wrong. He knew his blank hadn't been meant for this.

He had an old army blanket, and he lay down on top of the sleeping bag and covered himself with the blanket and tried concentrating on the birds singing sadly for the end of the day and the crickets cricketing happily for the start of the night. Nature's sounds. Wasn't there tranquility in all that? But his mind wouldn't quiet. He tried talking to God. A confirmed and proud agnostic since the ninth grade, his recent misfortunes had led him to try and reopen the conversation. Not out of hope for redemption but because he had new reason to suspect he might be heard. Who else but an all-powerful, all-knowing, and all-judgmental deity could have orchestrated his fate?

God didn't answer, and his conscience reminded him it had taken the loss of a spaghetti dinner to finally bring him to his knees. Why wouldn't God turn a deaf ear to a Johnny-come-lately genuflector?

What was next? Through all his losses, the one thing he had kept was his literary bent, and now that his elevated and self-satisfied perch as an outcast living off the financial fumes of the past was over, and he felt the terror of free fall, he remembered with bitter irony the wisdom of a philosophical hero: *And whomever you cannot teach to fly, teach to fall faster.*

3

"Good morning, Stew."

The voice from outside the tent was unwelcome but not unexpected. It was Slinky, his one good-hearted neighbor, playing alarm clock.

"You in there, Stew?"

He had been lying awake listening to the thrumming of the Sunday morning interstate traffic. I-287 skirted the south side of the woods, where it ran through a valley and was sided by twenty-foot-high concrete sound barriers. The barriers had been erected to spare the ears of the decent folk living adjacent to the highway. The accommodating air currents carried the traffic noise over the bordering houses and set it down on Scrapville. Those civil-minded engineers were good.

"Stew, you awake?"

Slinky was full of purpose but too polite to shout, and the tent didn't give him any place to knock. It was as if it were the days of Stewart's childhood, and Slinky was a neighborhood kid desperate for a playmate and calling for the block's studious homebody to quit his books and come out and join him.

Sunday was Stewart's day off, but he had something important to do on this one. Still he closed his eyes tighter. He might fall back to sleep, but he knew his neighbor wouldn't abandon him. He had treated Slinky with some decency, and in Slinky's unfortunate life, that was enough of an aberration to beget fierce loyalty.

"Stew, you home?"

He was ripe for that question, and he made it his own. He was here in this place, but was he home? Home implied a sense of contentment and belonging, and all his life he had been an admirer of the discontented. In high school, while his classmates revered athletes and rock stars, he became enamored of the lives of the wandering philosophers, from the Greeks to Marx and Nietzsche. He dreamed of living his own wandering genius's life, suffering the people around him, suffering himself, but sublimating it all into something special. A man out of touch with his times and the times at fault. That was the myth he had chosen to explain his self to himself.

At his two previous stops, a studio apartment in Jersey City and then a boarding house a block from the Harristown train station, he could still pretend. An apartment complex with a little seediness, and an old boarding house with eight-by-twelve rooms and a shared bathroom, living room, and kitchen fit his mythos.

But he had fallen fast, and facts being facts, this was home now–a two-man tent held in the ground by plastic stakes and even that flimsiness not set on terra firma. His squattage was still subject to the approval of a mysterious landlord whom he would meet today for the first time.

"Stewart!"

Finally, impatience in his neighbor's voice.

"Okay, Slink. Okay."

"We've got to get going," Slinky said. "We don't want to miss out."

Stewart concentrated and swallowed. It was his waking habit to check for any sign of a sore throat. Another of the obsessive habits he wished he could break. He had a great fear of getting sick while living like this, especially if it were to happen later in the year, in the winter. He was good at imagining an escalating chain of illnesses, from a scratchy dry throat to double pneumonia to a lonely death.

The Scrapville boys told vivid stories of despondent men found in abandoned houses or under bridges, their bodies unclaimed and their unattended burials in some potter's field. If he were to die in this place, he would prefer cremation. Maybe his ashes would share the fate that Shakespeare's feracious mind imagined for the great Alexander's–maybe he too would end up as a cork in a barrel's bunghole. Did ashes really turn into loam? Did they still use loam to make corks? Did they still use corks to stop a barrel's bunghole? Did barrels still have bungholes?

Breadcrumbs dotted the front of his T-shirt. He ate them for breakfast and then rolled out of his sleeping bag and into a hunched position. He was already conditioned to the tent's less than five feet of center height.

He pulled on his jeans and sneakers and flinched at lower back pain. Sleeping on the ground took its toll, and the cheap air mattress he tried only made it worse. He hung his blanket and turned out his sleeping bag and took off his wet T-shirt. Whatever he slept in always ended soaked with nightmare sweat. At least he had a clean T-shirt. A local credit union had held their grand opening the previous Friday, and following Slinky's lead, he had scrounged free coffee, two sugar cookies, and a T-shirt. Neither he nor Slinky were offered the pamphlets promising a bright financial future. His Visa CheckCard had long since run dry, though he kept it as a reminder of better times. All he could do now was stretch his scanty take-home pay as far as possible by making every expenditure stand trial for its life and recording every penny spent in a little black notebook.

He swallowed two capsules of the heartburn medicine his gastroenterologist had prescribed five years ago and still renewed for him. Without that medicine, his stomach caused him misery. He ran his fingers through his hair and that was it for his morning constitutional. Necessity had bred out some of his former fastidiousness. With his backpack in tow, he unzipped the tent's screen, undid the flap, and ducked through.

4

"You're alive," Slinky said.

Stewart nodded. The sunlight hurt his eyes, but after the tent's stuffy confinement, the fresh outside air felt good and he breathed deeply.

"You had me worried," Slinky said.

Stewart slid his pack over his shoulders and clinched the two front straps tight across his chest. He didn't like it when the pack bounced.

"Nice morning," Slinky said.

Almost everything Stewart owned was now on his back. At one time, his possessions required a two-story house with an attic, basement, and attached garage, and all that space so cluttered that his wife had hired a professional closet company to make things more orderly.

"Real nice day," Slinky said, a cheerleader trying to rouse some enthusiasm.

Slinky made for an unlikely booster. He was a casualty of life's unfairness. A lot of bad things had ganged up on him. His body was misshapen and his movements impaired by a form of spina bifida with a complicating lordosis. He was short and slight with stringy blond hair and a pallor so sickly that people sometimes mistook him for an albino. He got the nickname Slinky because he locomoted like the children's wire toy of that same name, in a sideways gait with one shoulder higher than the other and one half of his body always playing catch up to the other half. Stewart had asked his real name but was told that, if he preferred, he could call him Slink. That didn't seem much of an improvement, but Stewart made a point of using it to distinguish himself from the other Scrapville residents and their total heartlessness.

"How you doing?" Slinky asked.

"I'm okay," Stewart said.

He lied. He had the start of his sugar shakes and was out of his glucose tablets. It was New Jersey in August, and it was going to be too hot and too humid, and he already felt himself sweating under the press of the backpack. He had dreamt he was sleeping next to his wife, and when he woke to the aching reality of being alone in a tent in the woods, it was as if he suffered her loss anew. To top it all, his day's mission would begin with a crime and end with him seeking favor from a junkyard man.

"Got to get moving," Slinky said and hitched up a brown satchel that hung over his good shoulder. He carried his walking-around stuff in it. His distorted shape wouldn't accommodate a backpack.

"We wait too long," Slinky said, "and the boxes are gonna be empty. That won't be good. For me or you."

Slinky had a childlike excitement about him. He was anticipating the shared adventure. He had been a long time without a friend.

"Gotta serve the big man," Slinky said.

Stewart nodded to the presumed truth in that.

Slinky and the other camp residents lived in the woods at the discretion of a common landlord. That man, a six-foot four inch, three-hundred-and-thirty-pound giant called Scrap-Iron for his elemental toughness, owned a large junkyard and the adjoining woods that hosted the eponymous Scrapville. He charged each tenant a nominal $100 per month in rent but refused payment in cash, insisting on in-kind goods instead and putting his own arbitrary value on those. In a twist that fit the man, he required all the goods be stolen. Scrap-Iron liked to brag that he never missed an opportunity to promote sin, especially to those willing to learn. The big man also enjoyed the Sunday papers, and that was Slinky's responsibility: theft and delivery of the Sunday papers. Now, Slinky had a partner in that endeavor.

"Your stove still working well?" Stewart asked.

"It's good," Slinky said. "Thanks."

Slinky and Stewart met at the store when Stewart was stationed in sporting goods and went out of his way to help the even more hopelessly nonmechanical Slinky choose a propane camping stove. Since then, Slinky had made whatever department Stewart worked in one of the regular stops on his daily time-killing routine, right after a soda and a leftover newspaper at Burger-Land and right before a surreptitious snooze with an open book on his lap at the county library. When Stewart could no longer afford his place in the boarding house, a sympathetic Slinky invited him to pitch a tent in Scrapville. Slinky emphasized the invitation was on a temporary basis, subject to the landlord's approval. Scrap-Iron was gone on one of his mysterious southern trips and had told Slinky to watch over things. As tough as Scrap-Iron was on Slinky, he often said that he was the only one of the Scrapville boys who had a lick of common sense. He said of his other boys that if you shoved all their brains into an ant's ass and shook that ant, it would sound like three BBs in a boxcar.

Slinky extolled Scrapville's virtues to Stewart. He emphasized its privacy, anonymity, and bucolic setting. After just two miserable and degrading days in the transient homeless shelter, that description began to appeal to Stewart, especially given his only other alternative of going solo on the streets. The code of the streets was that you either traveled in a pack or you were tough. He knew he wasn't tough. So he took Slinky up on his offer.

For its peculiar residents, Scrapville did indeed have key advantages. It was adjacent to a railroad line, which meant straight and furtive access to town. It was close to a strip mall and its fast-food joints and their accessible bathrooms and fertile dumpsters. Most attractive of all, Scrapville provided a sanctuary from the captious world, the protection of a like-minded group, and the easy certainty of a charismatic and dictatorial landlord who made all the decisions.

But Slinky was testing fate with his invitation to Stewart. Scrap-Iron personally approved of each of his subjects, and no one joined his community without an audience. If Scrap-Iron thought Slinky exceeded his authority or if he didn't approve of Stewart, there would be pain involved. But Slinky was sure he saw something in Stewart that would appeal to Scrap-Iron. He was counting on the big man's need for elevated conversation. The coming meeting would prove or disprove that. Having the Sunday papers in hand would help.

***

"Let's Motorola," Slinky said.

The trail out of the woods started at the western edge of camp. Up and moving, Stewart wanted to hurry, but the path, its route dictated by the dense woods, snaked uphill, and Slinky for all his determination had trouble keeping up.

"You gotta be careful here," Stewart said, approaching the spot of last night's accident. "It can be slippery." He looked to the ground but saw no trace of his lost dinner. Some opportunist, maybe the tail-wagging squirrel, had enjoyed an unexpected feast. Nothing went to waste in the woods.

"We," Slinky said, re-emphasizing the newspaper-stealing mission as a joint venture, "don't want to miss out. On Sunday, those boxes empty fast."

Stewart wondered at Slinky's urgency. They had a task to do, and dedication was good, but there was more to it than that. He sensed something that he knew so well, a hint of fear, specifically a fear of failure and its consequences.

The trail emerged at a cinder-covered embankment that carried an old railroad freight line. A midnight train whistle would have been the perfect embellishment to Scrapville's lonesome existence, but that never happened. The trains ran sporadically but always in the early morning when, lying in his sleeping bag, Stewart could hear their air horn warnings and feel the ground rumble underneath him.

Stewart climbed the steep embankment to the tracks and stopped. His jeans hung loose around his waist and on his hips. He hitched them up and tightened his belt a notch. He hadn't weighed himself in a while but knew he was too thin. If he lost more weight, he'd have to punch a new hole in his belt.

It was already hot up there. Out of the woods and in the direct sun, it seemed a totally different ecosystem. Stewart took two Burger-Land napkins from his back pocket and wiped the sweat off his face. He needed glucose. He was acutely in touch with his body, and when he got the start of the shakes accompanied by a desire to fill himself with sugary food, he needed a glucose hit. A Snickers bar would have done nicely. A Snickers bar was another thing he didn't have. He remembered two pieces of hard candy he had from last night, taken from a bowl by the Ristorante's cash register, the candy there so Frank's discerning customers could cleanse their discerning palates. He dug the little spheres from a front pocket. The plastic wrappers wouldn't open, and he had to bite through them. He spit out pieces of plastic and popped the red-striped candies in his mouth. They had a strong peppermint flavor. He hoped that they would do double duty, stop his shakes and help his stomach.

Without turning to look, he knew Slinky was struggling. Uneven ground was especially hard for him. He didn't offer help. Slinky didn't like to be seen struggling, and he didn't like to be helped, as if any concession to his condition made it more manifest.

"Whew," a winded Slinky said, when he finally reached the tracks.

He was a pitiful sight. His myopia required heavy glasses, and they were more crooked than usual. The little color he normally had was gone, even from his lips. He looked like a victim of a bloodsucking vampire.

"I'm a little tired," Slinky said.

"Me too," Stewart said.

"I'm out of shape," Slinky said.

Stewart was about to repeat *me too*, until he thought more about being out of shape and how from Slinky's viewpoint it was literal truth. That's the strange way his mind worked. It got stranger when he had time to ruminate on something.

"Look," Slinky said, stalling for time and pointing to a wild canary that had landed on a nearby bush. The bird was a yellow to make Van Gogh jealous. They stood still and admired it.

"Sometimes," Slinky said, "I wished I had wings."

"Me too," Stewart said, without hesitation. Then he had an image of Slinky as Icarus, with delicate wax wings, flying toward the sun over the blue Aegean Sea.

Slinky needed some time. From the track's high vantage point, Stewart looked past him and back at Scrapville, that bivouac of the bedeviled and bemused. The camp was hidden in the thick summer woods. The only tent he could make out with ease was the big red one. The big red tent was for community storage: pots and pans, the big washtub, the cooking grills, the cheap plastic lawn furniture the boys brought out on hot nights.

Harder to spot were the other four tents arranged in a semicircle that faced a central fire pit and a makeshift flagpole. The blue tent belonged to the man they called the Soda Bandito for his skill at thieving from Burger-Land's soda fountain with cups scavenged from the strip-mall's trash cans. The two identical green tents belonged to Slinky and the youngest of the crew, a grimy runaway who could have been anywhere from fifteen to twenty and who was called Toad-Fucker for reasons Stewart didn't want to know. Stewart's camouflage-colored tent, bought with his employee discount, was the smallest. Next to the others it had a look of impermanence, like a child's backyard plaything. Scrapville's most-impressive structure sat deeper into the woods, a fort with solid wooden walls. The man known as Little Hercules, or just Herc, had built the fort from old railroad ties that had been stacked alongside the tracks. He fashioned a rope around his shoulders and waist in a makeshift harness and with the other end formed a bowline knot to loop around each crosstie. In a truly Herculean task, he dragged all the heavy, creosote-soaked wood along the rough and irregular path to his chosen site, the most remote and camouflaged spot in Scrapville. In the winter months, through the leafless trees, inquisitive track walkers could see the whole camp, even the flagpole, a straight birch trunk skinned and sunk a foot into the ground. Sometimes the flagpole did double duty as an anchor for a clothesline. Seeing all that, in the middle of their prosperous county, the good citizens' thoughts surely turned to what went on in those woods. Their imaginations weren't up to the challenge.

Down the tracks, about a quarter mile, was the strip-mall's back lot. The front parking lot, and its newspaper dispensers, was Stewart's and Slinky's destination.

"Scrap always wants both papers," Slinky reminded Stewart, for the third time.

"Yeah, I know. The *Times* and the *Record*."

Scrap-Iron favored *The New York Times* for its Science and Technology sections and the local paper for the comics, obituaries, and the police blotter. The obituaries and police blotter were a convenient way to track his old acquaintances.

"I just need a couple more minutes," Slinky said.

"Take your time," Stewart said.

He didn't mean it. He was anxious and scared, and when anxious and scared he needed to move.

5

The canary flew off, a yellow-bellied blur angling toward the woods. It disappeared among the trees.

His breath back, Slinky said, "Let's go."

He looked more willing than able, but with a side-winding step, Slinky started down the tracks. When Stewart hesitated, Slinky gestured with his hand, like a horse cavalry leader telling the troops to move out. Stewart followed dutifully.

The sky ahead was clear except for a teardrop-shaped dust cloud to the south, above the big cement quarry that operated there. After less than a minute, Slinky stopped.

"Shit," Slinky said.

Stewart's lifelong habit was to walk with his eyes to the ground as if he expected some pitfall at every step. At Slinky's curse he looked up. A man was coming straight at them and fast, with long strides.

"Who's that?"

"Ramon," Slinky said. "And he's trouble."

"Why?"

"I know him. He lived in Scrapville until a while ago. He was always trouble. Then there was bigger trouble, and he had to leave."

"What happened?"

"He beat up his girlfriend. Put her in the hospital."

"God. He did that in camp?"

"No. Over at the mall. In the parking lot one night. They were arguing, and he got mad."

"What," Stewart asked, "were they arguing about?"

"About what age someone had to be to get the Burger-Land senior discount. Ramon said fifty. His girlfriend said she thought it was sixty. Then he fractured her skull."

"That's terrible," Stewart said.

"Yeah," Slinky said. "The police came through the woods hunting for Ramon. There were six of them. It was like an invasion. Scrap knows all the police; they're buddies of his, but he still didn't like that."

"What happened?"

"Ramon wasn't in camp. But the cops caught him. He was at the laundromat, drinking beer and looking at pictures in the magazines."

"When was this?"

"About a month ago. Maybe a little longer."

"How come he's out?" Stewart asked.

"The girlfriend refused to press charges."

"She did?"

"Yeah. She loves him. But Scrap wouldn't let him back in camp."

"I can see why," Stewart said.

"Yeah. Scrap didn't like it. He said Ramon disrespected the camp."

As Ramon approached, Slinky pulled a scrimshaw-handled pocketknife from his front right pocket. He rubbed it between his thumb and forefinger and put it back. He'd never use it. The knife was more talisman than weapon. It was a gift from one of his foster parents, a woman named Muriel with whom he lived for eighteen months. She was as close to a mother as he would ever have.

"Ramon," Slinky said, "thinks this whole section of track is his. You want to avoid eye contact and make plenty of room for him to pass."

"He's territorial," Stewart said.

"Maybe that's it," Slinky said.

They both kept their eyes down and stepped to the side. It didn't work. Ramon stopped in front of them.

He was tall and wore shorts and was naked from the waist up with a long-sleeved shirt wrapped around his middle and tied there by the sleeves. His chest and arms shone with a light sweat. He looked like a well-trained light-heavyweight, his brown body all muscle and no fat, the kind of sculpted, vein bulging physique that exercise commercials promised.

Ramon squared up to Stewart, looked down at him, and asked, "Got a dollar?"

Stewart shook his head no. That was one of the learned lessons of his new life; don't give money out of weakness, unless you want to be a constant mark. Good advice in theory, but now, in reality, he felt a fast drip of fear.

Ramon looked to Slinky. "How 'bout you, Twisty?"

Slinky kept his eyes to the ground and shook his head. He was telling the truth. He didn't have a dollar. He had money left from his last check, but it was hidden in a mason jar buried behind his tent. He didn't carry it with him in anticipation of this kind of situation–so he could answer no and be telling the truth and not be proved a liar by a rough frisking. Slinky's monthly disability check was the only dependable cash flow in Scrapville, but he was forever being tapped by the other residents. How much of his generosity was from good-heartedness and how much from weakness? Stewart hadn't yet decided.

Ramon looked back to Stewart and stepped closer. "I need the coffee," he said. His nose was leaking, and he wiped it on his bare arm, as if a sleeve were there. He had an earring in his right earlobe. Its gold trim complemented his skin tone. Its fake diamond caught the early sun.

"Sorry," Stewart said.

"I need it, man," Ramon said. "B-Land has any size for a buck. You got a buck. You know you do, man."

Ramon lifted his feet up and down, marching in place, as if he were freezing cold or holding back a piss rather than yearning for a coffee. He wore black and red Nike running shoes that looked new. He wore no socks. His calves looked like they belonged on a track star.

Stewart couldn't run. Even if he embraced the "It's every man for himself" creed of the jungle and abandoned Slinky, he had his backpack on, and Ramon was twenty years younger and in good shape. Any attempt to run would trigger Ramon's predatory instinct, and he would chase Stewart down like a big cat preying on a lame gazelle.

"You know, man," Ramon said to Stewart, "I could tip you upside-around and shake your shit out."

Stewart's breathing grew faster and shallower. He pictured himself upside down and helpless with Ramon shaking him and Slinky watching, and that sent a wave of disgust through him.

Ramon's smile did nothing to lessen his menace. His teeth were a crooked mess, the gap between the big front ones wide enough to pass an olive through. Stewart thought how Ramon had probably never seen a dentist in his life, and he felt a twinge of pity for him.

Ramon leaned closer, and Stewart could smell him. It reminded him of the company subsidized health club he used to belong to, when the racquetball players invaded the locker room.

A life lesson ignored or not, he wasn't going to get beat up over a dollar. He reached into his pocket and touched his folded money. He knew he had a five and two singles, some change too but not enough to make a dollar. The trick was to pull out a single. To show more was to lose more. He pulled out the inside bill. A dollar. He handed it to Ramon.

"There's the tax," Ramon said. His feet moved up and down faster. His bright red shoestrings flopped. "Any size a dollar, but it's got the tax. You know, man. Gotta pay the tax."

Stewart fished in his pocket for a dime. He came out with a quarter and handed it over.

"You got a smoke?"

"I don't smoke," Stewart said. The flat refusal felt good.

"I need a smoke man," Ramon said. With a fast hand, he grabbed at Stewart's front pocket. Stewart spun away, but Ramon's untrimmed nails pinched his leg. A warm dribble of urine ran down Stewart's thigh. He hoped it wasn't enough to show through his jeans.

"I think," Slinky said, looking over Ramon's shoulder, "that someone's coming."

Slinky knew this dance as a never-ending round of demand, appeasement, and further demand. He had experience in this realm. He had known bullies all his life. Deformity attracted bullies. He didn't believe the psycho-bullshit that bullies were really weak themselves or feared weakness, and that's why they did what they did. Bullies did what they did because they were strong enough to do it, and they enjoyed it. They did it to the weak because abusing the weak was easy and a lot less risky than trying it on the strong.

"I think," Slinky said, squinting to see better, "that it's Scrap-Iron."

That got Ramon's attention. He looked down the tracks and toward the junkyard. For verisimilitude, Slinky craned his neck and looked to the spot where the woods met the back of the junkyard and its porous wooden fence. The eight-foot-high fence was a zoning concession to the surrounding area's slow march toward gentrification. Stewart looked too but didn't see any sign of Scrap-Iron, just heat waves reflecting off the steel rails into a low haze of morning pollen.

"I need a smoke, man," Ramon said, but with a wary eye still cast toward the junkyard. His tone was less demanding now, more pleading in it. That's how things worked in the jungle–just like that, predator could become prey.

"We don't have any cigarettes," Stewart said, sounding bolder now. Being a victim touched some hatred of inferiority rooted deep inside him.

"Maybe," Slinky said, "Scrap will have one."

He said that even though Scrap-Iron was a reformed ex-smoker and prohibited anyone else from puffing in his presence, in the garage, and even out in the yard. Slinky figured Ramon couldn't have much of a memory.

After a final nervous glance over his shoulder, Ramon spit into the weeds, mumbled something, and headed down the tracks with his dollar and a quarter, walking away from the junkyard and Burger-Land and its one-dollar any size coffee. Stewart and Slinky immediately headed in the opposite direction before Ramon could change his mind.

Slinky wanted to talk. Stewart didn't. It wasn't the time for words. His fear had started its slow but sure distillation into anger. And he was envious of how Slinky took the Ramon incident in stride, as if it were just another confrontation with ignorant brute force to be handled with street smarts and guile. Of course, Stewart thought, it was easier for Slinky. Nobody expected Slink to stand up for himself, while he still held some pretense to manhood.

"Ramon's scared of Scrap-Iron," Slinky said.

"I noticed," Stewart said.

"When Scrap threw him out, Ramon didn't want to go."

"What happened?"

"Scrap said, 'You're going. One way or the other.'"

"What did Ramon do?"

"He said, 'Fuck you, junk man.'"

"What did Scrap-Iron do?"

"He didn't say another word. He just spun around and punched Ramon in the chest. A short little punch, but so fast and so hard that it knocked Ramon right out of the garage and onto the driveway." Slinky shook his head, at the remembrance. "Ramon was laying there, wheezing and coughing, trying to get his breath back. I thought he was gonna die. When he got up, he had stones stuck in his back and didn't even know it."

"Jeez," Stewart said.

"Yeah. Later Scrap gave us a scientific demonstration of how to throw a punch. He said it was all about shifting your body weight and getting your legs and shoulders behind it and don't loop it, that the shortest distance between two points is a straight line. Scrap knows all about that stuff."

Stewart nodded to that, as if he knew something about the subject too.

"You know what Herc said about it?" Slinky asked.

"What?"

"He said Scrap punched a hole in Ramon's chest big enough to take a shit in."

The story jived with another one Stewart had heard about Scrap-Iron. How he had been, and maybe still was, depending on which version you heard, one of the biggest loan sharks in town. It was said that one time he punched a deadbeat so hard that he broke the orbital bone around the guy's eye socket. You had to punch hard to do that. It was said he even controlled territory in the "Hollow," the town's black neighborhood. You had to be tough to do that. What Stewart knew was that Scrap-Iron kept the gate to his junkyard unlocked but, because of reputation alone, was free from vandalism. He didn't even keep a dog. He preferred cats for their independence and intractable predatory ways. He did have a yard light, on a pole behind the garage, but Slinky said that was because Scrap and his boys liked to play at night.

Stewart hoped he would never personally witness any of Scrap-Iron's brutality. He had a deep revulsion for violence. Just its proximity made him quiver. But

Scrap-Iron had helped today. It seemed that, even from afar, the big man watched over his boys.

6

Five minutes farther along the railroad line, they angled down the right side of the embankment to a narrow path of crushed weeds. The path ran from the tracks to the strip-mall's macadamized rear lot. The spacious lot led to the backs of six different enterprises. From the rear, the stores were anonymous, but Stewart knew them all. From his right to his left, there stood: his store, Kentucky Fried Chicken, the Dollar Store, Burger-Land, Frank's Ristorante, and the Foodtown supermarket.

"You got to be careful on the tracks sometimes," Slinky said. "Not everybody's nice."

No shit, Stewart thought.

Maybe Slinky thought he was that naïve about the world and its ways, but the world's malevolency was something he considered a lot now. As a clueless American dreamer, you could live your whole adult life–starting with five or six years of being coddled at a warm and welcoming college and then graduating to a white-collar job while in your spare time attending cocktail parties and PTA meetings and talking over a picket fence to your equally moony neighbors–and never know there was a dark side. But if you found it, or it found you, say in the figure of a territorial psychotic on an isolated railroad line, you'd better be prepared. Even if you believed in a world where the lion lay with the lamb, it was better to be the lion. Or at least be under the protection of a lion.

***

The mall's back lot was the kind of place that nudged Stewart further down the road to the blue devils. Dumpsters lined its back edge and whoever threw the garbage out missed a lot. Animals favored the yellow Dumpsters behind Burger-Land and Kentucky Fried. During the day seagulls abounded, at night feral cats. Slinky claimed to have seen a coyote wandering about, but the boys said it was a long-legged, skinny-assed dog. The boys never gave Slinky the satisfaction of being right or of knowing something they didn't. The top claimants to the Dumpsters, day or night, were the human scavengers. For the non-particular and non-squeamish, the Dumpsters were an abundant source of protein.

"See that box over there," Slinky asked, looking to a big blue steel container in the corner of the lot, a gray plastic hinged door on its top and a white heart-shaped logo on its side. The container was meant for clothing donations.

"Yes," Stewart said.

"I used to sleep in there," Slinky said. "On the really bad winter nights, when the cold and wind cut through my tent and no matter what I put on I couldn't get warm and my back hurt like a toothache."

"It was warm in there?"

"Even on the coldest nights. In the middle of all those clothes and blankets it was nice. So soft it was like I was on a cloud. It made my back feel better. But I don't do that any more."

"Why's that."

"I almost got killed."

"How?"

"One night, when I was sound asleep, somebody made a donation, but it wasn't clothes."

"What was it?"

"They threw in a baby crib. They wanted to do something good, but it hit me in the head." Slinky rubbed the top of his head, as if it still hurt. "It knocked me out, and I was dizzy for two days."

"That's bad," Stewart said.

"Yeah," Slinky said. "Scrap checked my eyes with a flashlight and said I was concussed. He said the whack on the head might do me some good, might help straighten my shit out. The boys liked that."

It was the type of incident that set Stewart to wondering about life's vagaries. What was the chance that some good citizen would decide to donate a crib by tossing it into a clothing donation box *and* into that particular box *and* at the exact time that it contained Slinky *and* that the crib would hit Slinky in the head?

"You know," Slinky said, "when no one else was around, Scrap told me if the headache didn't go away, he'd send me to a doctor."

"That was nice of him," Stewart said.

"Scrap helped Toad out once too," Slinky said.

"When was that?"

"When Toad had to get his stomach pumped."

"Toad overdosed?"

"No. He was over at the recycle center, where he scavenges. He picked up a Coke bottle and took a big swig, but it wasn't Coke."

"What was it?"

"Motor oil."

***

Loading docks abutted the backs of the buildings. Several headless semitruck trailers stood against the big-box store's dock, where it was always busy. Burger-Land's dock was where Toad spent many nights with his laptop, one of Scrap-Iron's discarded machines. Scrap-Iron only used the latest technology. Toad tapped into Burger-Land's wireless signal to visit his favorite fetish sites. One time, at four a.m., the hotspot went down and Toad borrowed The Bandito's phone and called AT&T and complained about the service. They got right on it, and Toad was back up in twenty minutes. When Scrap-Iron heard about that, he said, "Only in America can a freak like Toad doing freak things get round-the-clock technical assistance."

The big-box store took the whole right half of the mall. Stewart and Slinky walked to the rear of it and then in the strip of shade along its far side, until Slinky stopped and poked his head out from the front corner.

"We've got to watch out for the security guard," Slinky said. "He's probably asleep in his car, but we still got to watch out."

"I've got to watch out for my boss," Stewart said. "If he spots me he'll grab me."

Stewart's coworkers had a habit of calling out on Sundays, and, if the boss spotted him, he'd get pressed into service. He needed the money, but today he had a higher duty. If he didn't impress his landlord, he wouldn't have a place to sleep tonight.

It was too early for most Sunday shoppers, and the mall's parking lot was nearly empty. Only a woman and her little girl were on the sidewalk, and they were headed toward Foodtown.

"The coast is clear," Slinky said.

Nervous as he was, Stewart winced at the cliché. He hated clichés.

They walked to the newspaper boxes, trying to project the nonchalance of regular citizens just come for the Sunday paper, but they were a duo about as conspicuous as masked men in a bank. Slinky moved his jaw side to side and made an aggravating clicking sound, as he did when he was nervous.

The blue box was for *The New York Times,* the yellow one for the local *Daily Record.* They positioned themselves in front of the paper dispensers with their backs to the rest of the mall. The last thing either one wanted was for someone to witness the coming theft, Stewart for the shame, Slinky for not wanting to be the guy who caused the police to revisit the woods and make another house call on Scrap-Iron.

Slinky did the yellow box. He pressed firmly on the right side of its handle and then, with a practiced method, using the palm of his left hand just as Scrap-Iron had tutored him, punched the other side. It was a surprisingly sharp punch, generated from such an invalidish frame. The box opened.

"Easy," Slinky said, "when you're taught by the best."

There was half a stack of papers left. Slinky took one, checking to make sure it had the comics inside. "You ready?" he asked Stewart.

Stewart nodded.

The blue box required a harder punch. "You really got to hit it," Slinky said. He repositioned Stewart with his legs spread to give him leverage. That was a bit of Scrap-Iron's advice on the well-thrown punch.

As Stewart leaned forward, he caught a flash of movement over his shoulder. It was the lady and her little girl whom he had seen on the sidewalk and who were supposed to be in the supermarket. As she passed, the girl looked back over her shoulder and up at the two perpetrators, her big brown eyes open wide, as if seeing some kind of freaks. Her mother grabbed her and pulled her along. Stewart cringed. He didn't like being one of life's bad examples.

The woman and her girl disappeared into the parking lot, and Stewart tried what Slinky had showed him, cocking his right arm in front of his chest, taking a deep breath, and punching the machine with the side of his closed fist. He was worried about the noise, and his punch was too weak.

"Harder," Slinky said.

Stewart's second punch worked, but it hurt his hand and made a great metallic bang, loud enough for the whole strip mall to hear. Slinky looked across the lot to the guard's little blue car. It didn't move. There were only two papers left. Stewart reached in and took one.

***

"I still think we could pay for those papers," Stewart said, on the walk back to the tracks. Being a thief didn't sit well with him.

When Slinky didn't answer, Stewart asked, "How would Scrap-Iron ever know?"

"I'd never tell him," Slinky said. "But he'd know. Just like I told you before, he'd know. Trust me. It's like Scrap can see inside a person." The point needed reinforcing, so Slinky added, with uncharacteristic brusqueness, "If you don't believe me, you could find out the hard way."

"I believe you," Stewart said and thanked Slinky again for his help. He wasn't in the mood for further risk.

"You can always count on me," Slinky said.

Stewart nodded and started working at appeasing his conscience–at least he hadn't taken the last paper for himself.

7

With pillage in hand, it was time to deliver.

The route to Scrap-Iron's place took them farther down the railroad tracks. The tracks were the main avenue through Stewart's life now, as the busy interstate had once been. The trains on this line ran only a few unpredictable days each week, observed a local speed limit of ten miles per hour, and blasted an early and loud warning to pedestrians. Despite all that, Stewart couldn't resist regularly checking over his shoulder. He always sensed bad things creeping up on him.

"I'm glad your boss didn't see you," Slinky said.

"Me too," Stewart said.

"You don't like it there, at the store?"

"No."

Slinky wanted to know more about Stewart and the journey that brought such a man to Scrapville. He asked, "Where'd you work before?"

"I was in finance."

"That sounds interesting. How'd you do?"

Slinky had probed along this line previously but without result. Now he had the bonding experience of successfully completing a mission with his new friend.

"I did okay," Stewart said.

He did more than okay. One of the biggest surprises of his life was that in business, in finance especially, he showed an aptitude. Something about its analytical nature suited him. He found satisfaction in the established rules and proven formulas that brought order to confusion and made things balance. When the market was hot, he had headhunters chasing him, dangling additional perks and stock options and pay increases.

"Did you like finance?"

Stewart shook his head yes and no. More to it than that. Study the pieces of any life's puzzle, and there's always more to it.

His problems in business stemmed from his success. Fear of failure drove his compulsive work habits. Compulsive work habits brought him success. Success brought him greater challenges. The greater challenges and exposure fed his fear. All this was a step-by-step prescription for high anxiety until, as he always did in a crisis, he crawled inside himself. Then his fear metastasized until he could see only one way out and that was to quit.

"So you left that job?" Slinky asked.

"Yes," Stewart said.

He quit because to quit or suffer a breakdown were his only choices. The lady psychologist said that he kept repeating the same mistake in his life, that he kept inventing false choices. But for all her learning and classy clothes and warm professional touch, she couldn't feel what he felt. Neither could Slinky. Even if he wanted to, how could he explain his self-destructive inner workings to Slinky?

"Do you ever wish you didn't quit," Slinky asked.

"Sure," he said. How could he not?

Quitting the all-consuming job meant a windfall of free time. Time for thinking that stoked his inner turmoil and reinforced his ego-protective conviction that he was meant to be a wanderer and an outcast. So he told his wife that he had to leave, and he didn't know where he would go or for how long he would be gone. Her reaction surprised him. She tried her best to get him to stay and work things out—even though he had become more burden than partner. He was surprised she loved him that much. When he finally decided to leave, she became very angry. That, he knew now, was another sign of her love. He knew he wasn't worthy of that much love. Marian was her name. A beautiful name. He used to call her Lady Marian. He hadn't seen her for two years and hadn't spoken to her in almost a year. He missed her. Now she wouldn't even know where to find him. He wondered if she would even want to.

"If you hadn't quit," Slinky asked, "where do you think you'd be now?"

Stewart needed to change the subject. They had reached the spot on the tracks where the woods ended abruptly at the rear boundary of Scrap-Iron's junkyard. He knew how much Slinky loved that yard, and he stopped and waved a hand at it. "If that yard," he said, "with all that old stuff, could talk, what would it say?"

"It would tell some stories," Slinky said. "That's for sure."

"From here," Stewart said, "you get a good view."

They were at the high point of the tracks, and from that height, looking down and over the yard's fence, the view was good. A well-worn dirt lane ran straight through the middle of the yard, with junk dispersed along the deep sides, more or less in sections. In the vehicle section were cars, from rust-ravaged Model A Fords to still shiny late model wrecks, all manner of bicycles and motorcycles and motorbikes, some trucks and even an airplane fuselage. The appliance section was a timeline of advancing convenience–wood, coal, and gas stoves, ice boxes, and gas and electric freezers and refrigerators, washtubs, and wringer and automatic washers. Sinks and bathtubs were so many they had their own place. Odd and singular things were scattered everywhere. Whatever product of American industry one could imagine, an example of it probably lay somewhere in that ten acres of the unfashionable, unfixable, and unfavored.

"We've got to move," Slinky said.

"You're the boss," Stewart said.

Walking again, Slinky pointed up to an ensign that flew from the top of an old boom-truck that sat in the middle of the yard. "There's Scrap's flag," he said.

The flag featured a horned Viking helmet and a Viking warship emblazoned on a background of red and white. Scrap-Iron was proud of his Nordic ancestry, especially the Vikings and their warrior ways and might-makes-right ethos. The antique truck was engineless and sunk in the ground up to its frame. It only served its owner's pride—its sky-boom allowed Scrap-Iron's flag to occupy the highest point between there and downtown Harristown.

"I bet," Slinky said, "that when you meet Scrap-Iron, you're gonna say you've never met anyone like him before."

"Probably," Stewart said.

"You know, he's into all kind of books," Slinky said. "Hard ones too."

Stewart nodded, though he wasn't sure what constituted hard in Slinky's literary judgment.

"He speaks Spanish and even some French," Slinky said. "He plays the banjo. He's done mechanic work all his life. He can do cars and trucks, and he can do electric, but no one welds like him. He even makes figures, cowboys and bulls and horses, from his welding. He used to enter them at the county fair but got tired of that because he won top prize every time. He restored an old jukebox, and he plays all his old-timey records on it. You should see how he paints a sign. He studies the plants and bugs in his yard. He's got a field mouse that lives in the garage and that's his friend. The mouse lets him touch him. You should see him studying a spiderweb. He's like a scientist."

Although he discounted some of that as hero worship, the buildup still made Stewart curious and anxious, as he was about to stand before this Scrap-Iron with his figurative hat in hand.

***

At the intersection of the railroad tracks and a two-lane crossroad, they went left, along the road and toward a big cinder-block garage that commanded the front of the junkyard. About a hundred yards behind the garage stood an old farmhouse, sagging from disrepair.

"Scrap built that garage himself," Slinky said. "He planned it and drew it up and did all the work–the masonry, the electrical, the plumbing."

"Wow," Stewart said.

"The only help he got was his girlfriend," Slinky said. "She carried the blocks."

"He's something," Stewart said. "That's for sure." He thought how that girlfriend was probably something, too.

Stewart looked up and said, "There's something about the garage that I wonder about."

"What's that?" Slinky asked.

"The roof. Why does it have all different color shingles?"

It was true; the garage's roof's multicolored shingles stood out like sprinkles on a cupcake.

"Scrap got the shingles free," Slinky said. "He likes to say they were donated."

"He got them for free?" Stewart asked.

"Yeah," Slinky said. "Scrap had Herc and Toad go around to construction jobs at night." His face lit up with the further telling. "He told them not to take too many shingles from any one job. That's why all the colors. Scrap borrowed them from a lot of different places."

That fit, but Stewart figured there was more to it. From what he had heard of Scrap-Iron, which despite his only being here a short time was plenty, the big man surely liked the way the varicolored roof drew attention to him and his nonconformist ways.

"You know about Scrap's house?" Slinky asked.

Stewart looked deeper into the yard and at the old house and its boarded-up windows and rotting clapboard siding. He couldn't imagine anyone other than the yard's cats living in that place.

"That's not it," Slinky said.

Stewart looked around but didn't see any other house.

Slinky told the story.

Scrap-Iron's grandparents and parents had lived in the big farmhouse. After his mother died, Scrap-Iron decided to build a new house. He dug and poured a basement between the garage and the old house, but, satisfied with the cellar's dimensions and having read a *Popular Mechanics* article about the natural winter warmth and summer coolness of subterranean living, he flat roofed what he had and quit right there. He had lived underground ever since, in what he called his bunker.

Stewart wondered again, what kind of man was this Scrap-Iron?

He wouldn't have to wait long to find out, because Slinky led the way through the yard's open gate. Posted there, on the gate, was a neatly painted sign with red letters on a yellow background.

Anyone found in this yard at night will be found there in the morning.

8

The garage's big overhead doors, front and back, were closed. Slinky led the way to the small side door. He stopped and motioned for Stewart to stand still and then tilted his head toward the garage, concentration on his face.

"The boys ain't here," Slinky said. "If they were, you could hear Toad."

"What time are they supposed to be here?" Stewart asked.

"The regular meeting's not until ten," Slinky said. He leaned his ear closer to the door again, making sure.

Stewart waited. This was Slinky's territory.

"Let's go in," Slinky said. "We're supposed to be here at nine, and we're already late. Scrap don't like late. If he's not in a good mood, we're gonna have to blame Ramon."

Slinky knocked.

"Come," a big and demanding voice said.

Slinky pushed the windowless door open and led the way through. Stewart followed.

In the sudden coolness and dim light, in what seemed a wholly different world, sat Scrap-Iron. He was recumbent on his throne, a reclaimed black leather recliner that at one time had surely adorned an upscale living room or study. He wore coveralls and was shirtless beneath them. With his great bulk wedged into the chair, he looked like a junkyard version of the famous seated figure of Zeus at Olympia.

"Hi, Scrap," Slinky said.

Scrap-Iron didn't look up and didn't answer. Through half-moon glasses that looked too small on his huge head, he studied a newspaper. A pen sat behind his ear, and the newspaper rested in his lap. A fluorescent lamp hung from the ceiling, its single tube providing barely enough light for reading. Scrap-Iron was working a crossword puzzle. Stewart recognized it as *The New York Times* puzzle, not the easy one from the local paper.

"Hi, Scrap," Slinky said again.

The big man still didn't respond. Instead, he focused on his task with such intensity that an invisible fence of concentration seemed to surround him. Slinky looked at Stewart and pursed his lips, counseling patience.

Scrap-Iron was clean-shaven, his face deeply tanned. Stewart guessed he was in his late forties. His bronzed arms hung over the sides of the chair, his biceps a match for any pumped-up weight lifter's. He had a receding hairline made less obvious by a close to the skull buzz cut. A wide scar ran down the right side of his head. It looked like an old scar, maybe surgical. Stewart learned later that it was from a steel plate, implanted there after a bad skull injury. The purported cause of the injury depended on who did the telling. It was either from an automobile accident or a baseball bat.

A sharp pain ran through Stewart's stomach. He hoped he wouldn't have to excuse himself. He was surprised at his own nervousness. It was as if he were back in the world of finance, making a critical presentation to some demanding vice president. Maybe, weighed against his current circumstances, Scrapville was enough of a prize to justify his jitters. The more he felt he needed something, the surer he was that he wouldn't get it, and he knew he wasn't Scrap-Iron's type. He had had enough interaction with the other Scrapville residents to know their landlord's preference was for quirky with a strong dose of deviance.

After a long and awkward silence, Scrap-Iron peered over his glasses at Slinky. His eyes were as intimidating as his biceps. He took no notice of Stewart, as if the stranger standing in front of him couldn't possibly be of interest.

"I need," Scrap-Iron said, "a seven letter word that means to complain bitterly." Coming from someone not accustomed to asking for help, it sounded more of a command than a request.

Slinky shook his head. He was prepared to meet any command, but words were not his thing.

"It starts with an i," Scrap-Iron said. "The third letter is a v."

Stewart focused his mental might. Words were his thing. It hit him quickly, a reward for many hours spent with his *Roget's*. "Inveigh," he said.

Scrap-Iron looked back at the puzzle. He did some quick work in his head and then took the pen from his ear and wrote in the suggested word. When finished, he laid the paper on his lap and blinked twice. All he said was, "Sumbitch."

Slinky looked to Stewart and smiled.

Scrap-Iron held up his pen and double-clicked it for Stewart's benefit. He said, "Anyone does a crossword with a pencil is a pussy."

Stewart nodded.

"So," Scrap-Iron asked Slinky, "what did you bring me here, a man with a brain?" He said it as if a man with a brain, presented to him in his garage, was the greatest of surprises.

"I brought you a Stewart," Slinky said. "He's smart."

"Are you?" Scrap-Iron asked Stewart.

"I like words," Stewart said. A humble answer. He was smart, and he knew it. It was the one positive thing about himself that he truly believed.

"Me too," Scrap-Iron said. He meant he liked words, and he was smart.

They both stayed silent for a moment, in mutual wonderment that they had something in common.

"You got college?" Scrap-Iron asked.

The question and the way the big man asked it seemed strangely anachronistic, as if a college education was still an extreme rarity.

"I do," Stewart said.

"I thought as much," Scrap-Iron said. "How much?"

"I have a bachelor's in business administration."

"From where?" Scrap-Iron asked.

"Seton Hall," Stewart said.

Scrap-Iron narrowed his eyes.

Stewart did a quick calculation as to whether he should tell of his advanced degree, whether that would further impress his prospective landlord or be a gilding that might irritate him. He decided to go all the way.

"And," he said, "I've got my master of arts in literature."

That was too much for Scrap-Iron. He tossed the pen in the air and let it land in his lap, for effect. He liked effect. He looked to Slinky. "So you caught me an intellectual. You do know how to get on my good side."

Though he was listening for it, Stewart didn't hear sarcasm.

Slinky beamed like a kid who had pleased a hard-to-please father.

"What do you think is the best American novel?" Scrap-Iron asked.

A common enough question, Stewart thought, even if asked by an unusual man in an unusual place. Though he would have preferred a more idiosyncratic response, he answered honestly, his voice reflexively taking on the deeper, authoritative tone of a highly trained professional delving into his field of expertise. "I'd say *Huckleberry Finn* or *Moby Dick*."

"Not *Gatsby*?" Scrap-Iron asked.

"No," Stewart said, "not for me. I just think there's much more to *Huckleberry Finn* and *Moby Dick*. *Gatsby*'s slight by comparison." As if he were at a faculty party and expecting immediate blowback, he equivocated some and said, "For my taste."

"Yeah," Scrap-Iron said. "You're right. *Gatsby*'s too pussy-whipped, like old F. Scott himself."

Stewart couldn't help but smile at that.

"*Moby Dick*," Scrap-Iron said, "is the best. It's a man's book, by a real man, about a real man."

Stewart gave a nod to that. Nothing really wrong with that although…

"*Huck Finn* now," Scrap-Iron said, "that's too niggary." He studied Stewart's face for reaction, winked at Slinky, and said, "For my taste."

Stewart didn't comment.

"Sit down," Scrap-Iron said. He motioned to a black bucket seat, torn from some sports car and set there on the garage floor.

Stewart did as commanded. He was happy that Scrap-Iron didn't offer to shake. The meaty part of his right hand still ached from punching the paper dispenser, and a blue stain was imprinted on the edge of his palm.

"How'd you do this morning?" Scrap-Iron asked Slinky, meaning, where are my papers?

Slinky hurriedly pulled the newspapers from his satchel. The hand the big man took the papers in was huge and battered and black in every crevice and under all the fingernails. Compared to Stewart's, it looked like an appendage from a closely related but different species of hominid.

Slinky's intermediary role was finished. He gave his back a break and took a seat on a section of the modular Naugahyde sofa that faced Scrap-Iron's chair, that sofa as out of place in the garage as was Stewart.

"So you're looking for a place to keep a tent?" Scrap-Iron asked.

"Yes," Stewart said, trying to prop himself up. He didn't like how close to the floor the car seat was. It further diminished him in the big man's presence, and he felt plenty diminished already.

"You could do worse than here," Scrap-Iron said.

Stewart nodded.

Slinky smiled and fidgeted. The big man talking up his place was surely a good sign.

"Walk through my yard," Scrap-Iron said, and tilted his head toward the garage's backdoor and the junkyard that lay beyond it. "If you don't hurry, like most people do, and, if unlike most people today, you have some power of observation, it'll teach you things worth knowing."

"I bet," Stewart said. He was surprised and impressed at how carefully the big man chose his words. He had the flattering but unsettling feeling it was all for him.

"Most people only see junk," Scrap-Iron said. "But you know what my yard's full of?"

"What?" Stewart asked.

"Desirable detritus," Scrap-Iron said.

The big man was showing off. Stewart knew his type, an autodidact. He admired the type. He figured Scrap-Iron had a mental Rolodex of fancy words and pulled one out when the audience was worth impressing. He should be flattered. But the big man was better at memorization than pronunciation. Detritus came out too long on the first syllable and too short on the second. Stewart's instinct was to correct him, albeit gently and in the spirit of a mutual love of learning and a mutual love of words. He himself had learned much through the salutary sting of embarrassment. He still remembered a professor in Music History 101 correcting him in front of the whole mass lecture hall, explaining that Wagner was pronounced Väg-ner. On that occasion, he had sunk deeper into his chair, but he never made that same mistake again.

In Scrap-Iron's case, Stewart's instinct for survival overrode his impulse to help.

"What do you think is better made?" Scrap-Iron asked, with a conspiratorial look in his eyes. "Old stuff or new stuff?"

Stewart was a natural fan of old stuff, but before he could conjure a suitably nuanced answer, Scrap-Iron made his case with tangible evidence.

He had two wheelbarrows in the garage, one his ancient hand-hewn favorite, the other modern and store bought. The old relic had a steel body, banged and bent around its top lip, but still solid and supported by a heavy tubular frame that extended into two long handles. Its hard rubber tire was guarded by the tubular frame and looked as if it might roll on forever. The modern one had a tin body, a pneumatic tire, and spindly pine handles.

"Grab that," Scrap-Iron instructed Stewart, directing him to the old wheelbarrow. Stewart pushed himself out of the bucket seat and stood and took the wheelbarrow by the handles and started to lift. Its weight surprised him. He had to tighten his grip and lift more with his legs.

"How much work do you think that nasty sum-bitch has done?" Scrap-Iron asked.

From the battered body and worn smoothness of the tire and rubber handgrips, the answer was clear. "A lot," Stewart said.

"And it still has a lot left in it," Scrap-Iron said. Then he looked askance at the new wheelbarrow. "Grab that one," he said.

Compared to the old one, the new wheelbarrow was feather light, more like a kid's toy than a workingman's tool.

After a knuckle rap that acoustically demonstrated the new wheelbarrow's tinniness, Scrap-Iron asked, "How much work do you think that pretty, powder-blue piece of shit can do?" As he liked to do, he answered his own question. "That new one, maybe it would be okay as a flower planter, but as far as real work, it ain't worth a bucket of piss."

Stewart nodded.

"Most of what's out there," Scrap-Iron said, tilting his head toward the yard, "people worked hard to craft. Most of today's shit, they work hard to sell. There's nothing like what the old masters built."

The *old masters*. That resonated with Stewart. He also believed in the old masters. He had learned something about them, and about suffering, from Auden's great poem, "Musee Des Beaux Arts."

"So," Scrap-Iron said, "you have that fancy degree in literature, but, here you are. Things must be bad in the literary world these days."

"I guess," Stewart said. "At least in my end of it."

"What I'm asking," Scrap-Iron said, "is how a guy like you ends up here, looking to set a tent among a bunch of unlearned and unwashed lowlifes?"

A blunt but logical question.

"I had some bad luck," Stewart said.

"Luck?" Scrap-Iron said, with a nipping laugh. "Luck's for losers. No winner believes in luck. Question the boys, sitting out there all night in the woods staring at a fire or jerking-off in their tents;

they'll hide behind luck, too. But they're all seriously fucked-up, and everybody knows it's their own fault."

"A lot of things can happen to a person," Stewart said.

"True that," Scrap-Iron said. "Take Slinky. He had a bad break. A congenital screw-up. I'll give him that." He spoke as if Slinky weren't present. "Who knows what happened? Maybe some important part of him ran down his old man's leg."

Stewart felt himself redden, for Slinky's sake.

"You know," Scrap-Iron continued, "what Slinky's got, that spinal twist? Hank Williams had that, too. The senior Hank. The genius one. But Hank's wasn't as bad. It didn't fuck him up as much as it does Slinky."

Slinky remained expressionless to the diagnosis and the music history lesson.

"But about you?" Scrap-Iron said. "I got to know whether to cut you any slack. So, back to my question."

"It's a long story," Stewart said. Sometimes a cliché worked best, and he was thrown off by the big man's sudden change of manner.

"I got time," Scrap-Iron said. He leaned back and folded his arms behind his head. His biceps flexed. Then he intertwined his thick fingers and thrust his hands forward, cracking his knuckles machine-gun-like and louder than any knuckle-cracking Stewart had ever heard.

Cornered, Stewart decided to go with his most sellable and practiced lie, how he was a victim of heartless corporate downsizing. The story wasn't true, but it easily could have been and never failed to win sympathy. When in the right mood, Stewart himself sometimes worked up a faint belief in the story, and an accompanying righteousness.

Scrap-Iron listened, attentive but poker-faced. At the end of Stewart's tale, he said, "So you lost the job. People are losing jobs all the time, and they don't end up on the skids. Something else happened, and you know what my money's on?"

"What's that?" Stewart said.

"My money's on a woman," Scrap-Iron said. For further clarity he spelled it out. "W-o-m-a-n."

Stewart didn't say yes or no. He didn't want to go there. He tried to keep his face expressionless.

"You were married?" Scrap-Iron asked.

"Yes."

"Divorced?"

"No."

Scrap-Iron tapped his teeth with his pen. "What happened? She just split?"

"No," Stewart said. "It was me."

"It was you?"

"I needed to take a different path," Stewart said.

"A different path?" Mockery in Scrap-Iron's smile, contempt in his voice.

"That's right," Stewart said.

"Bullshit," Scrap-Iron said. "You fucked-up, and she split."

Stewart's face heated. He never could stand being called a liar, even when he was. "No," was all he said.

"Yes," was all Scrap-Iron said.

It was a direct challenge. Stewart started to respond and stopped. He was afraid of pushing back and pushing his luck.

"My guess," Scrap-Iron said, "is that you couldn't keep Little Stewart in your pants. My guess is you had some depraved affair." *Dee-praved* is how he said it.

"No," Stewart said.

Scrap-Iron was obviously enjoying himself. He had the complete confidence of an omniscient with the upper hand. "Okay," he said. "Let's say it wasn't you. Then tell me, when did your wife start fucking someone else?"

That was too much.

"She was never unfaithful," Stewart said. "And neither was I. Never. There was no adultery." It all came out more belligerent than he intended.

"No adultery?" Scrap-Iron said. "Too bad. I've always been partial to adultery. Number six among the big ten but first in my heart. Adultery's been one of my life's joys."

Scrap-Iron smiled. It was a big lurid one, and though Stewart didn't know how he had overlooked it before, the big man's two upper front teeth were missing. His wider smile was a mug shot of dementedness. Later, Stewart found out how Scrap-Iron lost the teeth. It was one of the many wild stories about him. They had been knocked out by a jumbo-sized tomato juice can, wielded by a cuckolded motorcycle gang leader in a legendary bar fight. Stewart could easily imagine some bar brawling opponent, regardless of his size or ferocity, needing the help of a large juice can. And he could imagine himself hitting Scrap-Iron with everything he had and the big man not even noticing.

"So," Scrap-Iron said, "you're sure about the wife? I mean that she wasn't using it, you know, with someone else?"

Stewart didn't answer that. He didn't need a spot in the woods that bad.

"Come on now," Scrap-Iron said. "Don't get all red and shit." He sat straighter, and there was a loud sucking sound as his back pulled away from the leather chair.

"Tell your boy," Scrap-Iron said, to Slinky, "that I'm just busting his balls."

"So Scrap," Slinky said, sensing the right moment, "he can stay?"

Scrap-Iron stared at Stewart and cocked his head, as if still weighing the matter. After an appropriate wait, he said, "He can stay. For now. As far as where you put him, make sure you work that out with the boys."

"Good!" Slinky said. He was pleased not only that his new friend had a place to stay, but that he had been the instrument of his good fortune.

"Remember," Scrap-Iron said, "it's probationary." He sounded as if he enjoyed the concept of probation.

"Thanks," Slinky said.

By way of dismissal, Scrap-Iron said to Slinky, "Get the boys here on time today."

Scrap-Iron's mandatory Sunday meetings started at 10 a.m., but he expected all Scrapville residents there by 9:55. A little thing, tardiness, but it was the little things left unpunished that led to bigger things. Scrap-Iron learned that from successful football coaches. He had played football in high school, but briefly. A defensive lineman, his career ended when he was just a freshman and without his playing a single game–after he fractured the varsity quarterback's pelvis in a non-contact practice.

"Should Stew come to today's meeting?" Slinky asked. "I mean, now that he's one of us?"

"He can't do that," Scrap-Iron said. "He's gonna be the main topic."

9

At 9:55 a.m., Scrap-Iron's tenantry gathered around him in a semicircle, worshippers beneath the worshipped, the big man dominating the room like he dominated his entire insular world. Without moving from his recliner, he could answer his phone and bark orders and insults, ruling over his enterprise like a mighty earth god.

Slinky sat against the wall, on a stack of rimless truck tires. He was tired from the effort of getting the boys there and on time. It was like herding cats, but his were feral cats. The unusual position, his body half-sunk inside the tires, helped his ever-aching spine so much that he considered trying to duplicate the stack in his tent, for sleeping on the bad nights.

Toad sat in his black bucket seat. There was protocol in Scrapville, and though Toad was firmly at the bottom of that peculiar hierarchy, that seat was his seat. He had salvaged it from a wrecked Ford Mustang, the unobtainable car of his dreams.

The tall, wino-skinny and pony-tailed Soda Bandito and the fireplug-like Little Hercules made for uneven bookends as they sat on the end sections of the garage's Naugahyde sofa. The Bandito's section had wooden shims nailed to the bottom as make-do feet.

It was getting hot in the garage, and Scrap-Iron had opened both overhead doors about a foot, enough to add some light and allow airflow but still discourage outside interruptions. A big floor fan hummed in the far corner. On the wall above the workbench was a glossy color poster of an improbably built young woman who wore the skimpiest of pink hot pants and an outgunned T-shirt. She was bending over as if to pick something up from the floor while looking over her shoulder with eyes that asked, "Can you handle this?"

The scene not Rockwellian, but with a homey feel of its own.

***

Scrap-Iron held out his empty right hand, shaped to hold a beer can. "What am I missing?" he asked.

Slinky immediately started digging out of the stacked tires, and, once up, made his unsteady way toward the refrigerator. Toad jumped up, crossed Slinky's path, and beat him to the spot. Slinky looked to Scrap-Iron, but getting no direction there, turned, and went back to his spot.

Toad took a bottle of beer from the top shelf of the fridge, a long-necked Pabst Blue Ribbon, the only beer Scrap-Iron drank. The lower shelves were filled with cans of Budweiser. Those were for the boys, but only when Scrap-Iron said. Toad carried the PBR back to Scrap-Iron. As previously and forcefully instructed, he was careful to keep his unhygienic hands from near the top. He handed the beer to the big man, who took it but didn't open it. Something was wrong. Scrap-Iron fixed his unblinking eyes on Toad. Toad started to say something, stopped, and slunk back to his seat.

Scrap-Iron's eyes followed Toad, and Toad finally asked, with a whimper, "What I do?"

"Did I tell you to get the beer?" Scrap-Iron asked.

"No," Toad said, "but Scrap…"

"Is it your job to get the beer?"

"No, Scrap. But I just wanted…"

Scrap-Iron stared harder, a boring-in angry stare that struck Toad dumb.

"See that bug there?" Scrap-Iron asked while looking at a fruit fly perched on the arm of his chair. The garage had a recent infestation of fruit flies, drawn by the bananas Scrap-Iron ate for the potassium. His beefy legs were prone to cramping.

The boys turned their attention to the fruit fly. Scrap-Iron put a huge fist over the bug, about to crush it. He held his Damoclean fist there, perfectly still, until in a last-minute reprieve he pulled it back. The fly, unaware of its close call, stayed put.

"Toad-Boy," Scrap-Iron said, "I was gonna say that's how much what you want matters to me, about as much as this bug. But that would be wrong. See, this bug is," the big man slowed and pronounced the Latin name deliberately, syllable by syllable, "*Dro-so-phi-la me-lan-o-gaster.*"

After getting all that out, Scrap-Iron looked to Slinky. He got back the awestruck look he wanted. Then he put his face nearer the bug and moved his eyes side to side, studying the small yellowish fly and its brick red eyes with a naturalist's curiosity, like Darwin with a new beetle.

Pronouncing the Latin faster and with more confidence, Scrap-Iron said, "Unlike you, Toad-Boy, *Drosophila melanogaster* has some purpose in life. It's used in science. They study genes with it. Screwups. Mutations. You know Toad, if I had the time, I'd like to study your genes to figure out how someone gets as mutated-up as you. If I could figure that out, I'd probably win a Nobel Prize."

"Scrap…" Toad said.

"Don't give me that Scrap shit." The big man's voice was measured but full of menace. "You got that?"

Toad looked as if he got it.

"Slinky there," Scrap-Iron said, "he got up to get my beer. Like he should. That's his job. Then, without being told, you big-assed your way into the situation."

Scrap-Iron gave Toad a chance to comment on this. Toad didn't.

"I don't like that shit," Scrap-Iron said, seeming angrier for the lack of response. The big man was a true believer in social order. Civilization needed order, and here, in his world, he provided it. The boys accepted that and the associated benefits. Society put no value on them, but the big man did, even if he demonstrated it in his own way. Why else would he go to all the trouble?

"Listen, Toad," Scrap-Iron said, "I'm just a heartbeat away from getting my tired working-man's ass out of this chair. You want some of that?"

Toad bowed his head and shook it vigorously. His long, clumped hair didn't move. His hair looked as if it hadn't been washed in months, maybe years. It looked as if it wouldn't move in a Category 5 hurricane.

Everybody else sat silent, in uneasy stasis, waiting for the big man to cool. The Bandito took the elastic

71

band from his ponytail, massaged his hair, and retied it. Little Hercules stared at the cement floor and worked his forearms, moving his fingers as if he were milking a cow, admiring his flexor muscles. Slinky adjusted his back for comfort. Toad started picking at his earlobe, the red sore there perpetual.

Scrap-Iron opened his beer, tipped his head back, and in one long gulp drained the entire bottle. It seemed the time for a great belch, but none came. After a breath, Scrap-Iron said, "We've got important business to do."

The boys nodded.

"We've got new meat," Scrap-Iron said. "You all met him?"

Nods all around but nothing said. The boys had learned to never risk getting out in front of their landlord.

"He's real smart," Scrap-Iron said.

"Not as smart as you," Toad said.

"Smarter than you though, Toadster," The Bandito said. "But I could say that about a rock."

"Fuck you," Toad said.

"It be the best you ever had," The Bandito said.

"It be the first he ever had," Little Hercules said.

"Shut up," Scrap-Iron said.

Usually Scrap-Iron encouraged fights among his boys. He found it entertaining, simple brutes going head-to-head, holding no insult back, and trying their best to win his favor. It was crude entertainment, but you could only work with what you had. Now he had new material and the promise of more sophisticated fun.

"I want to know," Scrap-Iron said, "what you think of having an educated university man in your midst."

Slinky tried to think of something to say that might take the conversation in a positive direction. Maybe a few words about the value of different types and what Stewart could bring to the group. But he said nothing, for fear of saying something stupid and making things worse.

"He's a college boy?" The Bandito asked.

"Yep," Scrap-Iron said. He quoted Stewart, with deliberate affectation. "His bachelor's is in business administration, but his master of arts is in literature."

"Bullshit," The Bandito said.

"You don't believe it?" Scrap-Iron said.

"It's all bullshit," The Bandito said.

"And get this," Scrap-Iron said. "He's never been unfaithful to his wife."

"More bullshit!" The Bandito said. Everything in The Bandito's three marriages, from his doings to his wives' doings, made marital fidelity unimaginable.

"He thinks," Scrap-Iron said, "that he's better than you animals. And maybe he is, since that ain't saying much."

Slinky fought the urge to object to the unfair characterization of his new friend, but his hard life had bestowed an inherent understanding of risk and reward. As Scrap-Iron liked to say about himself, his mother didn't raise any simple children. Except in foster boy Slinky's case, it was twelve different mothers.

"If he thinks he's so hot," Toad said, "then fuck him."

"Boot his ass out of here," The Bandito said.

"Let us fuck him up first," Toad said.

Herc, as was his way, stayed silent. Scrap-Iron liked Little Hercules's taciturnity as long as it didn't hint at dissent.

"Well Toad-Boy," Scrap-Iron said, "I could do that. I could let you boys fuck him up. You know, for something to do. But I could do something else."

"What you thinking, Scrap?" The Bandito asked.

"We could have some fun with him," Scrap-Iron said.

The boys liked the sound of that. Slinky didn't. He feared Scrap-Iron was already planning something. Contrary to what appearances might indicate, the big man never acted on raw impulse. He planned and executed. In a different life, he might have been a general or with his mechanical bent, a great engineer.

"Here's what we're gonna do," Scrap-Iron said. "We're gonna help this boy broaden his experience. If he's lying, he's trying to make a fool of us. If he's telling the truth, he needs more familiarity with the corporeal side of the world."

"What's that?" Toad asked.

"You don't know shit, Toad-Boy," The Bandito said.

"Okay," Toad said. "Then what's it mean?"

"It's like," The Bandito paused to collect the right words. "It's like body stuff. Right, Scrap?"

"Right," Scrap-Iron said. "See, it's gonna come down to the basics. Like most things do. Now, what do I always tell you motherless morons about the basics?"

Scrap-Iron folded his arms, waiting for his answer. None came, but Herc's face showed that he knew.

"Herc," Scrap-Iron said. "What is it I always say about the world? Huh? Come on now."

"You say," Herc said, "that it's sinning that makes it go round."

"That's right," Scrap-Iron said. "And what's the best way to measure a man?"

"By his sins," Herc said.

"Very good," Scrap-Iron said. "You want to see how strong a man is, you measure the quantity and quality of his sins. You look at history, ever since Moses gave us the scorecard, and you'll see you can't go too far wrong with that."

"And we all do good here?" The Bandito said. "Don't we, Scrap?"

"You do," Scrap-Iron said. "I'd say with what you've been given to work with, you all do your best."

"Thanks, Scrap."

"But here's the question," Scrap-Iron said. "How do you think our new man stacks up?"

"Not so good," The Bandito said.

"I agree," Scrap-Iron said. "But I think we can change that,"

"How Scrap?" The Bandito asked.

"Well, being that our boy's so proud of being *Mister never unfaithful*, what would you all think of my hooking him up with Boxcar Betty?"

"Oh yeah!" The Bandito said, with no hesitation.

Herc grinned and nodded.

"You really mean it?" Toad asked.

Slinky had never heard of Boxcar Betty, but he was the junior member here, and from their reactions, everyone else seemed to know her and that her involvement meant great entertainment. That couldn't be good.

"Never unfaithful Stewart meets Boxcar Betty," Scrap-Iron said. "You think that would be fun to watch?"

Herc and the Bandito and Toad agreed that such a combination would be fun to watch. Such unanimity among the boys a rare occurrence in Scrapville.

"I'll set it up for next week," Scrap-Iron said.

II

10

"Move that podium!"

The boss's scream caught Stewart off guard. He jumped and fumbled a stack of store flyers. The woman working behind him laughed. She had strategically positioned herself near Stewart's greeting station, at the front of the girls' department, where she mindlessly rearranged blouses on a $9.99 circular rack. The boss's abuse of Stewart was one of the regular sideshows that helped her through her day.

It was a popular pastime among the store's staff to swap stories of how tight Stewart was wound and how the boss mercilessly busted on him. The stories didn't need much embellishing. "Tight as a frog's ass," the glassy-eyed guy who wrangled the store's carts liked to say. "The boy's tight as a frog's ass, and that's waterproof."

That observation from a guy so loose-jointed that he had missed only a half-day's work after he came racing down the mall's entrance ramp and, unable to stop his bicycle, crashed headfirst through a Buick's windshield. He wore no helmet, but a mandatory trip to the emergency room and a set of X-rays found him unharmed except for a deep bruise on his forehead. The car's elderly driver fared worse, suffering a size twelve sneaker to her face and the shock of a human missile crashing through her windshield and landing among her grocery bags in the back seat. Blessed are the loose-jointed, for they will be watched over.

"What a dum-dum," the boss said, when he stopped at the customer service desk. He looked at Stewart and shook his head in exaggerated exasperation. The two women working the booth smiled in sympathetic understanding.

It was Monday morning and being stationed as a greeter was a bad start to Stewart's week. In that function, he stood up front, just inside the store's automatic glass doors, wearing a bright blue store-emblazoned vest and a false smile, stuck out there in the open like a carnival barker.

There was an extra dose of humiliation in the greeting position. That job was for the old and infirm and the variously challenged types the store hired in order to look socially conscious and because the government subsidized their pay. The boss stationed him there to humiliate him. How else could you explain making a greeter of the only associate versatile enough to make keys, mix paint, and intelligently answer electronics questions?

Stewart hated the exposure. Every arriving customer eyeballed him as if he were a circus freak. They could tell that he needed the job. It was easy to tell who needed the greeting job and who did it to avoid sitting alone at home and decaying from loneliness and boredom. Even the dumbest of customers could tell. Standing there, he felt shrunken. He knew just what everyone was thinking, the same thing he used to think when he passed by a store greeter: "Shoot me if it ever comes to that." One of his new nightmares, made all the more vivid by the melatonin he took to help him sleep, was of his long dead father resurrected and walking through the store's front entrance to see living proof that his son hadn't amounted to much.

There was another thing about the greeter function that Stewart hated. The cliché of it. In his strange way of thinking, it was what he hated most. What could be more unoriginal than a professional man in decline ending up as a store greeter? Didn't his dramatic fall deserve a more exotic evocation?

"The podium's half in the aisle," the boss said, facing Stewart now, his back against the customer service counter and his elbows resting on it. A little lord, cocky in his little fiefdom.

"I'll move it," Stewart said.

"You bet you will," the boss said, for the women's benefit.

Stewart hated everything about the boss: he hated his stupid grin; he hated his cheap sport coat that was too big for him so that the cuffs came down to his knuckles; he hated his garish watch with the shiny metal band and an impossibly complicated face that looked like it belonged on the arm of a scientist or an aviator, not an assistant manager at a retail store in charge of tormenting his workers.

"The way you got it out in the aisle," the boss said. "Someone's gonna get hurt. Ain't you smarter than that?"

The boss being who he was, Stewart never got the professional courtesy of a quiet instruction. Instead, his humiliation was broadcast to customers and associates alike. He had thought of making a formal complaint. Company policy was on his side, but official billboard policy–We treat all our associates with respect–was one thing, and day-to-day management by the store's "coaches" was something else.

The boss walked away, back to jabbering into his stupid walkie-talkie, as if he were someone of importance and his lowly greeter not worth dwelling on, as if Stewart was like the other riffraff he managed.

Stewart collected the scattered flyers. The bending over made him dizzy.

He hadn't eaten breakfast; that's why he wasn't sharp. All he'd had that morning was a donut he had found in the store's cheerless break room–a peanut-glazed donut that was missing most of its peanuts. Hopefully some vulgarian hadn't licked them off. Post-donut hyperglycemia had let the boss get the best of him. That's what he told himself, but he knew it was something else. He hadn't slept all night. His mind had worked overtime, reliving his meeting with Scrap-Iron, parsing again and again the big man's every sentence.

"When did she start fucking someone else?"

That didn't need parsing, and recalling Scrap-Iron's cocksure delivery of it made him cringe. He knew that tonight, alone in his tent and trying to fall asleep, he'd return to the carnal possibilities that question fostered. He'd lie awake, obsessively imagining high definition images of his wife brought to pleasures she had never experienced before and by lovers so much more skillful than he that she would say it was as if it were her first time. By morning, he would be all crunched up in a fetal position, suffering again from the agonizing stabs of pain that ran down the side of his head, pain that felt like being jabbed behind the ear with an electrified ice pick. "When did she start…?" Maybe the torture of that question was his just deserts for getting himself in a situation to have such a discussion with such a man.

Last night, he had sought out Slinky and tried to get him to talk about what Scrap-Iron had discussed during his meeting with the boys, the meeting where he, Stewart, was the *main topic*. Slinky had been unusually reticent and vague. He said that Scrap liked to have fun with newcomers. He made it sound innocent, as if Scrap-Iron were planning some sort of a harmless initiation rite for his new boy. But Stewart wasn't convinced. Scrap-Iron's graphic assumption of his wife's adultery was meant to degrade him, to lower him to the level of the other Scrapville residents. For some reason, the landlord needed to do that, and whatever the reason, it couldn't be good.

He started moving the podium back, dancing with it and working its unwieldy bulk side to side. He wasn't much of a mover or a dancer, and the heavy podium made for an uncooperative partner. A pad and pen started to slide from the lower shelf, and when he tried to compensate, the podium twisted awkwardly and a sharp pain jabbed him in his lower back. Just what he needed, an injury to go along with a back already stiff and sore from sleeping on hard and damp ground.

The podium finally positioned, he set the flyers back on top so anybody walking by could grab one. It was early August, but the ads had already turned to autumn. They featured wholesome looking families of athletic fathers, perfectly proportioned mothers, and bright-eyed children, the happy campers raking leaves, playing football, and swinging in beautiful suburban yards. Everyone sported a cheerful face and appeared to be without a problem in the world, even the romping dogs and posing cats.

He knew the families were too good to be true. If his family had been featured in the ads, there would have been some empty space.

His mother died when he was three months old of post-partum depression. *Post-partum*, Latin for after-childbirth, which in this case meant after his birth, which meant, by any reasonable application of cause and effect, that he was the cause of his mother's depression and subsequent death. Explain to him the wrongheadedness of such thinking as often as you liked. He was a logical man, and the logic was solid. He sometimes wondered if he got his anxieties from his mother. Then he would wonder how he could be so heartless. He would often try and conjure an image of his mother, something to make her real to him. His father displayed no pictures of her, so in his mind's eye he adopted a particular painting of the Madonna that had always evoked so much feeling in him, one painted by the Italian master, Pompeo Batoni. It was titled *The Holy Family*. Both mother and child looked so vulnerable in that painting.

His father's persona wasn't the stuff of happy advertising. He wasn't a smiler. Maybe because he didn't have much to smile about. He had to raise a boy on his own, without an extended family to help. He had done his best, and if his best was hard on his son, it was hard on him, too. Stewart's most vivid memory of his father was the time he had misbehaved, and instead of yelling at him, his father broke down in tears. To see that weakness in his father shocked and scared him.

After his wife's death, his father had made safety and security his priority. They lived in an urban neighborhood but not a high-crime area. Nevertheless, doors were double-locked. A fire extinguisher was on every floor and enough bottled water and military surplus C-rations were stored in the basement to feed the two of them for a year in case of Armageddon, be it natural or man-made. His father once embarrassed him to death by bringing his rain boots to the bus stop where Stew stood with his schoolmates. He was about twelve then, and his father forced him to put the boots on, lest pneumonia befall him. All of it was done out of love, but doesn't love sometimes mean suppressing your fears lest they infect your babies?

He had no brothers or sisters, and his father wanted no part of dogs or cats. The mini-family's backyard was a small patch of crabgrass and not big enough for any decent swing set. What kind of ad would all that make?

11

On Tuesday, he woke early. He turned to his other side and cuddled into the comfort of the sleeping bag. He didn't have to be to work until one o'clock. He might sleep till noon. You took your pleasures where you could.

When his tent started shaking, he thought a tornado might have swept down on Scrapville. He crawled to the front and looked out the flap. There stood The Bandito, who looked down at him and shook his head in the kind of disgust he usually reserved for Toad.

"It's time to grind out some money," The Bandito said. "So get your ass out here, and let's get going."

Stewart did the only thing he could do; he dressed and got ready for a new unknown. Before he left, he swallowed two ibuprofens and put two more in his pocket. He knew he was going to need them.

The other boys were waiting, standing around the fire pit, looking anxious to get moving. Whatever the day brought, it was going to be a group venture.

"What's up?" Stewart asked.

"Time to start earning your keep," The Bandito said. He looked to the others. "Ain't that right?"

"That's right," Herc said. "No more freeloading."

"Let's go," Toad said. "He's gonna slow us down anyways."

"Where are we going?" Stewart asked.

"We got hustling to do," The Bandito said. "For some reason, Scrap wants you to go."

"Okay," Stewart said. "But I've got to be at work by one."

"We'll try and keep that in mind," The Bandito said.

"Yeah," Toad said. "Being that you're a big shot."

"Scrap's got rules," Slinky said. He wanted Stewart to know he wasn't being singled out. "One of his rules is everyone's got to hustle."

"Okay," Stewart said.

"You ain't been pulling your oar," The Bandito said. "I say you can't pull for a shit even if you want to, but Scrap says you get to try."

"Yeah," Toad said. "You ain't been pulling."

"I bet you been pulling," Herc said, to Toad. "You been pulling something every night. But it ain't an oar."

"Let's go," The Bandito said. "There's sheep out there, and we're the wolves."

***

The whole crew headed down the path through the woods and onto the tracks and toward downtown Harristown. Stewart brought up the rear, with Slinky.

"Scrap wants a hundred bucks today," Slinky said to Stewart. "We don't come back until we get at least a hundred."

"How are we supposed to get it?" Stewart asked.

"Lots of ways," Slinky said.

Slinky recounted a Scrap-Iron story to shed light on hustling and the importance the man put on it. He told about the time at the junkyard when a woman stopped by asking for a donation. She was from a local church and infused with the sanctity of her work. She was raising funds for, as she put it, wayward girls.

"Oh boy," Scrap-Iron told her. "I like them kind of girls, you know, the wayward ones. Them's my favorites." The woman was offended, but in spite of that pursued her larger goal with such determination that it genuinely impressed Scrap. "Listen honey," he told her, "you're a good hustler. Forget this do-gooding bullshit and get selling some pots and pans and I bet you could grind out some serious money. Make your husband real proud of you."

Slinky said the woman never came back. Scrap-Iron was a great deterrent to door-to-door vendors and proselytizers.

***

The walk took them to Harristown's Green, a two-and-a-half-acre historical park located in the center of town.

"A lot of history here, you know," Slinky said. He liked history. In high school he had memorized the presidents in chronological order and, more impressively, their vice-presidents. He had earned a little medal for that.

Slinky pointed to a bronze plaque that told the local history. He summarized it for Stewart's benefit.

The Green dated back to early 1715, when New Jersey was still an English colony under the rule of King George II and Parliament. It had served as an area for public executions.

"I'd liked to seen that," Toad said. "How'd they do 'em?"

"Hanging," Slinky said.

"You better be careful Toad-Boy," The Bandito said. "They find out all the shit you're up to in town, they might hang you, maybe right from that monument."

The Bandito pointed to the Civil War monument. It was a fifty-foot-high white granite obelisk, the names of great battles chiseled into it–Antietam, Vicksburg, Gettysburg…

"Can't you just see Toad hanging there?" The Bandito asked. "The birds shitting on him and pecking out his eyes?"

"We ain't here for a history lesson," Herc said. "Time to get to work."

"Okay," The Bandito said. "I'll start. Only one of us works at a time. You guys sit over there, on that bench. Make sure you watch for the cop."

The Bandito turned to Stewart. "You," he said, "watch and learn."

***

Five minutes passed until The Bandito sensed the right opportunity. A well-dressed woman with a baby in a stroller came down one of the concrete paths that radiated from the center of the park.

"Excuse me, Ma'am," The Bandito said, standing in the woman's way so that she couldn't pass comfortably.

"Yes?" she said.

"I'm sorry to bother your morning," The Bandito said and leaned toward the baby, not close enough to be threatening, just close enough to show he was taken by the child's beauty. "What a beautiful baby," he said.

"Thank you," the woman said. She was anxious to move.

"I got a boy too," The Bandito said. "But he's in Newark. I've had some trouble. Not drink or drugs or anything like that. Just some other trouble. You know. It can happen. I haven't seen my boy in almost a month now." The Bandito lowered his head to his chest, almost overcome with his grief.

The woman shifted her weight from one foot to another.

"My boy's named Bobby," The Bandito said. "I ain't got the train fare to go see him. It's seven dollars and fifty cents. That's one way, but I can figure some other way to get home. I was just wondering if you could, you know, help a little. It kills me to ask like this, but I miss him so much."

The woman hesitated. The Bandito lowered his head again. "I know it's tough times," he said. "For all of us." From his pocket he took a picture of a boy about ten. He had found the picture at a flea market, a freckled kid with a gap-toothed smile. The boys all said he looked like The Bandito.

The woman took her purse from the back of the stroller. "I think I got something here," she said.

"Anything will help," The Bandito said. "I miss the little guy terrible. He likes when I roughhouse with him some."

The woman dug through her purse. She finally gave up the digging, opened a wallet and handed The Bandito a five-dollar bill.

"God bless you," The Bandito said.

The woman hurried away. The Bandito gave the boys a big wink.

***

For two hours, the boys took turns hustling. Each had their tried and true specialty. The Bandito had his lost son story. Herc had a mother in a nursing home longing to see her only boy. Toad had enough for a hamburger but not for a soda, even a small one. Slinky, who when his heart was in it was the best hustler of all, played on his condition.

When the park's traffic slowed and most of the faces were familiar, it was time to move on. The Green would offer further opportunities. There was the fall coat giveaway where winter coats, many high-end and like-new, were donated. The best coats could be turned around quickly and for a good price. There were the free Thanksgiving turkeys that could be sold outside of Burger-Land. There was the Festival on the Green, an open-air event where businesses and organizations came together to advertise and offer promotional giveaways. There was the Christmas Festival where The Bandito's big city pickpocketing skills so exceeded the local citizens' wariness that he once lamented the lack of challenge. Scrap-Iron unsympathetically summed up the situation. "If they weren't meant to be shorn," he said, "they wouldn't be sheep."

As they left the Green, The Bandito said to Stewart, "Back there you was just learning. Where we're heading now, you got work to do."

Where they were heading was Saint William's church.

***

Along the way they passed the Main Street Mission and its cross-shaped sign—a horizontal Jesus, a vertical Saves. In the winter, they might have stopped there to scrounge a coffee or a hot chocolate and maybe a donut.

Two blocks east of Main Street, at the end of a tree-lined block, stood a towering stone church. Behind the church was a fenced in lot. Through the gate in that fence, in the middle of the lot, on top of four bricks, stood a fifty-five-gallon drum, rusted orange-red.

Stewart was confused now. He assumed the church would be the source of more largesse wrung from the good-hearted and naive. But their destination seemed to be this desolate back lot, behind the church and out of sight of the rectory.

The Bandito went right to work. With his knuckles he tapped the big drum, starting at the top where he produced a hollow echo and moving lower until at the three-quarters mark the sound changed.

"That's good," he said, at the deepening sound.

"What's good?" Stewart asked.

"We got a new batch," The Bandito said. "And you got work to do."

Stewart looked to Slinky.

"That barrel," Slinky said, "is where they burn the old envelopes."

"Okay," Stewart said. But he was still in the dark. Herc removed a brick and two lids from the top of the barrel. The first lid was solid metal, the second a wire mesh spark screen. In the lot's far corner, behind some ceramic flowerpots, lay a stack of paving stones and a half-handled shovel.

Next to the barrel, the Bandito shaped an open box with the paving stones. He set the wire mesh lid over it. He looked at Stewart as if he should know what to do next.

"Duh!" Toad said, when Stewart remained perplexed.

"Watch, college man," The Bandito said.

He dug the shovel into the drum, lifted out a full scoop of ashes and emptied them onto the wire mesh. With his hands he swept them through the mesh, careful to disperse them all. Nothing remained on the wire. He lifted another scoop of ashes out and did it again. This time four charbroiled coins were left–three quarters and a dime.

"Burnt offerings," Slinky said, with a smile. Then he put the coins in a large Ziploc bag and explained things to Stewart. "Volunteers empty the contribution envelopes for the church. Then they burn the empty envelopes in the barrel. Usually once a month. The only people who volunteer are all old, and they got old eyes and fingers. They miss a lot of coins. Especially the ones that get stuck in the corners."

Collecting those coins was now Stewart's job. Easy enough to learn, too. He worked for an hour. The Bandito made him go through all the ashes twice. Waste Not, Want Not.

Slinky did the final count. Thirty-two quarters, forty-six dimes, ten nickels, one penny. "The penny," Herc said, "must have been from some cheap bastard." Not their best day, but enough of a take, with the day's earlier hustling, to surpass their $100 target.

Scrap-Iron had assured the boys the Lord was on their side. He had quoted the Bible as proof: *Give your money to the poor, and you will have treasure in heaven.* The boys surely qualified as poor. Mostly, the boys were happy and relieved to satisfy Scrap-Iron. They knew him to be less forgiving than the Lord.

12

On Friday night, Scrap-Iron called the Bandito and summoned all the boys, Stewart included.

"Scrap wants every swinging dick at this meeting," the Bandito said to Toad, as he snapped the phone closed. "Even the new asshole."

It was amazing The Bandito never lost his phone. He always kept it in his back pocket with the top half sticking out–because he wanted everybody to see it and be reminded of his special status as Scrap-Iron's communications point man. Scrap-Iron had finagled the free cell phone through some program paid for by the taxpayers, a group that didn't include him. Scrap-Iron claimed to pay no taxes. He said the only thing he filed was his fingernails.

The unscheduled meeting made Stewart wonder if it was his initiation. He was torn between fear and a desire to get it over with. The boys hoped Scrap was ready for some real fun. If Scrap were sufficiently in the mood, he might even bring out the vintage steamer trunk that he kept in the garage's far corner under a canvas tarp. The trunk, secured by a padlock, contained his stash of toys, lovingly collected over the years: black powder and assorted fireworks; pistols ancient, old, and modern; a crossbow; a Samurai sword, a machete and an M1 bayonet; a pirate's knife, a Bowie knife, several switchblades and shivs; a Billy club, brass knuckles, and a sap; a bull whip and a hangman's noose; several sticks of dynamite. Pandora would have been proud.

***

But there was no initiation. Scrap-Iron was in the mood for fun, but not that kind of fun. One of the guys who worked in the yard–Scrap-Iron kept two steady workers whom he called his *punks*; they were locals with some mechanical inclination or at least a love for the cutting torch–had found a children's game in the backseat of a junked car. The game and its possibilities caught the big man's eye.

Meant for family fun, the game was called *Twister*. It was played on a plastic mat spread on the floor and meant to test one's balance and dexterity. The mat had four rows of colored circles–red, blue, yellow, and green. Based on the spin of an arrow, a player had to place a hand or foot on one of the circles and keep it there through the next instruction. Soon, a player had to assume more and more difficult arm- and leg-crossing positions, until even a well-balanced person might fall. It gave Scrap-Iron an idea for his kind of family fun.

"Here Toad-Boy," Scrap-Iron said and tossed the game box to him. "Set it up."

Toad opened the box and took out the plastic mat and spread it on the garage's concrete floor. He had to move his bucket seat to fit the mat in between the Naugahyde sofa and Scrap-Iron's chair.

When Toad looked up, perplexed by the instructions, The Bandito grabbed the box from him.

"The way you read, Toad-Boy," he said, "we might end up playing *Monopoly*."

The rule sheet held in front of him, The Bandito started. "Spread the mat face up on a flat surface. Okay, we did that. Now, the referee will spin the spinner and call out the moves."

"We don't need the rules," Scrap-Iron said. "I make the rules. Give me the spinner."

The Bandito handed him the spinner. It was an arrow-shaped needle, spun over a circle with four quadrants. Scrap-Iron spun the arrow. It landed in the right-hand quadrant and on a green dot.

"Toad," Scrap-Iron said, "put your right hand on a green dot."

Toad bent down to the mat and did as told.

Scrap-Iron spun again and ordered Toad to put his left foot on a red dot. It took a stretch but was easy enough for the young and flexible Toad.

"Okay, Toad," Scrap-Iron said, "get off."

"But Scrap," Toad said, "I'm doing good."

"Get your ass off before I boot it off," Scrap-Iron said. "This ain't about you."

Toad got off the mat and moved to the sofa. Unable to play a game that he was good at, he pouted.

"Slinky," Scrap-Iron said. "Your turn."

Slinky got off the tires, got himself pointed in the right direction, and made his way to the mat. The boys grew more attentive.

"Okay," Scrap-Iron said, "you ready Slinkster?"

Slinky forced a smile. Standing there, as if on a stage, his face ashen, he looked especially frail.

Scrap-Iron spun the arrow. It stopped, and he said, "Left foot, green dot."

Slinky put his left foot on one of the green dots.

Scrap-Iron spun again. "Right hand, red dot."

Slinky had trouble with that, but moving slowly and letting his hand free fall the last few inches, he touched the closest red dot.

Scrap-Iron spun again. "Right foot, blue dot."

Slinky started to move his right foot toward the closest blue dot.

"The blue dot that's all the way over here, by me," Scrap-Iron said. He had dictated a stretch that was impossible for Slinky.

"Scrap," The Bandito said, holding up the rules sheet, "that's not the way it's supposed to work."

"It works the way I say it works," Scrap-Iron said.

Slinky tried. He lifted his right foot and moved it toward the far blue dot. His foot didn't get there before he lost his balance and fell sideways, landing on his hip. The boys laughed. Scrap-Iron called out another combination, and Slinky fell again, harder this time. His involuntary cry of pain sounded like a puppy whose paw had been stepped on.

Scrap-Iron laughed, and the boys laughed louder. Stewart winced but held his tongue.

"Let me do it," Toad said. "He's too spazzed."

Scrap-Iron ignored Toad. He called out an even more impossible position for Slinky. Slinky got himself standing and looked to Scrap-Iron for mercy, but there was none to be had. He tried again but fell again, this time hitting his face and losing his glasses.

"That had to hurt!" The Bandito said.

Slinky rolled onto his side, in the middle of the mat. His back was twitching. His face was covered with sweat, and he was fingering the crucifix that had fallen out from under his T-shirt.

"I'm sorry, Scrap," Slinky said. "I'm not too good at this."

Stewart thought some of Slink's sweat was tears. He glanced toward Scrap-Iron. The big man stared back at him. No sympathy in those eyes. Scrap-Iron seemed to be more interested in Stewart's reaction to what was happening than he was to Slinky's painful plight.

Slinky struggled more, trying to get up. His pitiful wriggling motion reminded Stewart of the time he was a boy and joined the local Cub Scout troop. His Scout career lasted for one field trip to a nearby lake where one of the boys caught a sunfish and threw it on to the shore. The fish flapped and jumped, convulsing as it asphyxiated. No one moved to help it, and for fear of ridicule, Stewart held back too. The memory of that had haunted him ever since. It had seemed so cruel, a creature out of its proper place and suffering for it.

"Let's do something else," Stewart said.

"We're not done," Scrap-Iron said. He tossed the spinner to Stewart. "You put Slink through his paces."

"No," Stewart said.

"No?" Scrap-Iron said. He widened his eyes and put incredulity in his voice.

"No," Stewart repeated. He put the spinner between the chair's side and cushion, so no one else could get it.

The boys watched intently. This was something new and unexpected. Uncharted territory.

"Maybe," Scrap-Iron said, "you want to take his place?"

"Sure," Stewart said. "If it means he can quit."

"You're a regular do-gooder," Scrap-Iron said. "Aren't you?"

"It's not right," Stewart said. "It's not fair."

"And you think life's supposed to be fair?" Scrap-Iron asked.

Scrap-Iron turned to his boys. "Our new man here," he said, "thinks life's supposed to be right and fair." He turned back to Stewart. "You think they all think life's fair?"

Stewart didn't answer.

"Okay, Slinkaroo," Scrap-Iron said. "You're done. You did a good job, too. Now come here."

When Slinky made his way up and limped to Scrap-Iron's side, the big man leaned forward in his chair and gave his pathetic boy a gentle bear hug.

"You," Scrap-Iron said to Stewart, "don't have to play. It's a silly game anyway. I've got another game for you. You'll play that one on Sunday. And it ain't so silly."

13

On Saturday, the boss started him out at the greeter's position. Saturday meant the usual weekend rush and the familiar circle of gratuitous greetings and hollow responses. Maybe that was good. Maybe he'd be too busy to obsess on what was coming tomorrow.

The psychologist had suggested that he observe other people's flaws. She meant it as a form of therapy. If he saw the many imperfections in other people, he might be less critical of his own shortcomings, and he might better understand that imperfections were a part of being human. A necessary step, she said, as they worked on his low self-esteem. That advice didn't work as intended. Instead, it further fueled his chronic criticism of others, always worse when he was angry or scared.

There were flaws aplenty to observe, among his associates and the customers. *Ripley's Believe It or Not* could have recruited from the greeter's post. It was a ringside seat to an unending variety of *lusus naturae*: the attention-starved with their trashy tattoos, bizarrely colored hair and licentious dress; the shameless with their curlers, unshaved faces, and filthy T-shirts; the clueless and happy, who smiled their way through all this decline. He wondered: How did all of them live with their great imperfections? Even a greater wonder, some seemed to celebrate their imperfections.

***

Right after lunch, he greeted a familial group of boors. The father wore three or four day's growth of beard that crept down his neck like a lawn fungus. His pants were fastened by his belt because the button and buttonhole would never meet again. His navy-blue Yankees hat was a pitiful attempt to be part of something more successful than himself. The mother's face and figure sagged. Probably not ten years out of high school, her expression and posture showed total surrender to what Thoreau called a life of quiet desperation.

"Welcome to your hometown store," Stewart said. Technically, he was supposed to add: "where you get more for less and support your community." But only the new greeters did that and only for a day or two. It was too much of a mouthful.

The father gave a resigned nod. The three kids, a boy and two girls, were whining, and why not? Their parents were a simulacrum of things to come. As pitiful as the father's existence might be, Stewart fought a twinge of jealousy, for a life that had a woman to confide in and nest with at night, for kids to tag dreams to however improbable, for a life with moorings. For a life of at least *quiet* desperation.

Mostly, there were the unimaginative customers who responded to his insincere greeting with their equally insincere, "How you doing?" As if they cared. He didn't know which was worse, the slingers of false solicitousness or the ones with the hard look that said: "Don't bother me you piece of shit that if I stepped on I would be quick to scrape off the bottom of my shoe."

His worst times were when someone he knew from his former life came in the store. Then his shame went on display like the latest sale item. When he saw the shock of recognition in a familiar face, disgrace ran down his spine like a cold shudder. He could read their thoughts, how he, a man previously of their station or above, had been relegated to this. Most times, out of embarrassment, they pretended not to recognize him. Maybe his situation petrified them, sparking the thought that such a thing could happen to anyone. Maybe that's why they quickly diverted their eyes, the way people do from the grotesque. More likely, they assumed he had some great inherent flaw in his character that led him to this. He knew some must believe that because he did himself. To avoid further embarrassment, he would often run for the men's room or take a break, if he had one coming, sometimes even if he didn't. Those sudden disappearances had led to many of the boss's persecutions.

If he could, he would have avoided not just the boss and customers and associates, but every human being on the planet. The big tomcat that visited his tent would have been society enough. After a week of advance and retreat, he and the cat were friends now. A can of Grilled Chicken and Liver Feast in Gravy had sealed the fellowship. Now they appreciated each other. He could ill afford the cat food; it added up to twenty dollars a month, but like him the cat was alone against the world, alert to its bad intentions and doing what he had to do to survive. When you met a true kindred spirit in this upside-down existence, you stuck together. When he knelt to clean the gunk out of the corner of the big tom's eyes, and the appreciative cat raised his chin in a display of trust, it was more than worth the expense. It was one of those rare moments he could bank and draw upon when most needed.

Standing in one place hurt his back and wore him out more than opening boxes and stocking shelves or walking a department's aisles and assisting customers. Because he wandered too much, even though it was for the legitimate purpose of helping people, his boss insisted he stay in the greeter's designated spot. With some duct tape, the boss had outlined a box on the floor to mark his boundaries. It was a confining rectangle, about the size of a large pizza box. The boss enjoyed torturing him. If the rules allowed it, the boss would have Krazy Glued his feet to the floor.

The boss couldn't stomach having a subordinate who was his better. He had surely snooped through the personnel records, and when he learned of his lowly greeter's education and work background, he probably spread word of it in its most humiliating, how the mighty have fallen, interpretation. That's why his fellow workers addressed him as *professor*. He hated it when they did that; he knew their intent was to humiliate him.

What must have really pissed the boss off was his lowly greeter's salary history. In his best years, Stewart had earned triple what his current boss made. That alone was enough to make him the whipping boy who got blamed for everything. He hadn't put the podium in the aisle. The evening shift's greeter, the man everyone called Alzheimer's Al, had done it. But try explaining anything to a reactionary screamer. Stewart didn't betray Al to the boss because he felt sorry for him. One night, to test his affliction, Al's fellow associates decided not to remind him of his quitting time. The poor, addled bastard worked two consecutive shifts. Those were the kind of people he was working with. All of them, the boss and the associates, could go straight to hell.

The boss was all crudity and knew nothing about managing people. The personal attacks–his shirt collar was frayed or his hair wasn't combed or his pants were spotted–shamed Stewart the most and had the longest half-life. If his appearance wasn't what it should be, it was because of his circumstances. He fought a life and death struggle every day, while the boss's biggest worry was a hair out of place on a greeter who greeted the slovenliest people in America.

So, how would the psychologist suggest he divert his mind from all this? Maybe she'd offer the same idiotic advice, that he take a break and bounce a tennis ball against a wall. He could get a tennis ball in sporting goods and bounce it up against the Customer Service Station. How would his boss like that?

He had formulated something better, his own diversion, a favorite mind game to play while greeting. He imagined himself an automaton programmed for the sole function of recognizing approaching hominids and then spitting out a single line of code: "Welcome to your hometown store." He even made his voice robotic, putting an affected stress on each chopped syllable. If, on rare occasions, he got the impression his targets knew what he was up to, that was okay. If they were perceptive enough to sense that, they were perceptive enough to know that it was what his situation called for–a stubborn refusal to surrender any part of his human essence to the place or the anthropoid assholes it forced him to associate with.

When it got slow, still stuck in his duct-taped space like a dog hemmed in by an invisible fence, he thought about something Slinky had told him–how Scrap-Iron was always organizing group activities–how he gathered them all on clear nights and turned out the yard light and pointed out the stars and named the constellations; how he had an ant farm and lectured the boys on insect social intelligence; how he made the inner workings of an internal combustion engine seem a thing of beauty. Was that how Scrap-Iron saw him, a science project for his and the boys' amusement? If that was it, he wasn't going to cooperate. He wasn't an ant.

14

The boys were about to enjoy a fire, and Slinky decided to join them.

It was five o'clock, but the daylight hours were already starting to shrink and the camp was in shade. Toad and Herc sat along the ground, facing the fire pit, their backs to an old railroad crosstie set there as a permanent backrest. With their legs extended and feet crossed, the duo looked a picture of careless comfort. The Bandito was busy preparing the fire.

"Hi," Slinky said. "You guys look comfortable."

Herc and Toad gave him a halfhearted nod.

Slinky's objective wasn't comfort or camaraderie. He wanted to learn more about tomorrow's meeting and what Scrap-Iron had planned for Stewart. A campfire always got the boys talking, especially when the beer flowed.

"Sit," The Bandito ordered, with a roughhewn neighborliness. A fire always lifted The Bandito's spirits.

"Nice night," Slinky said.

It was. The worst of the heat had broken, and a gentle breeze weaved its way through the woods. It was a perfect night for sitting by a fire. The promise of a big bonus was there, too; the implements of a cookout stood by on a piece of blue tarp: two cast-iron frying pans, a large cooking fork and a spatula; a big black pot with a wooden spoon in it; and three cans of Boston Baked Beans next to it.

Cookouts were a sporadic event in Scrapville, dependent on the slippery confluence of the right night, spare cash, and aligned convivial spirits. The compensation of being rootless was that social obligations never interfered.

"Hope you're hungry," The Bandito asked.

"I could eat," Slinky said. He sat with his back against the railroad tie, at the end closest to The Bandito.

"I got something special," The Bandito said. He reached his leg behind him and with his bootheel kicked open the top of a red cooler. Inside, on ice, was a plastic-wrapped package of pork chops.

"Wow," Slinky said.

"We need beer," Toad said.

In the woods, nothing was free, and Toad wasn't famous for his subtlety. After pooling their funds and buying the pork chops and beans, the boys were tapped out. Slinky would have to spring for the beer, even though he didn't drink. Not such a bad deal, some beer for a pork chop meal and important information.

"I'll buy," Slinky said, "if you go get it."

"I'm tired," Toad said.

"Tired," Herc said. "What could you be tired from? Jerking off too much?"

"I'm just tired," Toad repeated. "Slinky can go."

"Slink's buying," Herc said. "So you're flying. Now get your lazy ass moving."

"Two six-packs?" Toad asked. He smiled with expectation, a yellow-toothed smile directed toward Herc, not Slinky.

Herc looked to Slinky.

Slinky nodded, reached into his pocket and handed Toad a twenty-dollar bill, fresh from its mason jar hiding place.

"You make sure," Herc said to Toad, "you bring him back his change."

Slinky nodded to that. It was eighteen days until his next check.

Toad headed out of camp, a little bounce in his step at the thought of the two six-packs. Slinky didn't drink, and Herc would stop at two. That meant plenty for him and The Bandito. As he approached the path at the edge of the woods, The Bandito yelled after him, "Get real beer. Not that piss-water."

He meant no light beer.

***

The Bandito knew how to make a fire. He started with a tinder pile of dried leaves and small sticks, and then stacked kindling around that. He shaped the kindling with care, the biggest pieces on the bottom and the smallest on top, so the fire would burn a long time.

He lit the fire with a long wooden fireplace match, scratching it to life against the sole of his boot and holding it to the edge of the tinder, using his body to shield it from the breeze. A flame sputtered, and he nursed it to life by leaning closer and blowing on it. When the fire erupted, he turned to Slinky and gave him a wink. Then he turned his attention to setting up his cooking space. Over the right edge of the fire, he positioned an iron tripod. On that he'd hang the pot of beans. Over the rest of the fire, he situated two grills, each with long metal legs that he stuck into the ground. He set one of his two big cast-iron frying pans on each grill, upside down, for a cleansing by fire. A large skewer fork was for managing the meat; a freshly snapped sprig, sufficiently green to prevent its combusting, was for poking and stirring the fire and arranging and rearranging its glowing embers to control the temperature.

***

The fire was going well, still at the too high for cooking stage, when Toad returned. He had two six-packs of Budweiser. He carried them by their plastic loops. Under his arm he had a giant-sized bag of potato chips.

"Who told you to get chips?" Herc asked.

"I wanted 'em," Toad said.

"I want to fuck Jennifer Lopez," The Bandito said. "That don't mean I get to."

"He's got no self-control," Herc said. "That's his problem."

Despite his circumstances, Herc was a convert to a healthy lifestyle. He took a dizzying array of vitamins and limited his beer drinking to two or three a night, which he considered abstinence. Once in a while he slipped off the wagon, but even then he didn't drink like the good old days. There was the time when he and a girlfriend had gone to a vintage drive-in movie and instead of buying a six-pack he bought a case of beer, figuring to take the rest back home for during the week. That was when a case of beer still came packaged in a real cardboard case with twenty-four bottles. His girlfriend didn't drink, but at some point during the second attraction Herc reached back and kept getting nothing but empties. He had drunk the whole case, twenty-four bottles, at that single sitting and before the double-feature ended.

"Toad-Man," Herc said, "I thought I told you to always get a bag. People see a freak like you carrying that beer back here, and they think the worst. We don't need that shit. Like Scrap says, we got appearances to keep up."

Toad just smiled bewilderedly until Slinky held out his hand for his change. Reluctantly, Toad fished the money from his jeans' pocket.

The Bandito got the fire settled to his liking–the flame low, the wood glowing red. With the flourish of a maestro, he arranged two and a half chops in each frying pan. He had a talent for hobo cooking. "It's all in the seasonings," he often said. He was also meticulous about picking the best meat. In the manner of poor people enjoying temporary economic power, he made the Foodtown butcher work for his business. In their first dealing, the butcher had tried to slough off his worst chickens on The Bandito, figuring him for a man of little funds and less discernment. The Bandito told the butcher that his birds had about as much meat on them as Scrapville's mosquitoes.

Herc and Toad got busy insulting each. Toad, as usual, was getting the worst of it. Slinky slid closer to The Bandito.

"What's Scrap got planned for us tomorrow?" Slinky asked. "Anything special?"

The Bandito was the one to ask. Each member of Scrapville brought his own strengths. Scrap-Iron planned it that way. When needed, Herc was additional muscle. Slinky brought reliability and a rare dose of common sense–told once to do something he seldom failed and never for a lack of trying. Toad was a *piñata* for abuse verbal and physical and for needed comic relief. When it came to depravity, The Bandito was the closest thing Scrap-Iron had to a protégé.

"We're gonna have some fun," The Bandito said, never taking his eyes off his cooking. "It's gonna be something different."

"Sounds interesting," Slinky said, and waited for more.

The Bandito spooned a little bubbling grease over the chops.

"We could use a little fun," Slinky said.

"For sure," The Bandito said.

"As long as it don't involve me," Slinky said, with a forced laugh. He rubbed his hip and pulled the waist of his jeans down far enough to show the Bandito the result of the Twister game. He bruised easily, and his hip was black-and-blue turning to purple. It still ached.

"Don't worry; it ain't about you," The Bandito said. "It's on the new guy. The big shot college man."

"Oh?"

"Yeah. Where'd you find that dude anyways? In the library's shithouse?"

"No," Slinky said. "Where he works over at the store. He's okay though. He's not a bad guy once you get to know him. He just a little, you know, shy."

"Well, come tomorrow morning," The Bandito said, with jumping eyebrows, "we're gonna get to know him a lot better, shy or not."

"What's that mean?" Slinky asked. He wanted details.

The Bandito tried to change the subject to cast-iron frying pans, how they needed to be kept well-greased and hot.

"How we gonna get to know him better?" Slinky asked.

"Scrap's working on it," The Bandito said. "Big time. He says we're gonna get to see a real show. Triple X-rated."

"What kind of show is that?" Slinky asked.

"You just got to wait," The Bandito said. "I can tell you this much though. It's gonna be good."

15

Quitting time offered Stewart a real diversion. He punched out and headed toward Burger-Land. He might find sanctuary there, in the quiet corner farthest from the lobby and the front doors.

The mall was busy. In the parking lot, cars circled, jockeying for the closest free space, their drivers determined to avoid any exercise. The red and white impatiens, planted in front of the buildings by cut-rate landscapers, were too sparse and too dry. They looked half-dead. Their droopy countenances reminded Stewart of the store's overnight crew.

He made sure to miss the sidewalk's every seam. With the proper attention, his stride fit just right, two comfortable steps inside each square. If he touched a seam, who knew what catastrophe would befall him. Given his recent misfortunes, the absurdity in his crack and seam avoiding ritual was not lost on him, but then again, if he hadn't been so careful, who knew what other tragedies might have befallen him? Worse calamities were always lurking. It wasn't the absurdity of his compulsions that bothered him most. What bothered him most was that his compulsions were so commonplace.

A light breeze carried a stench from the nearby water treatment plant. It smelled like the compost heaps of his former neighbors, the environmentally sophisticated couple. The county put the sewage plant here because this was the part of town for that kind of thing, for unwanted infrastructure and junkyards and déclassé department stores. For unwanted people too.

He passed the Kentucky Fried Chicken store where a life-sized cardboard cutout of the Colonel stood. The goateed dandy sported his own permanent greeter's smile, but then he had a lot to smile about, or at least his wealthy descendants did.

Stewart didn't have to worry about descendants. He wouldn't have any. His wife had wanted children but agreed to wait until he declared them financially prepared. The plan was she would take a leave of absence once they had a respectable nest egg. They were both good that way, he contributing to his 401(k), she to her 403(b). But the responsibility of children scared him. Children were a sacred commitment. How could he relieve his anxieties with dreams of running away if he had children? He still got pangs of guilt about causing his wife that pain–that she might think herself incomplete because of him. And he still got pangs of guilt for using his half of their nest egg to fund his wandering.

KFC's assistant-manager had made Stewart an offer, five dollars an hour, tax-free cash under the table, to stand at a busy intersection during the evening rush hour wearing a sandwich board advertising daily deals. The manager made the offer because Stewart was the most presentable among the dispossessed mall-crawlers. Stewart turned him down; he wasn't that desperate yet.

He passed the dollar store. When flush again, he would stop there and provision. What did he need?

Paper towels, hand sanitizer, tissues, AA and AAA batteries, candles, matches, Ziploc bags, garbage bags, deodorant, toilet paper, Band-Aids, toothpaste, antibacterial ointment, shampoo, soap, wet wipes, hard candy.

He liked the bargains at the dollar-store, but the narrow and overstuffed aisles gave him claustrophobia, and the Pakistani guy who owned the store kept a suspicious eye on him for as long as he was in the place. In one of his crazy dreams, he had given the owner's turban a yank and made him spin like a kid's whirly top. He must have gotten that idea from the long-haired, smart-mouthed teens who hung at the strip mall and rode their skateboards along the walkway in violation of all the rules. *Pull-start.* That's what the skateboarders called the dollar-store owner.

A pickup truck, raised preposterously high in the air, rumbled by. The truck's exhaust was purposefully loud, and its stereo system blared so that the curbside garbage cans shook. The truck bore a license plate that said it all–*A2TUDE*. He was surrounded by barbarians.

He thought how his father would react to the kid and his truck. He'd have used it as a lesson for his boy. "The manufacturer," his father would have said, "has got the best engineers in the world designing their trucks. Guys with world-class educations and world-class experience and world-class tools and support. Now that kid, probably earning minimum wage pumping gas somewhere, thinks he can improve on what they did."

What would his father say now, if he were alive and could see his son? At work or in Burger-Land, Stewart took particular note of loving parents, those who showered affection and positive reinforcement on their children. With each loving hair muss, kiss on the cheek, or word of praise, his heart ached a little.

It was time to divert himself again, and he contemplated lunch. Maybe he'd buy a kid's meal. He did that sometimes, mostly to get the toy that he would save to hand out to whichever kid he thought needed it the most. He alternated between the boy and girl toy. He liked seeing little boys and girls smile. Sometimes parents refused his offer of a toy, as if it might be contaminated with whatever afflicted him. But on the days when he handed out a toy and got a smile in return, he would try and make that his last conscious thought before sleep–the image of some kid smiling for the gift of a simple toy.

Just as he started to turn for Burger-Land's entrance, two bodies flew past him, one on each side, so close the violent air swooshes rocked him.

"Move it, ass-wipe."

That command came from the two skateboarders who had nearly run him over. It was his own doing. He had conjured the boys.

"You watch out," he yelled, to the backs of the sleeveless T-shirts. It came out high-pitched and weak, and as soon as he said it he felt more impotent.

One of the kids, the one with the stringy blonde hair to his shoulders, turned and while still riding his board, as if it were a maneuver he practiced regularly, squatted, grabbed his crotch, and laughed. That, along with the week's cumulative humiliations and the realization that he could have been badly hurt flipped the switch in Stewart that toggled between resignation and rage. People regularly complained to the mall's security officer about the skateboarders, but he did nothing because one of the kids was the son of a state trooper. Injustice like that infuriated Stewart, fury that could burn for hours, as if his insides were an airtight stove.

The kids, with the dexterity of youth and endless practice, stepped on the back edge of their boards and flipped them up and into their hands. There they stood, scruffy rebels, pleased with themselves and making sure Stewart understood they weren't afraid of him.

Scrap-Iron wouldn't need to keep a wary eye for skateboarders. They would keep an eye out for him. Why wouldn't they mess with Scrap-Iron? Because he would fuck 'em up. It was as crude and as simple as that. Predators had an instinctual respect and fear of stronger predators.

Two boys had challenged his manhood. He knew they would follow him into Burger-Land to continue their fun. What would he do about it? He reversed course and headed for safety of the woods.

16

As soon as he descended from the railroad tracks and started on the path to camp, Stewart smelled the tempting mix of wood smoke and broiling meat. A primal smell. When he was close enough to hear the grease's sizzle, it was enough to divert him from his usual furtive route and toward the center of camp. He knew he wouldn't be welcome, but his hunger propelled him.

When he approached, the boys looked up in surprise. The Bandito squatted over the big frying pans. His face glowed with sweat. With the big fork in his right hand and the poking and stirring stick in his left, he looked like a jazz drummer lost in his craft.

"Hi," Stewart said.

He wondered if everyone heard what he heard in his greeting—insincerity and opportunism. There was a great gulf between him and the others. He knew that they felt that he felt that he was better. And they were right. He did feel he was better. But not in so many ways as before. There were things to learn from adversity and people who dealt with it.

"You wanna sit?" Slinky asked.

Stewart didn't answer, and he didn't sit. He doubted Slink's authority to offer such an invitation.

"Take a load off," The Bandito said.

That was authoritative enough, and Stewart took the space Slinky had made for him.

"Now that we got pork chops, we're good enough for him," Toad said.

"Shut up," The Bandito said. "You hungry?" he asked Stewart.

"A little," Stewart said. He had become practiced in falsehood and understatement.

"You timed it good," The Bandito said, as he flipped the chops. "The meat's almost ready."

The Bandito saw in Stewart the welcome opportunity to show off his cooking skills on someone other than his unappreciative regulars, maybe even someone with a little taste. An artist needs admirers.

"Yeah," Toad said. "You got good timing."

"They smell good," Stewart said.

A light brown tinge had spread over the pork chops. Stewart's mouth watered.

"How long you been here?" The Bandito asked Stewart. "In the woods?"

"It's almost three weeks."

"That's it then," The Bandito said. "Your three-week anniversary. That's what we're celebrating."

In Scrapville, it didn't take much of an excuse for a celebration. The boys once partied all night to observe the installation of solar panels at the water treatment plant. That's when Herc talked about stealing a panel or two from the plant's array and using them to electrify Scrapville. Scrap-Iron nixed that idea. A pack of homeless guys living in the woods next to the plant and suddenly enjoying the benefits of sun power was too much of a clue, even for the local police.

Low hissing sounds came from the pork chops, punctuated by little grease explosions. The Bandito stirred the fire, and sparks flew and landed on his arm. In imitation of his leader, he ignored them, just as Scrap-Iron did when sparks flew from his welding torch.

Stewart counted four full chops cooking along with two halves. That made five in all. Were they planning on a guest? They surely weren't waiting for him. Could he be about to eat the chop meant for Scrap-Iron?

The Bandito licked the big fork. He closed his eyes and looked to the sky, concentrating, savoring. "You got to sear 'em just right," he said. "To keep the juices in."

Stewart was shamefully hungry. All he'd had today was a coffee for breakfast and four of Burger-Land's dry and stringy chicken squares and a diet soda for lunch. $2.36, recorded in his little black notebook. He coveted a thick, juicy pork chop, and this place, of all places, was the only place in the whole round world where he could get one.

The Bandito cut into two of the chops and inspected them for color and juiciness. Satisfied, he was moved to a brief but explicit lesson on the mistakes of overcooking and drying out meat. "It's like a broad," he said. "Dry ain't as good as moist."

***

When The Bandito declared the chops ready, Slinky moved to his knees, and, from an old KFC carton, passed out plastic forks and knives. Then he dispensed doubled paper plates and paper towels. All the appurtenances from the Dollar Store.

No *bon appétit*. Instead, The Bandito said, "Okay you hungry homos, hold out your plates."

Plates were held out and enthusiastically. Toad's too enthusiastically. He pushed forward and shunted Slinky's and Herc's plates aside. "Ass-wipe," Herc said. "Have a little class."

Each received a speared pork chop. Stewart thought his was the thickest. Slinky got one of the halves. He wasn't a big eater. The Bandito took the wooden spoon from the bean pot. He gave it a long lick, put it back in the pot, and stirred its bubbling contents one last time. He ladled out two great spoonfuls to each guest. He took obvious joy in his work.

"Goddamn," Herc said, to a still over-stimulated Toad. "Stop kicking around, or it'll be dirt and beans instead of pork and beans."

The food distributed, the conversation suddenly ceased, and a singular focus and lack of pretension ruled. Paper plates sagged into laps, pork chops were gripped with two hands for ready eating, and beans were spooned with maximum efficiency and minimum delicacy. Soon Stewart felt the best he had in a long time. Appetite, and its satisfaction, was a great diverting force. Much better than bouncing a tennis ball against a wall.

***

The meal done and the grills removed, the fire consumed the plates and paper towels. Compliments all around for The Bandito's cooking. Stewart made sure to join in the chorus, his praise sincere, heartfelt, and stomach felt. Toad still worked on his pork chop, making loud cracking and sucking sounds, like a dog trying to get the last bit of flavor out of a bone.

Slinky distributed a new round of beer. Stewart took a can for conviviality and appearances. Properly banked, the fire transformed from utilitarian to ceremonial, and it was time for storytelling. Not the story form Stewart had spent so much time and effort to learn but still tales colorful and informative.

17

"Toad," The Bandito said, "you remember the time we let you cook?"

Toad didn't remember or chose not to.

"I remember," Herc said. "How could I forget? I had the running shits for two days."

"Did not!" Toad said.

"Let me tell you," Herc said, "I was shitting through the eye of a needle without touching the sides." He rubbed his stomach at the memory of it.

Toad looked to The Bandito. "Why don't you tell us about your three crazy wives?" he asked.

"Good one, Toad!" Herc said.

"To start with," The Bandito said, "it ain't really three. The last one was just business."

The Bandito's third marriage was to a foreigner, a Russian woman. It was some kind of an immigration scam, and he pocketed an easy two thousand for his trouble. To The Bandito's disappointment, the marriage deal didn't include consummation. The woman was determined to stay in America but not that determined. Nor was the marriage ever formally ended. Technically, The Bandito was still married.

"How's about the first two then?" Toad asked. "Them count."

Toad had learned that the best way to avoid Scrapville's mockery was to play offense, not defense. Keep the focus on someone else.

"They didn't work out," The Bandito said. "So what? I was a trucker. That makes it tough. Ask anybody."

That was true. During The Bandito's first two marriages, he had been an over-the-road trucker and that was not the profession to encourage fidelity. Especially for The Bandito–there was something about truck stop whores in tight shorts and cutoff T-shirts that he couldn't resist. He used to carry a supply of meth with him to trade for sexual favors. He didn't have charm or good looks or loads of money, but the meth was more effective than all three. After his third treatment for venereal disease, his first wife divorced him. Three strikes, she said, and you're out. She was smart, and she handled all the divorce paperwork herself.

The Bandito ended his second marriage himself and as the aggrieved party. That was the story Toad wanted repeated.

"That bitch was crazy," The Bandito said. "I come home one night, all road tired and shit, working my ass off for her, and there she is, coming down the street on the handlebars of my neighbor's Harley, her dress blowing up in her face and nothing on underneath. They was riding all over town like that, just for kicks. That shit's messed up, man. I got even though. Before I left, I put a gallon of bleach in the Harley's gas tank."

Stewart doubted everything the boys said, but who could or would make up a story like that?

Herc was the claimant of a normal home life. A high school diploma earned, even if mostly shop classes. His old man a bit of an asshole but no more than ordinary and not violent. His mother a saint who no one ever said a bad word about. His mother was full of love and worry and still sick with disappointment over him. He had to call his mother one of these days. His problems all from an early love of drink and hatred of authority. At fourteen, he was already drinking heavily. He had done some jail time but for nothing serious. His last arrest was his first in a long while, and he was stone sober for it. He told that story.

"I was minding my own business. This cop from town, one of the muscled-up steroid boys, messed with me. He says that with my attitude I was due for a beat down. We were in front of the Dunkin' Donuts. So right in front of the chicks that always hang there, I says to the cop, "Man, you couldn't beat my dick if I gave you a baseball bat." The girls all laughed. The ball-less bastard of a cop called for reinforcements."

For his smart mouth, Herc got his choice of a five-hundred-dollar fine or a ninety-day jail stint. It might as well have been a million dollars. Scrap talked to the cop, and after the cop talked to the judge, the fine got reduced to two hundred, for court costs. Scrap paid it and added it to Herc's account. Herc had to tell the cop he was sorry. He crossed his fingers when he said it.

Toad was anxious to talk. He waited for Herc to finish only for the fear of a slap.

"My old man," Toad said. "There's a prick that needs a beat down."

"Toad-boy," The Bandito said, "I hope you ain't gonna show us your ass again."

Toad did. But first he told again how his father was handy with a homemade cat-o-nine tails–nine heavy leather strips knotted on the ends and secured with heavy-duty staples into the end of an old broom handle. Toad still had the scars to prove the story. The boys were always accusing him of making stuff up, so the scars were once again displayed. The sight of Toad's uncovered and scarred backside, so soon after dinner, met with screams of, "No more. We believe you. We believe you!"

Slinky was a reluctant talker. Not that he didn't have a lot to talk about, having had a dozen different foster families, enough to produce a normal distribution of treatment from good to unmentionable. The boys were most interested in his deformities, especially their impact on his sex life and what imaginative positions his condition mandated. Slinky was good at answering but not answering. One surprise, he was quite a swimmer. In high school, the gym teacher gathered two classes together so he could demonstrate his form from the diving board. Some embarrassment at the time, the gym teacher going on about his courage and all, but a spark of pride in Slink's eyes when he retold it.

When everyone's eyes turned to Stewart, he hesitated. He was never a happy kid, but what could he tell them of his life that wouldn't sound like weak whining? Instead he told his screwed by the system, victim of heartless corporate downsizing tale—the unfairness of the system a theme the boys readily accepted.

***

Inevitably, the stories turned to Scrap-Iron, everybody but Stewart with ready material. The tone one of hero worship. Some of the tales first-hand, some hearsay garnered from long time junkyard customers and Scrap-Iron folklorists. Some direct from the big man himself.

The Bandito had known Scrap-Iron the longest and had the deepest reservoir of stories. Like the one about how, when times were hard, Scrap became a bus driver. Scrap could drive anything with wheels—trucks of any size, cranes, bulldozers, front-loaders. Everyone but Stewart had heard the bus driver story, but everyone wanted to hear it again. How some of the passengers loved Scrap, they even called into the main office to praise his extraordinary level of service, but some hated him and complained about missed schedules. Such a divergence of opinion made the bus company curious. They put a spotter on the bus. Turned out that for his favorite customers, usually the young ladies, Scrap would take the bus off its route, even down narrow side streets, and deliver them right to their front door. He did this with total disregard for schedule, bus company policy, or traffic laws.

Then there was how Scrap stole from all his employers, the bus company no exception. He'd take every third fare and declare loudly and proudly, "That one's for me." He'd make sure the whole bus was watching before putting the coins in his pocket. Some riders loved it, undoubtedly wishing they could do the same to their employer. The company didn't love it, and after their spotter's report, they fired Scrap. Another job lost, but do you think Scrap gave two shits? No. He always preached to never get dependent on any job:

"Always have options. Don't let them get their hooks in you." The minute Scrap felt himself getting dependent on a job, he'd up and quit—unless there was a final opportunity for some fun, say the chance to sabotage things.

Like the time he worked in the auto plant. Wasn't it at Ford? Anyhow, it was on the assembly line. Scrap started a carpool, driving three other guys back and forth every day in his old Chevy. He made his riders pay but would only accept items they stole from the plant. There was a lot of stuff in an auto plant that could be used around his own shop. One day, he eyeballed a valve used on the door assembly line. The valve attached to a pneumatic paint gun that shot deadener inside the doors, tar-like stuff, to take the tinny sound away when a door closed and give it a more solid, quality-like sound. Scrap wanted the valve to use for his own heavy-duty paint gun. He assigned the job to one of his riders, a big Polish guy named Walter, who quickly stole the valve for him. That was good for a month of rides. Unexpected consequences though. The foreman couldn't shut the assembly line down; it would be a disaster at that busy time of year, so he had to continue to run it and stack the unfinished doors along the plant's walls for later retrofitting. Scrap saw how much chaos and confusion that caused and was so pleased that a couple weeks later, just for fun, he had Walter steal the replacement valve. Scrap liked nothing more than causing chaos and confusion. He always said confusion was a saboteur's best friend.

More drink and freer tongues and meaner stories. The one about the lady who asked a teenaged Scrap-Iron to feed her horse while she was away on vacation.

The lady loved the horse, and the horse loved her. Whenever she fed the horse a treat, she would call him her baby boy and follow-up with a big, wet kiss on his nose. Scrap altered that routine. After every treat, he bit the horse on its nose. When the lady returned and tried to kiss her four-hoofed baby boy, he bit a piece of her lower lip off.

More drink and cruder stories. The time Scrap was working out-of-town on a big welding job in Oil City, Pennsylvania. The company put him up in a tiny room that shared a bathroom with two other rooms on the same floor. Soap and toilet paper were the shared responsibility of all three tenants. Scrap bought his share, but the others didn't. Stuck without toilet paper once too often, he decided to teach a lesson. He wiped his ass on the bathroom's lacy white curtains. Scrap said he had no more problems after that; there was always a roll and a spare.

Yep, that's Scrap!

***

Stewart stayed later than he had planned. Against all expectations, he enjoyed the camaraderie as well as the food. He was starved for fellowship, and even flawed fellowship was better than none at all.

Leaving a group was always difficult for him. Something about getting up and walking away from people made him very uneasy. But he was tired, and the half can of beer he had drunk wasn't sitting well.

"I'm sorry," he said. "I have to go. I'm a little tired."

"Okay," The Bandito said. "You're fed good though, right?"

"It was very good," Stewart said. "Thank-you again."

"Now," The Bandito said, "you get your rest. Tomorrow, you're gonna need it."

18

Back in his tent, Stewart felt dizzy. He kept his light off and found his aspirin and melatonin by touch. He took three chalky, generic aspirins and two melatonin capsules. He needed sleep.

The more trouble he had with sleep, the more he valued it. Perhaps because it was the closest thing to a total and permanent loss of consciousness, the closest thing to death, that state that Shakespeare described as: *The undiscovered country from whose bourn no traveler returns.* At his lowest moments, he had thought of suicide. He doubted his own seriousness but was at least thankful for the option. As Nietzsche said: *The thought of suicide is a great consolation: by means of it one gets through many a dark night.*

On top of his sleeping bag, even in the tent's contained heat, he felt chilled. He curled up in the insulated bag but didn't zip it.

Scrap-Iron had something bad planned for him tomorrow. That was clear from the way The Bandito spoke of it with a sick anticipation. Scrap-Iron probably wanted to explore further the nitty-gritty details of his new boy's decline and fall. The big man had lit up with the discussion of Stewart's failed marriage, and this time he would do it in front of everyone. It went further than ordinary schadenfreude. For some reason, Scrap-Iron needed to degrade him. How messed up was that?

He thought again about writing a letter to his wife. He had contemplated such a letter before, even going so far as to buy some stationary at the dollar store. But he had never put pen to paper. Now he occupied his mind by imagining what he would say to her.

He would be gracious. He always was. He would take the blame for what had happened. He always did. But was anyone ever one-hundred percent responsible for the crazy doings between two people?

There would be a section about what a good wife she was. He would touch on their mutual successes—their educations and career advancements and buying the house, and how they had supported each other through it all. He would reminisce about the long hours both had worked to make their mark in their vocations. His wife was an English teacher and a great one. He would recall the many nights they spent at their kitchen table, drinking coffee to stay awake and studying to add to their credentials and advance themselves.

He would remind her of their first apartment, a second-story flat with windows that let the cold air blow through until the curtains stood out like they were flags in a windstorm. That was the apartment above a lawyer's office with only a bathtub and no working shower, and that meant they couldn't invite her mother to stay overnight because her mother wouldn't take a bath, only a shower. That was the apartment with the first-floor burglar alarm that went off at the slightest provocation and usually in the middle of the night so that he had to go down and reset it while carrying a miniature baseball bat because you never knew if this time a burglar really was in the house, and he would give his life rather than have any harm come to his wife.

He would mention the Volkswagen, their beetle that never heated properly in winter and toward the end had a hole in the floorboard that water splashed through every time they went through a big puddle. When he drove her to her night classes in the middle of February, he had to keep one hand free to wipe the frost off the inside of the windshield. He thought of that and laughed out loud, lying there in his miserable sleeping bag in his miserable tent while for just a moment the warmth of reminiscence was some anesthetic to his pain.

He would have to address the bad things. His slide into depression and then his leaving. Why he couldn't talk to her about his problems. Why he didn't trust her to be his confidant and healer. He'd tell her he couldn't puncture the seal on his emotions for fear that it would release all his anger. Where did his anger come from? She should know that none of it was directed toward her. It was important that she know that.

Who was his anger directed toward? The psychologist had told him to examine that question. What Stewart decided was that a lot of people handled a lot of things that were worse than he had experienced and without all his anger and problems. Maybe he was just weak.

The last two years had surely been hard on his wife. He would acknowledge that. It wasn't fair, and he wasn't proud of it. How had she told her mother? How had she explained to her friends? His main mistake was that he had never taken the time to explain things to her. Did he just lack the courage? He should have explained to her what it was like to live every day with fear in your heart, a haunting fear that you would be proven a failure. If he could have told her that, today he might be a different man living in a different world.

Back then, he had to protect himself. Every being has the right to protect itself from its vulnerabilities. He had to quit rather than expose himself. Self-survival was a primal instinct, after all. He'd done what had to be done. Truth was, the thing he feared most was exposing his true self to her. She had always thought of him as intelligent, resourceful, honest, and strong. She thought way too much of him. How could he have told her that she was wrong about him? He ended up showing her. Ultimately, she saw his weakness, but if he had stayed longer, she would have had an up close view of the pitiful human being that he really was. He had to save her from that.

He would make sure to tell her that he knew that she could take care of herself. He wouldn't have left if he wasn't confident of that. Before they married, she had told him she never would commit to marriage if she didn't have her own independent income. She was the strong and resourceful one. Would she have wanted him hanging around, living off her, shrinking before her very eyes? He wanted to spare her that. He could tell her all that and not be dishonest.

What did he think he was in for when he left? She would want to know that. That had to perplex her. What he thought was that he would be on an interesting journey where he would discover just who he was and things would work out because things always did. It was as simple and naïve and stupid as that. He thought his life would magically adjust to some form that fit him just right. He never thought he would replace her.

She needed to know that. He still loved her and always would. He hadn't so much as thought of another woman since he'd left. He hoped she hadn't suffered too much. He hoped she wasn't lonely.

Would she want to hear his story of devolution and degradation? Would that make her feel better? No. She wasn't that kind of person. Did he want her sympathy? Would it be sympathy or pity? He tried imagining he was next to his wife, cuddled to her, as they used to do on cold nights. Did she now cuddle with someone else? Maybe. Who could blame her if she did? He wouldn't think about that.

He imagined her getting the letter in the mail. She would study the envelope and be shocked that it was from him, that the address was in his handwriting. She would pause over it before opening it. But she would open it. Then she'd read it over and over, slower each time, looking for hidden meaning. Would she see his earlier self in the letter? The young man who used to talk to her about his dreams? Would such a letter lead her to try and find him? He didn't know. But he wouldn't tell her where he was, not in his current situation.

The thought of the letter made him wonder again what would happen if he were suddenly dropped back into the same situation–back in his old job with his marriage still intact but knowing what he knew now. How would that change things? Deep down he feared he would react the same way. Put that same stress, real or self-imposed, back on him, and the same cracks would appear. Stress it enough and flawed material eventually cracked.

All his imaginings didn't matter because he wouldn't write the letter. Not writing the letter gave him a sick, empty feeling.

***

The melatonin started working, and he felt the first fading of consciousness. The last things he heard were the treetops rustling and the flagpole's metal fastener clanking. The breeze must have freshened. He had always been a dreamer, and the melatonin accentuated that. It also made his dreams more vivid. That night's dream was no exception.

He was back in his boyhood A-frame house, a regular setting for his dreams. He was in his unheated, upstairs bedroom. The cramped room barely wider than a large man's wingspan. It was the depth of winter. The warmth from the first-floor's space heater didn't reach the upstairs, and when he poked his head from his heavy cover of blankets, he could see a foggy cloud of his condensed breath. In his dream, it snowed inside his bedroom. Everything was always worse in his dreams. His father called him to come downstairs, his voice carrying up the narrow curved stairway that ran from the kitchen to his bedroom. His father was in the living room, sitting in his wooden rocker. The dream was detailed enough that he could make out the cheap gold leaf that decorated the rocker's headrest and even the holey soles of his father's favorite slippers. The living room wallpaper was still its ugly floral pattern. From nowhere, Scrap-Iron appeared and squeezed into his father's now vacant rocking chair. He was too big for the chair, and the arms snapped off. Scrap-Iron picked up one of the broken arms and started batting Stewart around the living room. Then the petrified little Stewart stood over the living room's space heater and pissed himself. The smell of his urine burning away on the heater's old manifold was as strong and pungent as on the distant day that he had really done that.

He woke then, drenched in sweat and shaking. The dream so real he had to reassure himself that it was just a dream. Later, the remembrance of his father's holey slippers would make him cry.

It was getting light out. The meeting with Scrap-Iron was just a few hours away. Was the dream a portent of something to come? He'd know soon enough.

19

Slinky arrived at Stewart's tent with the Sunday papers in hand. The morning's theft already done as a favor to his friend.

"Stew?"

It only took that one call, and Stewart poked his head out. "I'm up," he said.

"I'll wait out here," Slinky said. The ducking in and out of a small tent was difficult for him.

They talked through the open flap while Stewart finished dressing.

"I got the papers already," Slinky said.

"Thanks," Stewart said.

"I got both of them. I figured you had enough going on today."

"I'm okay," Stewart said. "Whatever it is, it's not going to be a big deal."

He always hid his fears from others, despite what the psychologist had advised. She stressed that everybody had fears and it was better to share what he was feeling—that things were less frightening when shared and out in the open.

On the walk to Scrap-Iron's, Stewart never spoke a word. Slinky stayed quiet too. A fast learner, he knew when to leave well enough alone.

***

"Here he is!" Scrap-Iron said, when Stewart entered the garage.

Stewart nodded. Here he was.

"You know who this is?" Scrap-Iron asked.

The boys knew, and they grinned with expectation of what was to come.

"It's the star of the show!" The Bandito said.

Slinky took his place atop the tires. Stewart started to take an end spot on the Naugahyde sofa.

"Sit there," Scrap-Iron said, motioning to the bucket seat that Toad sat in.

"But Scrap," Toad said, "that's my seat."

A sideways glance quieted Toad. Scrap-Iron was good at non-verbal communication. Toad sulked but got up and moved to the sofa. Stewart appropriated the bucket seat. To not do so would offend Scrap-Iron. Out of common courtesy, he looked to Toad and said, "Thanks."

Toad ignored him.

"My man, Stewart," Scrap-Iron said.

Stewart nodded.

"My man—the Professor," Scrap-Iron said. "Who would've thought that I'd have my very own in-house professor of literature, just like those kings who used to have their own in-house artists? You'd figure that in a crew like this I'd have my perverts and degenerates, but who would suspect a professor? Now that's something, ain't it?"

That was a particularly aggravating twist, Scrap-Iron calling him *professor* just as his work colleagues did. Maybe the big man picked that up during one of his visits to the store. Maybe it was coincidence. Maybe the name fit, even if misapplied by Philistines.

"Now, Professor. I've got something to read to you. I'm in need of your professional analysis."

"Okay," Stewart said.

Scrap-Iron reached over the side of his chair and lifted a slim, leather-covered briefcase onto his lap. It looked like the briefcases the finance firm used to award as gifts to their best performers, those who made the Achievers Circle. Stewart had one of those cases packed away somewhere back in his attic.

Scrap-Iron undid the case's brass clasps, letting them snap open with a loud flair. Inside were a bunch of thin paperbacks. There were some Louis L'Amour Westerns, but mostly old-fashioned pornos, racy relics of the pre-Internet age, the brightly colored covers depicting deep cleavage, skirt stretching hips, and long shapely legs.

Scrap-Iron chose a book. Its cover featured a heavily lipsticked blonde woman, naked but for her red high heels and three strategically placed black dots. The cover was worn soft with use.

Here we go, Stewart thought. This was today's show, Scrap-Iron getting over on the uppity literature professor by reading him cheap, paperback smut. It fit, Scrap-Iron poking fun at what he, Stewart, held in high esteem and doing it in front of everybody. Not the way he would have preferred to spend a Sunday morning but something he could handle. He had read Henry Miller and had even considered offering a night class on X-rated literature: Literary Pornography in the 20th Century and Its Impact on the Sexual Revolution. That would have been a class without the usual worry of meeting the minimum enrollment requirement. It might even have gotten his adjunct position renewed.

Scrap-Iron opened the book, positioned his reading glasses, and indelicately cleared his throat. A nasty little boy look covered his face. He was ready to read.

As he read, his index finger traced the words, and his lips moved. Stewart tried not to listen. He could make the appropriate gestures of cognition and appreciation based on the big man's dramatic tone and leering looks. Unfortunately, he couldn't help but listen after Scrap-Iron kicked his foot to demand his full attention during what Scrap-Iron called the "good part" that started: "the full girth of his massive pulsing manhood stretched her…"

It went from bad to worse as the sex scene descended the ladder of abstraction, from the conceptual to the concrete, from the inferred to the anatomically detailed. Stewart was surprised that the author, at least in the art of describing sexual congress, seemed to know his business.

"That's really good," a beaming Toad said, when Scrap-Iron finished. In his bouncing enthusiasm, Toad almost fell off the slippery sofa. "I mean that's good writin' Scrap. Especially that part about the screaming woman and the smell of burning rubber."

Like an officious judge, Scrap-Iron stared over his half-glasses and down at Stewart. "Professor," he asked, "that last part, the climax, didn't you find it very evocative?" He emphasized *evocative* to give it its due as just the right word at just the right time. "I mean didn't you find it impressive, the way it appeals to all the senses—sight, hearing, smell, touch, even taste?"

When Stewart didn't answer, Scrap-Iron leaned toward him, lowered his voice to a confidential whisper and said, "But it was nasty, huh?"

Stewart nodded to that.

Two sacrileges in one. It was the Sabbath, and truly good books were what he really worshipped. But objection was not an option. The big man was dangerous and mercurial, and unlike the other powerful people Stewart had known, not just with pen and paper.

Scrap-Iron took off his reading glasses. The frames had already made deep red grooves along his temples. He smiled at Stewart and said, "You want the book for your library?"

Stewart demurred. He felt relief though. At least the stupid exercise was over and with less pain than he imagined. Like his father had told him when the grade school kids made fun of him: "Sticks and stones will break my bones, but words will never harm me." What was strange though, was that he loved words so much that they could harm him. What was even stranger was that a man like Scrap-Iron liked words too and used them against him.

"Our tablet," Scrap-Iron said to Toad. "Get it."

Toad bounced up and walked to the workbench. The boys fidgeted in their seats. The show wasn't over. Stewart figured a tablet meant a small computer and a turn to video porn. Like Slinky said, Scrap-Iron utilized all the latest technology.

Toad crawled under the bench. He scuttled around there, his pants creeping down so the raised tops of his whip scars showed again. He came out with a gray rectangular object about the size of an open newspaper. The way he handled it indicated it was made of something light, maybe plastic or cardboard. He propped it on top of the bench. It looked like a Halloween tombstone from the Dollar Store, but what Toad had retrieved was a listing of the Ten Commandments, rendered on faux stone.

"You look confused, Professor," Scrap-Iron said. "You shouldn't be. We take the Commandments seriously here." He looked to the boys. "Don't we?" he asked them.

The boys all agreed that they did.

"Matter of fact," Scrap-Iron said to Stewart, "that's the purpose of today's meeting. You and the Commandments."

20

"There's no human behavior," Scrap-Iron said, "that can't be explained by that little tablet. And those Commandments thousands of years old. What more do you need to know about man's nature and the stupidity of trying to change him?"

Scrap-Iron waved an open hand at his boys, his incarnate examples. "It's been a while," he said, "since I checked on you sinners and how you're doing with the big Ten. That's because I know you boys so well that I have confidence in you. But now I have a new boy, and I must take stock of him. This is gonna take some care. I'm not used to working with the highly educated and lettered."

"I'm not sure what you mean," Stewart said.

"Well," Scrap-Iron said, "let me explain it in my simple way. Our goal here, as individuals and as a community, is to break at least one of the Ten Commandments every day."

"What?" Stewart asked.

"Yeah," Scrap-Iron said. "And, I got to admit, my boys are pretty reliable."

A rare compliment for the boys and well-earned. They glowed like little girls just told how pretty they were.

"The one I'm worried about," Scrap-Iron said, "is you. See, any team is only as strong as its weakest link."

"I'm no saint," Stewart said, sizing up the situation, hoping to deflect attention from himself, his clean living, and his sure failure to live up to Scrap-Iron's perverse standards.

"That's not for you to determine," Scrap-Iron said. "We can't judge ourselves now, can we?" He sat forward, furrowed his brow and quoted Scripture. "I judge between cattle and cattle, between the rams and the goats. Saith the Lord."

With his right hand, the big man dug inside his chair's side pouch. He threw napkins and old crossword pages and a Phillips screwdriver on the floor. He wasn't a patient man. Finally, he came out with a pen-like device and pointed it toward the tablet and pushed a button. A red laser beam shone on the tablet.

"Aha," Scrap-Iron said. He held the laser pointer up for all to see, surprised and happy that the thing still worked.

"There's one thing we're special proud of here," Scrap-Iron said. "You might say we specialize in it. That's our sinning." He shifted into his more cerebral voice. "It's our forte. You might say it's the common thread of our community. See, Professor, I'd rather rule here, over my simple trespassers, than serve somewhere else as a lackey to the sophisticated."

Scrap-Iron waited for some reaction to that, and when it didn't come, he asked, "That sound familiar? It should, to a literary man like you."

Stewart nodded. He had picked up on the reference to Milton's *Paradise Lost*. He had to admit to himself that Scrap-Iron likening himself to the devil fit.

"What the tablet's for," Scrap-Iron said, "is to serve as our touchstone, to keep us focused on the fundamentals. In any endeavor worth doing, it always comes back to the fundamentals. I can personally confirm that The Bandito and Herc and Toad are Commandment-breaking machines. I can personally attest to their breaking every single one, except the Fifth. Slinky there, he does his best, and that's all I can ask of him. You got to adjust your expectations, and Slink's my special needs pupil."

Genuine pride in Scrap-Iron's praise of his boys and their transgressions.

"I take it you know your Commandments," Scrap-Iron said.

Stewart nodded and then on second thought moved his head slowly side to side. He never liked to exaggerate his knowledge.

"The most important thing," Scrap-Iron said, "is that you want to be a full-feathered member here and not just a fledgling. That's why you deserve a comprehensive review. Your first interview was just preliminary. I need to better measure you, so I can properly set your goals."

Scrap-Iron painted red laser circles around the First Commandment.

I, the Lord, am your God. You shall not have other gods besides me.

"Número uno, and I can vouch that everyone here has broken it. That includes you, Professor."

"I never…" Stewart said.

146

"Oh yes," Scrap-Iron said, "you've broken the First Commandment. You have a false god."

"Worshipped a false god?" Stewart said. "No, I never did that." He forced a laugh. This game was madness, but he still couldn't ignore the bizarreness of such an accusation.

"You show up here on Sunday now?" Scrap-Iron asked.

"Well, yes…"

"You and Slinky bring your tribute, right?"

"We brought you your papers, but…"

"*QED*," Scrap-Iron said.

"What?" The Bandito said.

"Never mind," Scrap-Iron said. He moved the pointer down to the Second Commandment.

You shall not take the name of the Lord God in vain.

"That's an easy one," Scrap-Iron said. "We all break that one every day. But just to be safe, Professor, I want you to say 'I swear to God that Toad-Fucker is a simple bastard.'"

The boys perked up at that, in anticipation of fancy-tongued Stewart talking such talk. Stewart hesitated. Scrap-Iron stared at him, all lightness and humor suddenly gone from his demeanor.

"I swear that Toad-Fucker is a simple bastard," Stewart said.

Scrap-Iron shook his head slowly, as if he were a patient owner of a puppy who had just chewed on his slippers. "You got to say *swear to God*," he corrected. "You've got to be precise when you're taking the Lord's name in vain. You do believe in the Lord?"

"I swear to God that Toad-Fucker is a simple bastard," Stewart said.

"Thanks," Toad said.

"You're making progress," Scrap-Iron said. "You got a long ways to go, but like I always say, take it one sin at a time."

Scrap-Iron finished his beer and wiggled the empty bottle at Slinky. Toad stayed seated this time. Stewart's progress continued as the laser light touched the Third Commandment.

Remember to keep holy the Lord's Day.

"Another easy one," Toad said.

"For a degenerate like you," Herc said, "they're all easy."

"Now, Professor," Scrap-Iron said, "you work at that store on Sundays, right?"

"On some Sundays," Stewart said.

"That's sufficient," Scrap-Iron said. He was anxious to get through the easy ones. He lifted his pointer and focused it on the Fourth Commandment.

Honor your father and your mother.

"What do you have to say about your father and mother?"

"Nothing bad," Stewart said.

"More bullshit," Scrap-Iron said. "Everybody's got something bad to say about their father and mother."

Stewart found it hard to imagine the big man having a mother. It seemed more likely he would have sprung out of some evil god's head, already full grown and sputtering curses, like Athena sprang from Zeus.

"It's our fathers and mothers that ruin our lives," Scrap-Iron said. He looked to Toad. "What you got to say about your old man?"

"He was a motherless cocksucker," Toad said, without hesitation or need for reflection.

"So, Professor," Scrap-Iron said, "you got to have something for me."

So far, Slinky had been right, you couldn't bullshit the man. So Stewart told a truth.

"My father," Stewart said, "he was distant."

"Distant?" Scrap-Iron said. He didn't sound impressed.

"There were times," Stewart said, "when he didn't talk to me for days. You know, if something was really bothering him or I'd made a mistake."

"That's bad?" Scrap-Iron said.

"You'd be surprised," Stewart said.

"I'm sure I would," Scrap-Iron said. He paused, as if deciding whether to go on. He did. "When I was a kid," he said, "I was big for my age and still pretty clumsy. One time my old man carved this pumpkin for Halloween. He spent an hour or two on it. Gave it teeth and a big smile and eyes and everything. He was good at that shit. He set it over our outside gaslight, so everyone who came in the yard could see it. Everyone told him what a good job it was and that he was an artist. He was real proud of it. But I lifted it off to get a better look at how he did it, and I dropped it on the driveway. It broke into pieces. It was like it exploded. I laughed. I couldn't help it. You know what my old man did?"

"What?" Stewart asked.

"He killed my hamster."

Everyone silent at that. There was no kidding in Scrap-Iron's voice.

"That hamster was my buddy," Scrap-Iron said. "His name was Hannibal. I had just read a book about Hannibal the general. That's how I named him. You know how my old man killed him?"

Nobody hazarded a guess at that.

"He threw him into an empty plastic swimming pool with his buddy's rat terrier. He made me watch. You ever see a rat terrier work?"

Scrap-Iron turned inward for a quiet moment. So did Stewart. In his mind he saw a hysterical and hyperventilating boy forced to watch a merciless execution of his beloved pet.

Scrap-Iron shook his head, as if to bring himself back to the present. "In your case," he said to Stewart, "I guess 'distant' will have to do."

The laser dot circled the Fifth.

Thou shall not kill.

"So," Scrap-Iron said, "we get to the big one."

The boys nodded in respect.

"You know," Scrap-Iron said, "Thou shall not kill is really the Sixth, but the tablet we have is the Catholic version."

"I'm not Catholic," Stewart said. He said it as if he had found a loophole.

"No matter," Scrap-Iron said. "Here we make do with what we have. We're what you might call, ecumenical." The big man got that pronunciation right and smiled at his verbal ostentation. "Anyway, it all comes out the same in the end.

"Thou shall not kill," Scrap-Iron said. "I don't count breaking that one among my lifetime achievements. My old man did. In the war. They say most soldiers never talk about that kind of thing. But my old man bragged about it all the time. For our situation here, the Fifth's what I call aspirational. Everybody needs something to aim at. You know, reach the unreachable star and all that."

Stewart, for the first time, questioned not only Scrap-Iron's soul but his sanity.

The laser dot jumped to the Sixth.

You shall not commit adultery.

"Okay," Scrap-Iron said, his normal voice and enthusiasm back. "Now we've come to my personal favorite."

He looked to Stewart but got no reaction.

"I know," Scrap-Iron said, "it's not your favorite. Probably because you haven't tried it. You were *never unfaithful* to your wife. Ain't that right?"

"Never," Stewart said.

Of adultery, he was innocent. Completely so and he was not going to lie.

"Never unfaithful," Scrap-Iron said. "That sounds like a movie title. Well, maybe we need a sequel. How about, *It's Never too Late.*"

The boys liked that.

"Of course it takes two to tango," Scrap-Iron said. "But I got just the gal for you." He winked at the boys. "Don't I?"

"Oh yeah," The Bandito said.

"Boxcar Betty," Scrap-Iron said. He said the name as if it were all he needed to say.

The boys laughed knowingly. They enjoyed being co-conspirators.

What was developing didn't seem just a perverse game to Stewart any longer. He said, "I'm not..."

"You'll enjoy it," Scrap-Iron said.

"But," Stewart said, "I'm not…"

"What you're not gonna do," Scrap-Iron said, "is tell me what you're not gonna do."

He stared hard at Stewart, daring further objection. When none came, he said, "We'll be coming back to number Six. We got important work to do on that one."

The laser highlighted number Seven.

Thou shalt not steal.

"That one's done," Scrap-Iron said, and reached over the side of his chair and shook one of his newspapers.

"Now, number Eight."

The laser highlighted the Eighth Commandment.

You shall not bear false witness.

"Tell me something, Professor," Scrap-Iron said, to Stewart. "Did you ever do something and then blame it on someone else? Or did you ever tell your mother you didn't do something that you did?"

Stewart's eyes went to the garage's concrete floor.

"Okay," Scrap-Iron said, "that takes care of number Eight."

The laser touched the Ninth Commandment.

You shall not covet your neighbor's wife.

"That one's such bullshit," Scrap-Iron said. "Every man in the country breaks that one every day."

"Except," Toad added, "for the fags. Right, Scrap?"

"Yeah, Toad-boy. But they're after the neighbor's husbands. The Commandments just ain't caught up to them yet."

"Maybe," Toad said, " 'cause they were carved in stone. If they'd started on the Internet, they'd been easier to change."

"That's pretty good, Toady-boy," Scrap-Iron said. "Once in a while you surprise me, but then even a blind squirrel finds his nuts sometimes."

Toad beamed, for being back in the big man's good graces.

"Now for the last one," Scrap-Iron said, and highlighted the Tenth Commandment.

You shall not covet your neighbor's goods.

"Another lame one. Show me one asshole who doesn't covet his neighbor's goods. Where would America be if we didn't covet our neighbor's goods? Coveting your neighbor's goods is the American way. Right, Professor?"

"I guess," Stewart said.

"So you don't contest Nine and Ten?"

"I guess not," Stewart said. He looked like a captured POW, beaten down and ready to confess to anything.

"So," Scrap-Iron said. "We're left with the Fifth and the Sixth. I can't, in good conscience, hold you to the Fifth. Like I said, that one's aspirational. But the Sixth now, that one's too important to be missing from your résumé. I mean it's the source of great literary work and the favorite of popes and presidents."

"I'm not..." Stewart said.

"I told you," Scrap-Iron said, "don't talk about what you're not gonna do. You're too negative. You gotta be more positive. Besides, the time is right. The arrangements are already made. In fact, you're gonna do it right here and right now."

"What?" Stewart asked.

Scrap-Iron looked to Toad and The Bandito. "Set up the cot, and set up the light," he said. "I'll call Betty and tell her that we're ready for her."

21

Toad worked with uncharacteristic enthusiasm. He pulled an Army cot from the garage's far corner, where it stood behind the compressed air tanks that Scrap-Iron used for his pneumatic tools and for filling tires. Toad unfolded the cot's frame and set it in the center of the garage. He beat the dust out of the tick mattress without taking it outside and without regard for his colleagues' lungs.

Scrap-Iron sometimes used the cot for his naps, though he barely fit on it. He also used it for special occasions, like the time he presented the boys with a prostitute as a Christmas gift. He had even turned the garage's heat up for that fleshly Christmas Eve fest. Professional and non-discriminating, the woman was willing to service the Bandito, Little Hercules, and even Slinky, who abstained, claiming his medicines precluded his participation. Pro or not, the woman drew the line at Toad. "Toad man," Scrap-Iron had said, "She don't want any part of your raggedy shit." Toad's response: "That's okay. She's got a right to choose her own friends."

As Toad worked with the cot, Scrap-Iron got busy setting up his fancy video camera, handling it with a professional's care and attaching it to his tripod equipped with fully adjustable handles, pan and tilt locks, and 90-degree tilt adjustment.

"I need more light," Scrap-Iron said.

The Bandito took a mechanic's trouble light from the sidewall's pegboard and looped its long cord over a crossbeam so the light dangled over the cot. He adjusted it several times until the metal guard stopped turning and bulb faced the cot. He plugged the light into an outlet near the workbench, and the scene took on a look eerily close to a cheap porno set.

"Love is like a weed," Scrap-Iron said. "It can blossom in the strangest places."

The garage walls seemed to close in on Stewart. He couldn't believe what was happening was real.

"Professor," Scrap-Iron said, "I want you to think of yourself as a craftsman. And I want you to think of that cot as your workbench."

"I'm not..." Stewart said and stood up.

Scrap-Iron put his arm around Stewart and let it rest there. It weighed on Stewart's shoulder like a lead drape. Stewart didn't finish his thought. He didn't have the strength.

"The only problem," Scrap-Iron said, "is that your co-star isn't here yet."

A surge of hope. Maybe, Stewart thought, whoever this Boxcar Betty woman was, she wouldn't show, and the whole thing would be called off. How reliable could she be?

"You better hope she shows," Scrap-Iron the mind reader said. When the benumbed Stewart didn't react to that, the big man asked, "You know why?"

"Why?"

"Because Toad's her understudy."

"He ain't doing me," Toad yelled.

"He's doing someone," Scrap said. "And if Betty don't show, it's you."

Scrap-Iron stepped to his workbench and picked up a large plastic jar of petroleum jelly. He used it for adding a protective sealing coat to O-rings inside of water pumps. He didn't say anything. He had a natural comedian's sense of timing and understood his audience and how the lowest level of comedy would most appeal to them. He bounced the jar in his hand and then tossed it to Toad.

The boys loved it.

"I almost hope," Herc said. "That Betty doesn't show."

22

And then she was there.

She came through the side door like a star appearing on a stage. She wore a bright, flowered sundress and platform heels that thudded on the cement floor.

"You're late," Scrap-Iron said.

The woman smiled, lifted up a foot, and said, "Try hurrying when you're wearing these."

"I knew she'd make it," a relieved-looking Toad said.

"Let me," Scrap-Iron said, "make the introductions."

With a familiar casualness, he put a hand on the woman's hip and turned her toward Stewart. "This," he said, "is Betty." He corrected himself. "Excuse me, this is the famous *Boxcar Betty*."

Stewart acknowledged her with a slight bow.

Betty smiled. She looked sober and surprisingly normal. Older that Stewart expected. That showed around her eyes. But she wasn't haggard. She had even groomed herself for the occasion. Her short brown hair shone as if just washed.

"Meet Professor Stewart," Scrap-Iron said.

"Hello Professor Stewart," Betty said.

Stewart didn't answer. Betty looked right into his eyes and further unnerved him. He wanted to scream: *This is lunacy and we both know it and we should both refuse to participate, whatever the consequences.*

"You want to know," Scrap-Iron asked Stewart, "how she got the name Boxcar Betty?" His smile suggested it was some story.

"Never mind that," Betty said. "He seems like a sweet guy. He doesn't need to know about all that."

"Okay," Scrap-Iron said. "Let's get down to business. Now, I'll be your cameraman and director and producer. The video is important, for posterity. The Professor might want to show it to his grandkids someday."

"Good," Betty said, as if they were talking about filming a birthday party or some religious ceremony.

"I'll do my best," Scrap-Iron said, "to get your top performances. Of course, as talented as I am and as talented and experienced as Betty is, there's one thing that's up to you, Professor. You got to rise to the occasion."

Then the director led his performers to the cot, Stewart by the arm and half dragged.

There was no escape. No use in appealing to God. If God watched over him, he wouldn't be here in this absurd, humiliating, dangerous situation.

"Oh yeah," Toad screamed, for the imminence of the action.

"I'm only gonna say this once," Scrap-Iron said and turned to Toad. His tone of voice was all business. "Except for the two stars," he said, "I want complete silence once I say *Take!* The moaning and groaning, and there better be moaning and groaning, are a big part of a good take. So the rest of you keep your mouths shut. There's artists at work here."

He turned his attention to Betty. "You know the confidence I have in you. So do you want me to direct you, or do you want to go with the flow?"

She wanted to go with the flow.

"Okay," Scrap-Iron said. "As long as the flow includes the important things."

"Did I ever let you down?" Betty said. She said it with attitude, as if her expertise in such matters should never be questioned.

Stewart's heart pounded in his ears. He couldn't possibly do this. He worried about fainting, and then he tried to faint. Boxcar Betty took him by the hand and positioned him closer to the cot.

Betty turned to Scrap-Iron and said, "Give us some room."

Scrap-Iron obeyed. He backed off to his video equipment and started playing with it again, working on the angle and focus.

Betty was up against him, and Stewart tried to move away, but the back of his legs hit the cot and there was nowhere to go. His left leg started shaking. He could see it shaking through his pants leg. He smelled lilac on Betty.

"Try and relax," Betty said and gently pulled his T-shirt toward her. She seemed to sense for the first time that her partner was unwilling and maybe unable. She whispered in Stewart's ear, "I lead and you follow. Just like a dance."

He would follow her lead, wherever she led. What choice did he have?

"Turn off that fan," Scrap-Iron said. "It's too loud, and I want to see sweat."

Instead of getting off his seat, Toad reached out and yanked the fan's red extension cord until the plug came out. Normally Scrap-Iron would have slapped him for that—he had spliced and taped too many cords because of such laziness. But now he was busy with higher things.

"Let's do it," Scrap-Iron said. "Take one!"

Betty took Stewart by his shoulders and with a slight push sat him down on the cot. The frame squeaked. Betty reached behind herself and unzipped her dress. She seemed as relaxed as if at home and getting ready for a nice warm bath.

Scrap-Iron kept playing with his camera. The boys stood up and formed a semicircle, just five or six feet away. Slinky couldn't see over them so he joined them. He couldn't help it.

"I'm good now," Scrap-Iron said. "Keep going. Action!"

Betty slipped off her heels and lost a half head in height. It was as if the floor beneath her had sunk. With Stewart sitting and her standing, she wasn't much taller than he was. She stepped out of her dress and let it drop on the concrete floor. A new wave of her perfume hit Stewart, and its discordant blending with the garage's grease and kerosene smells made him light-headed.

Betty bent down and pulled Stewart's sneakers off without untying them. Scrap-Iron grunted as if he liked that. As Betty bent, Stewart diverted his eyes from her full breasts.

Her body looked younger than her face. In bra and panties, she looked in surprisingly good shape. She looked like an exerciser. Not a hint of shyness about her, standing there in such a place, in such a state, in front of such an audience.

Stewart tried putting himself in his robotic greeter's mode. That didn't work. He tried deep breaths.

Betty pushed on his chest, and he was flat on his back. She leaned over him. Her still restrained breasts near his face now. He could see dark blue veins on them. Her eyes were bloodshot. She cupped his chin in her hand and said, "Okay, baby." It was meant to sound sensual, but Stewart took it literally. He felt like a baby.

With both hands, Betty took hold of his T-shirt, lifted him by it, and pulled the shirt over his head. Before it was completely off, she whispered in his ear, "You got to try and relax."

"Wait a minute," Scrap-Iron said.

"You ready or not?" Betty said. The way she instantly came out of role and her aggressive tone shocked Stewart. He had never heard anyone talk to Scrap-Iron like that. And Scrap-Iron took it. Between Betty and obsessively messing with his equipment, Scrap-Iron actually looked flustered. The strangeness of that, Betty seemingly in charge, settled Stewart just a little.

"Okay," Scrap-Iron said, "I'm ready. Keep going with Take One."

"Take One's gonna be the only take," Betty said. "So get it right."

She stood straight and then pulled Stewart's pants off, both legs at once. Like a shy little boy, he caught his boxer underwear and held on to keep them from coming off. Betty giggled at that. Stewart was scared. When they married, his wife had been as inexperienced and shy as he. In their lovemaking, she always let him lead, if what he did could be considered leading. Eventually they were comfortable with each other and enjoyed each other, but they were never adventurous.

Because of the narrowness of the cot, Betty couldn't lie next to him. Instead, she crawled up and straddled him. She kissed his cheek and licked his ear with her tongue. Stewart tried concentrating on the wooden crossbeam above—it was an old guardrail that Scrap-Iron had borrowed from the Garden State Parkway. Stewart tried thinking about the life cycle of that crossbeam, from sapling to tree to guardrail to garage support. He tried to think of all the cars and passengers that had passed it by.

Betty gave him a soft poke in his chest. "Fake it," she whispered. "If you have to."

He had to.

"Speed it up," Scrap-Iron said. He was neither a fan nor a practitioner of foreplay.

Betty sat up straight, arched her back for maximum effect, and unsnapped her bra. She held it in place a few seconds and then took it off with a flourish and tossed it aside, aiming it at Toad, but sailing it over his head. Toad whooped, and, without abandoning his camera, Scrap-Iron reached out with a kick that just partly caught him.

When Betty's breasts came free, they fell toward Stewart like an avalanche. With them came more perfume. He felt no stimulation. But he had recovered enough aplomb to try and pretend he was simply an actor in a play or movie.

"Let's go," Scrap-Iron said. "Time to ride."

Betty removed her panties, slowly and provocatively, one still shapely leg at a time. She positioned herself for the boys' maximum enjoyment. Intentional or not, it had the effect of turning the boys' attention from Stewart and exclusively to her. Even Scrap-Iron couldn't resist and took his eyes from his camera to get a peek.

Betty wanted to make Scrap-Iron jealous. She was still pissed at him. The last time they were together, he had commented that, "she was getting a little age on her." He said it matter-of-factly, as if he were talking about a horse. She hadn't forgotten that.

"Maybe," Scrap-Iron said, "we should strap a board to the Professor's back, so he doesn't fall in."

"Maybe," The Bandito said, "he should stick his head in, wiggle his ears, and spit."

"Maybe," Betty said, "the peanut gallery should shut their traps." Then, in one smooth and decisive motion, she pulled Stewart's underwear off. The speed and angle she did this with had the effect of giving him some modicum of modesty.

"It's okay," Betty said. "You can do it. Just keep tight against me."

Stewart did as he was told. At that time in that position, he would have done anything this woman said. He had heard of the bliss people felt when they surrendered all to a greater power, and he felt something like that now, not bliss, but surrender and a semblance of calming resignation.

Betty made all the appropriate moves and noises. She knew what it was that excited men, whether it was faked or for real. Men weren't hard to figure out or hard to fool, even Scrap-Iron, who fancied himself such a smart cookie. Having fun now, she turned to Scrap-Iron, who was busy working his camera.

"This boy's so good," she said.

Nobody knew better than Stewart that that wasn't true, but it sounded genuine.

The boys all wide-eyed now. This was different than one of Scrap's movies. A live show was better.

"I want a penetration shot," Scrap-Iron said.

"I want it right where it is," Betty said.

The moment overwhelmed Stewart, and to his amazement, he felt the first swell of passion.

"There we go!" Betty said. She sounded genuinely excited, not sexually, but as if she were teaching a little boy to ride a two-wheeler and for the first time he had ridden without training wheels.

Scrap-Iron got his requested shot, and, against all odds, everything else he demanded. At the conclusion, Betty, perhaps a little too theatrically, collapsed on Stewart. "That's it," she said to Scrap-Iron. She said it without rising, all her weight still on Stewart, as if she were too spent to rise.

A surprised and satisfied audience, the boys were unnaturally quiet.

"Whew!" Betty said to Scrap-Iron, after she raised herself to a sitting position. "You got your money's worth and so did I."

"Okay," Scrap-Iron said, so involved with his equipment that he wasn't sure what he had got.

Stewart found his pants, fumbled with them, but got them back on. He shoved his underwear into one of his pockets.

Betty, still naked and in no apparent hurry to cover up, stood and punched Scrap-Iron on the arm, hard. The force made her jiggle.

"You never said you had this big a job for me," Betty said. "I should renegotiate or at least get a bonus." She gave Stewart a wink, tilted her head toward Scrap-Iron, and said, "I mean, I'm not used to such a big job."

She was laying it on thick. Maybe too thick.

Stewart was too shaken, drained, and disoriented to be sufficiently thankful his ordeal was over. Later he would think again, what a strange place the world was. The good-hearted hooker was a cliché he hated. So overused in literature and on-screen. Yet here was a woman who, not long ago, he would have averted his gaze from to avoid the lower parts of the world, and now she had rescued him and done so with the skill of an artist.

After Betty dressed, she gave Stewart a kiss on the cheek. "See," she whispered, "you didn't even have to fake it."

"Thank-you," was all Stewart knew to say. He wanted to say more, but he was physically and emotionally numb.

III

23

To Stewart's surprise, Scrap-Iron seemed to lose interest in him. Now that the thing was done, the big man was absorbed with adjusting the settings on his video equipment. Albeit on shaky legs, Stewart was able to just walk away.

The boys were confused. The morning's doings were meant to humiliate Stewart and entertain them. That's what Scrapville's initiation rites were all about, entertainment through humiliation. That was a cost of being a newcomer and a benefit of being a veteran. They had been entertained this morning, that was for sure, but Stewart seemed more of a star than a dupe.

Stewart wasn't confused. He knew what he had to do. He had to get away and never come back. To be put on display, like some barnyard animal, was the worst humiliation of his life. To be under the thumb of a man who would do that kind of thing—that was the ultimate in lack of control. Staying here as Scrap-Iron's serf would be like being a child's plaything, if the child were a sociopath. When Scrap-Iron was a boy, he probably pulled wings off of flies.

Slinky followed him out the garage's side door, but Stewart walked away as fast as his legs would take him, so Slinky would know he wasn't invited. Slinky didn't take the hint.

"Wait up, Stew," Slinky called.

When Stewart ignored him, pretending he didn't hear, Slinky yelled so loud that Stewart couldn't ignore him. Stewart stopped, but not until he was safely away from the garage, where the street met the railroad tracks.

"I've got to talk to you," Slinky said.

"I've got to go," Stewart said. "I'm getting out of here."

"You sure?" Slinky asked.

"Am I sure? Of course I'm sure. You saw what happened in there, didn't you?"

"I saw," Slinky said.

"And," Stewart said, "so did everybody else in camp."

"I'm really sorry about what happened," Slinky said.

"What are you sorry about?" Stewart said. "You didn't do anything."

His forgiveness was feigned. Slinky must have known about Scrap-Iron's plans. But all Stewart wanted now was to get away and be done with all this.

"I should have said something," Slinky said. "I should have told you what I knew. Or at least what I was worried about. Whatever Scrap-Iron had planned for you, I knew it wouldn't be nice, and I should've warned you. A friend should have said something."

"It doesn't matter now," Stewart said. He didn't have the time or will to go over all this, especially for the purpose of absolving Slinky of guilt.

"Stew, I didn't think Scrap would do anything like that. I really didn't."

"I believe you," Stewart said.

A look of relief crossed Slinky's face. His friend's forgiveness was important to him. Stewart started down the tracks, and Slinky followed.

"I knew he was going to do something," Slinky said. "You know, some kind of initiation, like he did for all of us, but I didn't think…"

"Forget it, Slink," Stewart said. "It's not your fault. Scrap-Iron's a mental case."

"You know, Stew," Slinky said. "This place could still work for you."

"What?" Stewart said and stopped abruptly. "Are you crazy? After what just happened?"

"I know it wasn't right," Slinky said. "It was bad. But now, it's like you passed your test. We all had to do something."

"I don't want to talk about it," Stewart said. He started walking again.

"I know," Slinky said. "I don't talk about what Scrap made me do. But now that you've done it, and you're in the group, see, that changes things."

"Not for me," Stewart said.

"Then where you gonna go?"

"Anywhere but here."

"There's worse places," Slinky said. "It might not seem like that to you now, but the woods are a lot better than the shelter. You know that, right?"

Stewart knew about the shelter. The two nights he had spent there were plenty. The place was so crowded that they turned people away, and you ended up sleeping on a cot not two feet from a complete stranger. The smells and noises made you think you were sleeping in a barnyard. The staff insisted on inspecting your bags, and reveille came at seven a.m. with bright lights and the blasting of an awful song that stuck in your head like a flake of popcorn caught behind a tooth. "Good morning morning, hello sunshine, wake up sleepy head." And then there were the crazies, like the guy next to him who had stayed up all night arguing with himself, taking both sides of the debate as to whether Marlon Brando was the greatest of all method actors.

"You gotta think about it," Slinky said.

Stewart knew what Slinky was thinking. Slinky was still selling Scrapville because he wanted him to stay. Stewart knew why. He had felt the dismal ache of loneliness; in fact, he had become a connoisseur of loneliness, and now he understood how people would accept most anything to avoid it—bad spouses, bad partners, bad friends. And loneliness was all over Slinky.

"I spent a month in the shelter," Slinky said. "When I had nowhere else to go, before I found Scrap and his woods. It seemed like a year."

Stewart looked over his shoulder. The boys weren't coming. That was good. He would pack and run.

"A lot of jerks in the shelter," Slinky said. "They had this strict schedule too. They wake you up early every morning, and you have to be out and not back until six, maybe even later in the summer. That was tough on my back. But the worst thing was all the assholes."

Stewart nodded to all that. He hated being roused out of sleep. To sleep ten to twelve hours on his days off was one of the few things he still took pleasure in. And he knew about the jerks at the shelter. He had learned something about the downtrodden. The downtrodden were no different from any other group of people; they had their fair share of jerks. His father had often told him he didn't know a thing about the wicked ways of the world or the wicked ways of men. His father was right.

"The woods aren't great," Slinky said. "I'm not saying they are. But they're better than any shelter. Especially being that your initiation is over. The initiation's the hard part."

Stewart was still focused on getting away. It was early enough in the day that he could pack and be gone before dark. He thought he might roll up his tent and store it and his stove and lamp with Slinky, in case he needed it in the future.

"Where you gonna go?" Slinky asked again.

That was the question, and Stewart didn't have the answer.

"Where you gonna stay tonight?" Slinky asked.

"I don't know," Stewart said.

"You know," Slinky said, "it was trouble at the shelter that got me to Scrap's place."

Stewart had never asked how Slinky had met Scrap-Iron and found his way to the woods. He knew he was going to find out now.

"I was looking for a knife," Slinky said. "Something bigger than my little pocket knife. Someone told me to check out the junkyard, how there was a whole trailer full of knives there and that the old knives were better than the new ones anyways. That's how I first met Scrap. He asked me what I wanted a knife for."

"What did you want it for?" Stewart asked.

"Protection. There was this guy at the shelter. He kept saying what he was gonna do to me. He said he was gonna keep doing it 'til my eyes popped out. He wasn't kidding. I was real scared. When I told Scrap what I needed the knife for, he told me forget about it."

"He said forget it?"

"Yeah. He said that guy or someone else would take the knife away from me and carve me a new asshole. Then he told me about his woods. He said I could stay there if I wanted and I didn't need a knife and no one would mess with me. All I needed was a tent and his introduction to the boys, and then I was safe."

"So you moved in?"

"Yeah. Scrap made Toad go to the store with me and carry back and set up the tent I bought. Scrap even lent me some money until my check came. And now no one messes with me."

A little triumph in Slinky's face.

Stewart thought some more about the shelter and how he would have to practically beg for a spot there, and he thought about the complications of storing his stuff with Slinky and then having to find a more permanent place until it all seemed like an impossible task.

"I really think," Slinky said, "that things could be different now, between you and Scrap."

"Why's that?" Stewart asked. "Because he had his fun with me?"

"Yeah," Slinky said, "there's that. Scrap likes to mess with people. But you'll be more like one of the boys now. You might not know this, but the more he messes with you, the more he likes you. Plus, he can talk to you about books and words and stuff that he can't talk to the other guys about. That's why he keeps saying I did good by finding you. You should keep that up, talking about that smart stuff. That's your edge. He says you're real smart. I wish he'd say that about me. Just once."

They had reached the spot where the weed-trampled path ran off to the mall's back lot.

"I've got to think about things," Stewart said.

"You should think about things," Slinky said. "That's good."

"I've got to be alone for a while," Stewart said.

"Okay."

"I'm going over to Burger-Land," Stewart said. "I'll see you later."

24

He headed straight to Burger-Land, first for a cleansing, then to think.

He would use the men's room for a sponge bath. With warm water, a soap dispenser, and an endless supply of paper towels, he could do almost as well as with a shower. All he needed was to be left alone long enough.

He had a system. First he would lever out a long sheet of paper towels, wrapping them around his left forearm. Then he would wet three sections and dab one with soap from the wall-mounted dispenser. In a locked stall, he'd strip bare and wash and rinse and dry himself, neck to foot with extra care for his crotch and under his arms. Finished with that, he would stand at the sink, and, as fast as possible because he hated that blind and vulnerable bent over position, wash his face and hair. Flossing and toothbrushing, which he always took great care over, he did in his tent with the aid of a bottle of water. He didn't like the thought of some stranger coming in a public bathroom in the middle of his dental hygiene. After he dried himself, he would carry the used towels out with him and throw them in the lobby's garbage bin. The Bandito had once flushed a thick handful of towels down the toilet and plugged things up. The Burger-Land manager tried to plunge it open but couldn't. The manager was mighty pissed at the plumber's bill and threatened to banish The Bandito for life. A big part of living on the edge was not inviting unwanted attention.

***

As he pulled open Burger-Land's glass door, a current of cold air hit him and then a sudden euphoria swept through him. These infrequent and unpredictable surges usually came first as a feeling of well-being, followed by a burst of exaggerated optimism. Maybe it was his brisk walk from the tracks that had brought this one on. In the grip of euphoria, he saw the world very differently. Now he changed his mind about the sponge bath, deciding to preserve that sensory memory of Betty. Later on, when trying for sleep, he would center on it, as well as the silky softness of her back and the warmness of her skin against his. He'd been a long time without meaningful human touch.

As humiliating as it was, the morning's experience could have been worse. All credit went to Betty, but he could still take pride in his survival. More and more often, he was surviving things he thought he couldn't. How about this for cliché—he was a survivor. Most amazing of all, he had just made love to a woman, something he had convinced himself would never happen again.

He felt weary. That was a warning. The shakes were coming. He needed to refill himself. Betty had drained him. It was as if his insides had been vacuumed out. He bought four chicken pieces and a small soda, not bothering to ask for the senior price. At the disgusting convenience center, he filled his cup with ice and regular sugary coke. He imagined the convenience center scrubbed clean, its mixed spills of ketchup and soda and who knows what purified with a pounding blast from a steam hose and the cleansing continuing until it had purified all of Burger-Land and then the whole mall before expanding to Scrapville and the whole world.

He sat in his favorite seat in the far corner with his back to the wall and the whole place, counter and lobby, in front of him. The corner smelled bad. He wondered who had sat there before him. He was out of hand sanitizer. His back hurt. He must have strained it when Betty was rocking on him. That was okay. It was a good hurt. A virile hurt.

There was the usual assortment of mall crawlers in Burger-Land. The place was cavernous and seldom filled to capacity and then only at lunchtime and only on weekdays. The management was loose and only causing trouble would get you booted. The lost and near-lost would sit there for hours, nursing and refilling a small coffee or soda, hoping for some incident that would enliven their day. Maybe there'd be an angry confrontation between a customer and the counter help, maybe somebody would need emergency services. Anything to animate their bleak, pulseless lives.

To leave or not to leave. He needed to decide, but instead he thought of his wife. What was she doing at that very moment? It was on Sundays, especially in the early days of their marriage, when he and his wife slept late, and he would make French-pressed coffee, and they would spend the morning and early afternoon in bed, reading the newspaper section by section. They shared the paper with the efficient back and forth of a surgical team. After the newspaper, they sometimes made love. When he thought of that, and what had just happened with Betty, he felt as if he had some obligation to notify his wife. He wanted to call her. To tell her what? That he had been forced? That he had proven he was still a man? He had a sudden longing for his wife.

He filled his cup again, this time mostly with ice. He walked to the end of the lobby and looked out the big plate glass windows. Part of him hoped the skateboard kids were out there. He felt ready for them, even if it meant martyrdom.

Might Scrap-Iron back off now? Had he had enough fun? Did he really admire his new boy for his intelligence? It was possible. The big man showed a love of learning that he had seldom seen in his night students. It might make sense to stay in Scrapville, just until he found something better. Out there, beyond Scrapville, was the unknown. To leave, he had to have someplace to go, someplace both within walking distance to work and better than the shelter. Hadn't he had his fill of the unknown? The unknown didn't usually work out so well, and the thought of striking out again, all alone, petrified him.

He had surely paid his dues. Scrap-Iron had got his show. Maybe he should try adding a dose of flattery. He had seen the glint of satisfaction in the big man's eyes when he was flattered, even by his simple boys. He could use the big man's narcissism against him. How about telling Scrap-Iron he felt satisfaction in meeting his expectations? Hadn't he risen to his expectations? Maybe someday over a future campfire, the boys would be telling the story of Stewart and Boxcar Betty. After a few beers and with typical exaggeration, it would make quite a story. He would be a Scrapville legend.

He devised a plan. The past was the past. In the language of finance, the past was a sunk cost. It would be a delicate balancing act, dealing with such a man. If he thought it might work, he could admit to Scrap-Iron that there was merit to his views and that he, a professor too long removed from the real world, had needed to get stronger. He could even thank the big man for his help. A weird thought—did he really owe a debt to Scrap-Iron?

With Scrap-Iron sufficiently placated, he could stay in the woods until a better situation presented itself. Everything depended on being smart. As he had heard Scrap-Iron say, after the boys had praised his great physical strength: "The strong take away from the weak, but the smart take away from the strong."

Like it or not, his situation called for flexibility. This world wasn't black and white, but profoundly gray. He had to leave, but on his terms. Now that he better understood the big man, he could better manage him. This all required careful planning and execution. That was good. It gave him something new to ruminate on.

25

Scrap-Iron sat on his king-sized bed with his back to the wall, next to him, a quart of ice cream and a tablespoon. Not just any ice cream. Strawberry ice cream bursting with sun-freshened strawberries. He'd eat the quart at this one sitting. He was practicing moderation. In his youth, he'd eat half a gallon at one sitting.

His real treat was about to come. He was ready to preview his latest directorial triumph. *Betty Schools the Professor*.

His bedroom was his screening room. A sixty-inch widescreen television dominated the room. It was complimented by a Blu-Ray player and a surround-sound system with large floor-standing speakers. Scrap-Iron said being underground made for the best acoustics.

All the other furnishings were Spartan. No head or footboard to his bed, just the frame, box spring and mattress. On the wall behind his bed, a large, framed poster of Raquel Welch as an improbable but aphrodisiacal cavewoman in the movie *One-Million Years B.C.* Not a thing on the other walls except for cobwebs. To support his weight, the bed frame had the extra support of solid wooden blocks, one under each corner and one in the middle. Next to the bed, a nightstand and his police band radio. Behind the nightstand, in easy reach, his *Persuader*–a 12- gauge Mossberg shotgun, fully loaded with double-ought buckshot, five rounds in the magazine tube and one in the chamber. Any stranger found in his bunker at night would be found there in the morning.

One of Scrapville's prime perquisites was Saturday night at the movies. Scrap-Iron had a professional projector system and showed all the movies on the back of the garage's front overhead door, which he had painted with a reflective type of acrylic paint designed especially for projection walls.

For the regular Saturday showings, Scrap-Iron preferred classic and character-driven fare. His favorites were *Dr. Strangelove* and *The Man Who Shot Liberty Valance*. The boys preferred action films, heavy on sex and violence. Scrap-Iron made sure his double features had at least one film tailored to his boys' primitive tastes. On movie night, he let the beer flow and made available his vintage popcorn machine, with a severe warning that someone must clean the glass sides afterward. The boys loved movie nights.

Next Saturday he would premiere *Betty Schools the Professor*. But he was an artist and a perfectionist, so first there would be some editing to make sure he properly accentuated the good parts. All art must be distilled.

***

With a pad and pen next to him, he started the video.

There were two or three minutes of Stewart and Betty getting ready. Most of that too jumpy, and he made a note to shorten it. Then Betty was slipping off her dress with a sly wink at the camera. The camera liked her, and she loved it.

In his first close-up, Stewart looked ten years older and haggard. When Betty first touched him, he looked as if he were about to be devoured by a crocodile. Scrap-Iron liked that look. It was the look of pending humiliation and the look of good parts to come. It made his toes curl with anticipation.

But the good parts didn't come. Betty stole the show. She had tricked him into focusing on her. Her female self-absorption on display again. That was bad enough, but the problem that no amount of editing could fix was that Betty had actually made the little bastard Stewart look good.

Scrap-Iron watched with increasing anger. He had trusted Betty too much. He had lost focus on his objective and become absorbed in his art. That was because he was an artist. You couldn't change your inner self. And things looked different through the camera lens. That's why nature filmmakers in dangerous environments sometimes took stupid risks without even knowing it. It was easy to get lost in the artificial space behind the camera.

Whatever the cause, the effect was to completely ruin his work and his plan, and waste all the effort he had put into this. He'd have a talk with Betty. He hadn't got what he'd paid for. That's what happened when you trusted someone. If he didn't know better, if the thought wasn't impossible to entertain, he'd think she'd enjoyed herself. And the boys, those assholes, instead of serving as witnesses to Stewart's degradation, they looked as if they were watching a porno film at the seedy theatre out on Route 46. He was surprised they didn't ask Stewart for his autograph. The boys would never see the video.

He should be playing the video over and over, pausing it, going frame to frame and using super slow-motion, delighting in the close-up details of Stewart's abasement and impotence. That's what this evening should have been about. He had been looking forward to that. Instead he played the climatic action over and over again, not because he enjoyed it, but because he couldn't stop himself.

He had been betrayed, and that was bad wrong. But he would get what he wanted. Didn't he always? But there was no room for another mistake. The stakes had been raised. Once you started to lose face, it was an irreversible process, even if your disciples were morons. Maybe more so. It might take a little while, but whatever plan he came up with next would be foolproof and totally humiliating for Stewart.

He would deal with the Professor. He had broken weaklings before. It required pushing them to their limits. He had been taught that by the best. As a boy, his father's furies against weakness had terrified him until they fascinated him. When his father saw his first son, Scrap-Iron's older brother, Buck, couldn't take his share of abuse, he wrote him off as weak, as less than a man. When he saw Scrap could take it, he started treating him like a man. Scrap-Iron had adored his older brother—until he realized the old man was right about Buck. Buck was too squeamish to even give their diabetic father insulin injections. The younger Scrap-Iron had to administer the shots. At nineteen, Buck joined the Marines to try and prove something, but he ended up getting himself killed and didn't even do that in a way his father would have approved of. He got hit by a pickup truck while walking across a highway in South Carolina. Now the only time Scrap-Iron allowed himself to think about his brother was when he thought about weakness.

He finished the ice cream and concentrated. With his mind dedicated to getting even, he felt better already. Getting even was something he was especially good at. His worst fear was that Stewart might disappear before he could get even. That couldn't happen, and what came next for the Professor had to be big and bad. If not, Stewart would have won. The current score was easy to tally. Stewart had got laid and at his expense. What kind of a humiliation was that?

26

By the time Stewart made it back to camp, his shifting moods had left him unsure of anything except that he wanted to be alone.

How bad was that morning's experience? Some men wouldn't think it bad at all. Some men would brag about it. *There is nothing either good or bad, but thinking makes it so.* That's what The Bard said. Or was he just rationalizing again? Maybe Dostoevsky was more apropos. *Man is the being who can get used to anything.*

He was thinking too much again, but before he could duck into his tent, Slinky intercepted him and put an end to that.

"Look what I got," Slinky said.

He had a box of cookies. Coconut macaroons. He knew they were Stewart's favorites. It was an offering meant to gain an audience and soothe a guilty conscience.

"Come in," Stewart said. If he had to talk, he didn't want to do it out in the open.

"I've got tea too," Slinky said. He dangled two tea bags to demonstrate. Earl Gray Breakfast tea, part of his stash pilfered from the hospitality station in a local car dealer's lobby.

They ducked into the tent. Stewart poured water from a plastic jug into a saucepan. He put the saucepan on his propane stove and lit the burner with a match. The push button sparker had already stopped working. He figured the perpetual dampness of the woods had caused that. Nothing lasted for long in the woods.

Every time the stove's flame sparked and popped to life with its distinctive little poof, he rejoiced a little. It was an amazing piece of utilitarian magic, how this little bit of technology could warm a cold life. He had an appreciation now for things he never thought of before, like how fire truly was the discovery for the ages. True appreciation requires hardship.

He had two ceramic cups. He preferred decaffeinated tea, especially later in the day, but for hospitality's sake he accepted Slinky's caffeinated offering. One of his cups had a dark crack along its rim. He took that one for himself.

When the water started to boil, he shut off the flame and made the tea. He made his plain, Slinky's with two artificial sweetener packets donated by Burger-Land. He purposefully poured boiling water over his cup's cracked rim to kill any lurking bacteria.

The cookies were good. He knew he'd eat too many.

"One other thing about this morning," Slinky said.

"No, Slink," Stewart said. "I don't want to talk about that any more."

"Okay," Slinky said. But then, before Stewart could object, he got his thought out. "I just wanted to say you really did good. I mean with that Betty. You were really…"

"Slink, I said I didn't want to talk about it, and I mean it."

"Okay," Slinky said. "I'm sorry."

They stayed quiet, slapped a few mosquitoes, sipped tea, and listened for any activity in camp. Stewart made sure to turn his cup to avoid the cracked rim and whatever germs might survive a boiling.

"So," Slinky said. "Are you gonna stay a little?"

"For as little as possible," Stewart said. "As soon as I find something else, I'm gone."

"Okay," Slinky said.

"Keep that to yourself," Stewart said. "About me leaving. It's nobody else's business."

Slinky drew his thumb and index finger across his lips, as if he were zipping them closed.

27

Scrap-Iron finished his ice cream and then called The Bandito.

"I want you to check and make sure the Professor is in camp. Don't fuck around. Get right back to me."

The Bandito walked to Stewart's tent and heard Stewart and Slinky inside. He called Scrap-Iron back with the good news.

"He's here, Scrap. In his tent. I heard him talking to Slinky."

"Listen," Scrap-Iron said. "You make sure he doesn't leave. Don't say anything to him or Slinky. Just make sure the Professor doesn't leave. That's your only job. I'm calling a special meeting for tonight."

***

Scrap-Iron had never called a Sunday evening meeting before. Sunday evenings were dedicated to the chess games he played against himself. With his hand-carved chess set, it was Norse Vikings against Norse Mainlanders, and slow on the beer until he finished, lest he dull his thinking. Scrap-Iron took his chess seriously. He forced himself to play both sides to the best of his ability, but he always rooted for the Vikings.

Tonight he would continue his real life chess game with the Professor. He controlled the board. He had the pieces, and he had the strategy. Now the strategy had to degenerate into action.

His first priority was to readdress Stewart's humiliation. That had to be done immediately. He couldn't have Stewart strutting around camp like the cock of the walk. He needed to break Stewart and do it in front of the boys. His instinct was to do it in his tried and true fashion—with physical intimidation and the proper dose of pain.

He could use one of his favorite ambushes, the arm-wrestling match. He had a successful history with that. There was this body-builder type who used to visit the junkyard. An effusive young man, he was harmless but loud and inordinately proud of his muscular arms. All summer he wore the same sleeveless T-shirt with two red arrows on the front that pointed from his chest to his biceps. Above the arrows it said, Gun Show. In a spectacular display of foolhardiness, this man enjoyed teasing Scrap-Iron. "You got to get to the gym, big man," he would say. "Getting a little soft around the middle there." He did this foolish thing in front of the boys. Scrap-Iron challenged him to an arm-wrestling match. Besides his great strength, Scrap-Iron was schooled in the techniques of arm wrestling. He never did anything halfway, and he loved combining the physical and the mental. As the match started, Scrap-Iron got a high grip on his opponent's hand and locked him in a straight-up position. No matter how much the young man tried, he made no progress. When his surprised opponent's face had turned a bright red from maximum effort, Scrap-Iron grinned and asked, "Still think I need the gym?" Then he applied all his strength, and in one sudden and violent thrust, broke the young man's arm, snapping his humerus bone with the sickening sound of a stick being broken across a knee.

Just a few years ago, he might have done Stewart in some similar way. But that would mean only short-term satisfaction. Broken body parts heal. The mature Scrap-Iron was a long-term thinker. He knew that the key to breaking a man like Stewart wasn't physical but mental. Stewart didn't have pride in his physical being. How could he? He had probably been physically humiliated all his life, from the time he first left his mother's side to play with another kid and that kid instinctively sensed a weakling placed on this Earth for his exploitation and entertainment. Physical humiliation would be nothing new for Stewart. What Stewart still had pride in was his goodness and his sense of himself as better than others. Take that away, and what would he have left? Nothing.

Scrap-Iron was pleased with himself. Maturation had refined his thinking. It had taught him how to maximize benefit and minimize risk. That was the cool-headed and cold-hearted way the criminal masterminds did it, in books or film, and he admired them for it. Even if society didn't admire them, or perhaps because they didn't, he rooted for the criminals worthy of his appreciation–for Raskolnikov, for Moriarty, for Hannibal Lecter.

What would a weakling like Professor Stewart be to such men? A bug to be crushed.

28

The boys sat in the garage, waiting. At first they were excited, and then they were bewildered. They thought Scrap-Iron had summoned them to view the Stewart and Betty video, that Scrap had found the good parts so good that he couldn't wait until movie night to show it. But the projector wasn't set up, the garage wasn't infused with the buttery smell of fresh popcorn, and the popping machine stood dormant in the corner.

Stewart had also expected the video. He had prepared himself for it, hoping the viewing was the final act of his initiation rite. He could handle that one more thing. He'd have to, to buy some time. One crazy feeling had built in him on the way to Scrap-Iron's place. He felt a warm anticipation at seeing himself and Betty on the screen.

***

Scrap-Iron entered through the small side door. The boys' hellos went unrequited. The big man just sat in his chair and drummed its arms with his fingertips. The boys took on their landlord's somber mood. When Scrap wasn't happy, nobody was happy.

"Listen up," Scrap-Iron said. "No tongues, just ears."

He had something important to say. Without further preamble he said it.

"Pack up all your shit. Tents and everything. You gotta get out. All of you."

The boys sat straighter. All their focus now on their landlord and benefactor. Scrap-Iron was practiced in getting the attention of the habitually inattentive. You dealt with them just like you did kids and animals–don't complicate things; make it all about them and their needs.

Even Stewart felt a sudden sense of disorientation at the prospect of being turned out and so suddenly. Lately his nightmares had evolved. They were more about abandonment, about having no place to stay, no place to feel safe. In the dream that recurred most often, he was a grown man still living at home and unable to support himself while his father kept threatening to throw him out into the cold and cruel real world.

"What do you mean, Scrap?" The Bandito asked.

"I didn't make myself clear?" Scrap-Iron said.

"Why do we gotta leave?" Toad asked. He sounded like a whining kid.

"Ramon," Scrap-Iron said.

"Ramon?" The Bandito asked. He said the name as if he had never heard of his former campmate.

"Ramon," Scrap-Iron said.

The boys looked at each other as if the answer to this mystery was somewhere among them.

"What's Ramon got to do with us any more?" Herc asked.

"One of my cops called me," Scrap-Iron said. "Ramon tangled assholes with the law again and got himself arrested. Because he's a dumb bastard. To save himself, he tried trading everything he knows about all of you, telling a bunch of shit about all that goes on here."

"We didn't do nothing to him," Herc said. "And what do the cops care about what he says anyway?"

Herc harbored bad feelings for Ramon stemming from a small thing that turned big, as happens between men of shattered and sensitive pride. Burger-Land had had a two-for-one Wednesday deal on their double-sized hamburgers, and Herc, wanting protein but watching his caloric intake, donated his free one to Ramon. Ramon was insufficiently appreciative. Worse yet, when he was done eating and without asking, Ramon tossed his wrapper onto Herc's tray. Herc didn't like the disrespect. He would have settled things right then and there inside Burger-Land, but feral men, like feral animals, learn to avoid fights with dangerous foes. It wasn't that Herc didn't think he would win, but that there was too much chance of getting hurt. He could lose teeth or break a limb or lose an eye. Living in the woods required he be physically whole.

"This cop," Scrap-Iron said, "called me and told me Ramon talked some shit to one of the sheriff's daughters. A thirteen-year old girl."

"A real perv," Herc said. "I knew it."

"When he got picked up," Scrap-Iron said, "he was scared of a beat down, so he told the cops that he knew about all kinds of bad things going on in the woods. Like you guys were some kind of master criminals and account for half the crime in town. He said if they let him go he'd tell them all about it."

"Like what we do at the mall?" Toad asked. "On the docks, on big delivery nights?"

Scrap-Iron looked Stewart's way. "Let's not get into specifics," he said.

"If he said anything about drugs," Herc said, "then that's a goddamn lie." Reformed Herc was sensitive about drugs.

"Ramon's not known for telling the truth," Scrap-Iron said. "But my cop says that if what he's talking about gets to the town's big shooters, they got no choice but to do something. If that happens you're all fucked."

"What we gonna do?" Toad asked.

"What you're gonna do," Scrap-Iron said, "is pack up and run. I'll get you over to Pennsylvania. Then you're on your own."

"But Scrap," The Bandito said. "We got no place to go in Pennsy. We don't know nobody over there."

The boys all nodded to that.

"Pennsylvania?" Herc said. "Shit. Don't they got bears out there?"

"You mean leave here and never come back?" Toad asked.

"That's exactly what I mean," Scrap-Iron said. "So you better get your asses in gear."

Stewart thought Toad was going to cry. Toad could go from threatening nemesis to scared little boy in an instant.

"Scrap," The Bandito said. "There must be something you can do."

The thought of Scrap-Iron not having an answer to any dilemma was foreign to the boys. It already seemed foreign to Stewart.

"There is one thing," Scrap-Iron said.

"What?" The Bandito asked.

Scrap-Iron shook his head at his own idea's dim prospects. "I could," he said, "I might… "

"Yeah, Scrap?" the boys asked, over each other.

"I might be able to get Ramon released tonight before he can talk to anyone else. That's important."

"Why's that important, Scrap?" The Bandito asked.

"Because tomorrow a new shift of cops and supervisors come in. If Ramon talks to them, you're done."

"Can you do that?" The Bandito asked. "Get Ramon out?"

"My guy has ways," Scrap-Iron said. "A paperwork mix-up. Shit like that happens all the time."

"But they'll just pick him up again," Herc said. "Ramon's too dumb to hide and too lazy to run."

"It'll take them at least forty-eight hours to get him back," Scrap-Iron said. "It's not like he's a priority. That'll give you time to pack up and get."

"But we don't want to get," The Bandito said.

"I don't want to get old and die," Scrap-Iron said. Silence.

Scrap-Iron leaned back and focused on the burn scars on his arms as if he had just discovered them.

The longer the quiet lasted, the more Stewart felt an overwhelming desire to help. He liked nothing more than to use his brain to solve difficult problems, especially when in the solving he could win praise from some powerful figure. This need to please had got him into troubled waters before, especially during his corporate days when being the one to have a good idea usually meant getting the responsibility for implementation and follow-up. But it was an instinct he couldn't resist.

"Okay," Scrap-Iron said, as if things were settled. "You guys get packing, and I'll get the van." He started lifting his bulk out of the chair. Every time he did that, the chair creaked and cracked as if it might come apart.

"Maybe there is something," Stewart said.

"Ah," Scrap-Iron said, "we hear from our Professor."

"What you need," Stewart said, "are pressure points."

"Pressure points?" Scrap-Iron asked, and not derisively, more like he liked the sound of the phrase or the possibilities it suggested.

"It's like," Stewart said, "the carrot and the stick. You get Ramon released, and then you use positive and negative pressure points to keep him from talking."

"Is this something you learned in college?" Scrap-Iron asked.

"It could work," Stewart said.

The boys all looked to Scrap-Iron, not understanding, but hoping against hope.

"Give me an example," Scrap-Iron said.

"Well," Stewart said, "as a positive you offer Ramon a chance to return to camp or at least a chance to enjoy some of the benefits of camp. That's the carrot. I'm sure he misses camp."

"How about the stick?" Scrap-Iron said. "I think I'll like the stick better."

"Okay," Stewart said. "You tell him that, if he talks, he can never come back to camp because there won't be a camp."

"What you're saying," Scrap-Iron said, "is that if I can get Ramon released, I can use that time to persuade him not to talk."

"Yes," Stewart said. "That's it." He already felt good about his contribution.

"It's a half-assed idea," Herc said.

"Half-assed?" Stewart said. His face and neck warmed at the criticism.

"We should get Ramon released," Herc said. "Just like Scrap said. So he can't run his mouth to the wrong cops. But why should we take any risk because of Ramon?"

"What are you suggesting?" Scrap-Iron asked.

"Scrap," Herc said, "you know what an asshole Ramon is. I mean he's hopped up most of the time. He gets any grief from the cops or that sheriff and he'll talk and there ain't no carrot or pressure stick gonna change that."

"Herc's right," The Bandito said. "I don't think the asshole even eats carrots."

"And you, Professor?" Scrap-Iron asked. "You disagree with that tactical assessment."

"It's a risk," Stewart said. "There's risk in any plan."

"Ramon talking ain't a risk," Herc said. "It's for sure."

Herc would oppose any idea he proposed. Stewart knew that. Herc was proud of Scrap-Iron's interest in his idea and jealous of any alternative.

"Okay then, Herc," Stewart said. "What do you propose?" As if sparring at a faculty meeting he added, "Specifically?"

"Specifically?" Herc asked. He had some trouble with the word; it came out as *spesaphysically*. That agitated him further.

"Yes," Stewart said. He was going to add *specifically*, but after Herc's butchering of it, he wasn't sure he could get it out right.

"What I propose," Herc said, "is something that you, mister Professor, ain't got the balls for."

Stewart face reddened more. "And just what is that?" he asked.

Herc looked to Scrap-Iron. The big man nodded.

"We got to shut Ramon's mouth," Herc said. "I got no doubts about that. But we got to shut it for keeps."

"What are you talking about?" Stewart asked.

Herc looked back to Scrap-Iron. The big man nodded again. It was put up or shut up time.

Herc put up. He walked over to the workbench and from beneath it he pulled out the Ten Commandments tablet. He held it up for all to see. Then he jabbed a finger at the tablet, punching a hole clear through the Fifth Commandment.

"That's what I'm talking about," he said, spittle flying from his mouth.

Scrap-Iron broke the ensuing silence. "That," he said, "is what I call specific."

29

"I need a beer," Scrap-Iron said, as if the turn of events was so dramatic and unexpected that he required fortification.

Slinky rose to get the beer. The boys looked to the refrigerator, but Scrap-Iron didn't offer.

"You know what we're talking about here?" Scrap-Iron asked.

Before answering his own question, he waited for Slinky to deliver the beer. He took a long drink and wiped his mouth on his arm, letting the silence build suspense.

"What we're talking about," Scrap-Iron said, "is breaking the Fifth."

"Yep," Herc said.

"That's the big one," Scrap-Iron said. "The Fifth requires justification."

"There's no moral justification here," Stewart said.

"That's yet to be decided," Scrap-Iron said. He put his beer between his legs and rubbed his hands together. He was back to enjoying himself.

Stewart felt as if he were cast in a movie and one in which he didn't want a role. Maybe Scrap-Iron was just testing his boys to see how far they would go for him. Maybe he would rein them in when the time was right.

"Justify me this," Herc said. "Why should we all be fucked because of one useless asshole who's a snitch and a pervert?"

"Listen," Scrap-Iron said. "The Fifth is a complicated Commandment." He tossed his bottle cap into a plastic bucket next to the workbench. It was half full of caps. He used the caps in his artistic welding projects.

"Thou shall not kill," Stewart said. "Sounds pretty simple to me."

"Well," Scrap-Iron said, "when things seem simple, they're usually not. And if the Fifth's so simple, then the great have been sinning all through history."

"You're trying to confuse things," Stewart said.

"Back to simple then," Scrap-Iron said. "Sometimes a culling is necessary for the survival of the herd."

"Then you're gonna declare open season on Ramon?" Stewart asked. "Maybe you should issue your boys hunting licenses?"

"You're assuming it's the boys that will have to do it," Scrap-Iron said.

Stewart's eyes narrowed at the implications of that.

"One thing I don't assume," Stewart said, "is that any of us has the right to kill Ramon."

The boys attentive to the back and forth. Something important was about to come out of it.

"You," Scrap-Iron said, "are assuming you have the right to keep the boys from protecting themselves."

Stewart shook his head in frustration.

"I'm assumin' something," Herc interrupted. "I'm assumin' we got to shit or get off the pot."

"The man has a point," Scrap-Iron said. He guzzled the rest of his beer, turned to Toad and said, "Get me another one, and get everyone else one. There's a hard decision to make before anyone leaves here."

Toad distributed the beers. A bottle of long-necked PBR for Scrap, a can of Budweiser for each of the boys.

The Bandito popped his can open, took a swig, and asked, "So Scrap, what do we do?"

There was a little boy innocence about the question, a complete willingness to be led. God help us, Stewart thought.

"C'mon, Professor," Scrap-Iron said. "Help me here. Didn't you take any strategy courses in all that college?" Scrap-Iron loved strategy and tactics. He excelled while playing war games on his computer, pitting himself against Napoleon at Austerlitz and Robert E. Lee in the great Civil War battles.

Stewart thought back to Slinky's advice to engage the big man on topics that he loved. It was good advice for getting along in a bad circumstance. When it came to going along to get along, Slink was no dummy.

"The goal," Stewart said, hoping to change the trajectory of things, "is to get the desired result but take the least drastic action possible."

"This pressure spot stuff," Herc said. "It's all bullshit. And time's wasting. Whatever we do, it's got to be done fast. I don't want to end up in the Pennsylvania boonies, in the woods shitting next to a bear."

"I don't think," The Bandito said, "that the bear would like that either."

"Well," Scrap-Iron said, "I'm gonna tell you boys all I can about this thing. Then it's your decision. In any hard choice, you got to weigh the consequences of doing it against the consequences of not doing it. In this case, it's your lives on the line, so it's got to be your scale. Nobody else can calibrate that scale for you. And nobody should put a thumb on the side of mercifulness or the side of mercilessness. Let the scale decide."

Scrap, the subtle nudger. Scrap like the torque wrench he used for tightening lug nuts, a powerful tool but capable of a nuanced touch—not so little torque that the nuts could come loose on their own, not so much torque that the nuts wouldn't break loose when needed.

"Let's do it," Herc said. "Let's cut all the bullshit and do it. That's what my scale says."

The Bandito nodded.

"You're together then?" asked Scrap-Iron.

"I still think," Stewart said, "that we could scare him off."

"First of all," Herc said, "even if we scare Ramon, he's too fucked-up to stay scared. Second of all, if whatever we do sends him right back to the cops, then we're all screwed good. Except for you, Professor. You can just go back to wherever it was you came from. For the rest of us, I say we got to do what we got to do."

"Yeah," Toad said.

The boys looked to Slinky.

Stewart tried making eye contact, but Slinky avoided him.

"I guess," Slinky said. "I don't know what else we can do."

"So," Scrap-Iron said and looked to Stewart. "Are we all off the pot?"

Still on the pot, Stewart felt how lonely of a place that was.

"This ain't majority rules," Scrap-Iron said. "See, that's okay for little things. You know, like electing a president. That kind of shit. This is serious. This requires a unanimous vote. We don't do this any other way."

"Everybody's got to agree," Herc said.

"Agreed," The Bandito said.

"Me, too," Toad said.

All eyes back to Slinky until he nodded.

"No good," Scrap-Iron said. "You got to say it."

"Okay," Slinky said.

"What's that mean?" Herc asked.

"I'm in," Slinky said. "I agree. Jesus. Ramon's got to go. Break the Fifth. The whole thing."

Stewart couldn't believe it. *Lord of the Flies* playing out before him. His options were rapidly closing. If Scrap-Iron truly meant it, it wasn't going to be easy to get him off this craziness of killing Ramon. But there was no way he was going to get involved with a killing. He had to at least buy some time. Time meant options. If he got away before morning, he could call the police and anonymously tip them about Scrap-Iron's plan to kill Ramon. He would save two lives, his and Ramon's.

"I wish there was another way," Stewart said. He uncoupled his hands. The sides of his fingers were bright red from the squeezing pressure. He didn't even know he had been doing that.

"You know what my mother used to say?" Scrap-Iron asked.

Stewart shook his head.

203

"My mother used to say," Scrap-Iron said and held both hands out, palms up. "Wish in one hand. Then shit in the other. See which one fills up faster."

To say it felt like a Scrap-Iron punch to his stomach, but with an in-the-moment pragmatism, and knowing he wasn't going to stick around and play any part in this, Stewart said, "Okay." Any deception was permissible in this spot.

"You're in?" Scrap-Iron asked.

"Yes," Stewart said. "I'm in."

Scrap-Iron smiled.

"Okay," Scrap-Iron said. He let out a big breath, as if all this was too much work.

"Now what?" The Bandito asked.

"Now," Scrap-Iron said, "we get to the part that God's in."

"What part's that, Scrap?" The Bandito asked.

"The details," Scrap-Iron said.

30

"Okay," Scrap-Iron said. "It's got to be done by tomorrow. We can't wait any longer than that."

No disagreement.

To be sitting there, involved in something as sordid as this, even if he were just playing along, made Steward sick to his stomach.

"Is Ramon still staying in that old railroad car?" Scrap-Iron asked. "The one on the side track east of here?"

"Yeah," The Bandito said.

"You're sure about that?"

"I saw him coming from it just the other day," The Bandito said.

"Okay," Scrap-Iron said. "That's good. Now remember, he sleeps half the day. I could never get him going before noon. And he's always comatose in the morning from all the shit he's had the night before. Catch him at sunrise, first thing, when he's asleep in the railroad car; he'll be like a rattlesnake on a cold morning. Easy pickings."

Nods at the sense in that.

"Now think it through some more," Scrap-Iron said. He thought everything through. "What means would best suit our purposes?"

"You mean how to do it?" The Bandito asked.

"That's right," Scrap-Iron said. "First, think about Ramon. Think about him in his total assholiness." Scrap-Iron spread his arms in a big circle, as if such a totality would be hard to mentally encompass. He let the boys think a moment longer, then gave further direction.

"Most personal tragedies," he said, "are self-imposed. What fatal end would Ramon be likely to impose on himself?"

"I don't get you," The Bandito said.

"Put it this way," Scrap-Iron said. "If you woke up tomorrow and heard Ramon was croaked, what manner of death would least surprise you?"

"He's a druggy," Herc said. "He could OD anytime and croak, and no one would be surprised. The only surprise is it ain't happened already."

"Good," Scrap-Iron said. "That works for us."

"The other thing going for us," Herc said, "is that no one is gonna care. You know what the cops say when they find a guy like Ramon dead?" Herc answered for himself. "Good riddance."

Scrap-Iron liked the look on Stewart's face, and he liked the way things were progressing. The boys were sinking to their lowest denominator and dragging Stewart with them—while he sat above it all formulating strategy for breaking the greatest of the Commandments. It was good to be alive.

"We're getting there," Scrap-Iron said. "At sunrise, Ramon's in an isolated rail car with no one around and no security cameras and no bystanders. That's the way he likes it, and that's the way we like it. In the morning, he's dormant from all the shit in him. Now he gets an overdose."

"How?" the Bandito asked.

"With," Scrap-Iron said, "a little help from his friends." He made the motion of sticking a needle in his own arm and depressing the plunger. "*Adiós, mi amigo.* Just like it was eventually gonna happen anyway. No blood, no mess. No one a bit surprised, and no one cares. No checking and no forensics. No *CSI*, no *Unsolved Mysteries*. It's wrapped in a bow for us."

"That means we don't have to pack and go?" Toad asked.

"Almost," Scrap-Iron said.

"Almost?" The Bandito asked.

"First thing," Scrap-Iron said, "is to get Ramon sprung. That'll take me one call." He pulled his phone from his chair's side pocket and showed it to the boys.

The boys nodded. They were confident in him.

"So," Scrap-Iron said, "we know what we've got to do. And we know why we've got to do it. We know when we're gonna do it, how we're gonna do it, and where we're gonna do it. So the question I have for you masterminds is this: When you've got the what, why, when, how and where—what are you missing?"

Stewart knew but didn't show it. The less he was involved, the better.

Herc shook his head in affirmation; he knew too.

Scrap-Iron pointed to Herc.

"We're missing who," Herc said.

"You got it!" Scrap-Iron said. "My friends: what, why, when, how, where and who. Sound familiar, Professor?"

Stewart nodded. He didn't know if Scrap-Iron was referring to Kipling and his six honest serving men. But it wouldn't have shocked him.

"For the who," Herc said. "I volunteer. It be a pleasure. You won't need a needle either. I'll slap a Full Nelson on him. Then snap his neck."

Herc had been a middleweight wrestling champion in high school. Quietly, he stood and snuck behind Toad. He put his arms under Toad's armpits and pushed them through and around the back of his neck. He intertwined his fingers and applied pressure. Toad screamed and wiggled, and Herc pressed down harder until Toad, despite his youth and wiriness, was helpless.

"Turn him loose," Scrap-Iron said. This was serious business. He didn't have time for horseplay or an inadvertently broken neck.

Herc let go, and Toad rolled his head side-to-side and front to back, like a man trying to work out a severe kink.

"You'd do the job," Scrap-Iron said to Herc. "I don't doubt that for a minute. But there's something bigger, a strategic issue you got to think about. Sometimes you have to sacrifice yourself to something bigger."

Scrap-Iron hooked his thumbs in his overalls and pulled them away from his chest to give the boys time to think. It was for effect. He didn't have much faith in the boys' problem-solving abilities.

"The doer," Scrap-Iron said, "shouldn't be the person who wants to do it. It should be the person who doesn't want to do it."

The boys perplexed at that.

"It's what the Professor there," Scrap-Iron looked to Stewart, "might call a paradox."

"Tell us, Scrap," The Bandito said.

"Let's say," Scrap-Iron said, "we get this good deed done, and everything goes to plan. Who do you think is most likely to get second thoughts about it and talk to the cops? Is it the person who most wants Ramon dead or the one who least wants him dead?"

The boys thought about that for a minute. Despite looking disappointed, Herc answered for them. "I'd say the one who wants it least."

"You got it," Scrap-Iron said. "That's the weak link, the person most likely to have regrets. And that person must be the doer because then he has everything to lose if the story comes out."

"That's brilliant shit, Scrap," The Bandito said.

"And," Scrap-Iron said, "every chain has a weak link. Now, our chain has six links. Who among us is the weak one?"

All the boys, even Slinky, turned and looked at Stewart.

Stewart said nothing. Instead he wondered for the millionth time how he ever landed in Scrapville. But there was one thing he knew that Scrap-Iron and the boys didn't. His link was a lot weaker than they thought. He wasn't going to participate in any of this madness. He wasn't going to kill anyone. If he could, he was going to prevent a killing.

"I guess," a frustrated Herc said, "that sometimes the team has to come first."

"I'm sure," Scrap-Iron said to Stewart, "that you've thought about breaking the Fifth Commandment. Who among us, if the truth be told, hasn't thought about that?"

"It's not been my lifelong aspiration," Stewart said.

Scrap-Iron smiled at that.

"Scrap," Herc said, "I got a question."

"Shoot," Scrap-Iron said.

"The Professor there," Herc said and looked skeptically at Stewart.

"Yeah?" Scrap-Iron said.

"I mean," Herc said, "this ain't gonna be easy. It's gonna take some big ones."

"You don't think he's got big ones?" Scrap-Iron asked. "Didn't you see him this morning?"

"This is different," Herc said. "You know, Scrap, for something like this, he's probably got the balls of a bull canary."

"I believe in giving a man the benefit of the doubt," Scrap-Iron said. "Remember, we've already underestimated him once. But I get what you're saying. This is too important to leave doubt in the equation. So I will accompany our man on his mission. Let's say I'm going to be there for quality control. I'll make sure things go as planned. And, before you ask, only two can go on the mission; more than that complicates things and adds unnecessary risk."

Disappointment but no dissent.

"You know," Scrap-Iron said, "when you think about it, who can say what worse shit was coming Ramon's way? Who knows what bad we're saving him from? We're probably doing him a favor."

Scrap-Iron nodded as if he had convinced himself.

"Professor," Scrap-Iron said. "Meet me in the morning at the flagpole. I'll be there at first light. I don't have to tell you not to be late. Do I?"

"No," Stewart said.

"Toad-Boy," Scrap-Iron said, "another beer for everybody. The Professor too. But Toad, you don't get one."

"Why not?" Toad asked.

"Because," Scrap-Iron said, "you gotta stay awake tonight. You got watchdog duty. In case the Professor tries to run."

Stewart felt like a man being dragged into hell.

IV

31

There was no walking off by himself this time. As the boys headed down the tracks and toward camp, they kept Stewart in the middle of the pack, contained there as if he were a babe among a species that shielded their young from predators.

Herc rapped the back of Stewart's head with a knuckle. "You shouldn't of never messed with Scrap."

"What did I do to him?" Stewart said.

"It's what you did to Betty," Herc said.

"Yeah," The Bandito said, "you screwed Betty right in front of him. You're lucky you ain't dead yet."

Stewart mum for the lack of any notion of how to reason with such logic.

Herc spat and wiped his mouth. He tapped Stewart's head again. "I'd say you're the one screwed now."

***

Herc and The Bandito carried their beer to Herc's fort. Boredom not the enemy tonight. Lots to talk about. Tomorrow figured to be a big day in Scrapville. It wasn't everyday someone got snuffed.

Toad wanted to join Herc and The Bandito, but as watchdog he had to stick with Stewart and remain vigilant and wasn't allowed any beer. He always got the shit duty.

Slinky was solicitous of Stewart. "I can stay with you," he said. "If you need someone to talk to."

"I need some time by myself," Stewart said. Survival trumped manners.

"You're sure?" Slinky asked.

"Yeah," Stewart said. "But there is something you can do for me?"

"Name it."

"Would you go over to the mall and get me a six-pack of beer?"

"Sure."

As strange as this request was, coming from Stewart, Slinky welcomed it. He was glad for some favor to do, for anything to help soothe his conscience, which had turned from bad to worse.

"That's more than I need," Slinky said, when Stewart handed him cash.

"I want the sixteen-ounce cans," Stewart said. "Budweiser."

"Okay."

"On second thought," Stewart said, "instead of the six-pack, make it the eight-pack. You know, one of those boxes of eight the boys get. Is that okay? Can you carry that?"

"Absolutely," Slinky said.

***

When Slinky delivered, Stewart thanked him but didn't invite him to stay.

"Come get me if you need me," Slinky said.

Stewart left his tent's flap open. Through the screen he could see Toad sitting against the camp's railroad tie with his feet crossed, his back to the fire pit, and his eyes locked on his tent. Toad was good at one-dimensional tasks.

With the beer in hand Stewart stepped out of his tent. He stopped in front of Toad and tore a can from the box and popped it open. Toad's eyes went to the escaping foam. Stewart licked the foam from the can and feigned a big gulp.

"You want a beer?" he said. "I mean being that we're both stuck here."

Toad, distrustful of generosity, stared at the beer and at Stewart.

"Is it cold?" he asked.

That was the kind of aggravating thing Toad did— to qualify his acceptance of something offered, even when it was obvious that he was desperate for it.

"Nice and cold," Stewart said and handed a can to Toad. He set the rest of the eight-pack on the ground between them.

Toad popped his can open and guzzled.

"You gonna sit?" he asked Stewart after a little while, as if Stewart were making him nervous.

"It must be everything that's going on," Stewart said. "But I need to do something. I'm jumpy. I'm going to organize my stuff."

Toad tipped his beer can toward Stewart, as if to say do whatever you please as long as you stay put.

Despite the heat, Stewart closed the tent's screen and flap behind him. Survival trumped comfort. He watched Toad for a moment, and then, for good luck, took a last sip of his beer and said to himself, "Drink up Toad-Boy."

He would pack everything while Toad anaesthetized himself into a deep sleep. Seven sixteen-ounce cans of Budweiser should be an adequate soporific. He would leave an hour before first light and head west. He had an Amtrak schedule, not the latest but good enough. The earliest train west on Mondays left at 5:48. For about the tenth time, he reached in his pocket and confirmed he had cash for the ticket.

There was a religious retreat near Bethlehem, Pennsylvania, where he and his wife once spent a long weekend meditating and escaping the pressures of their upwardly mobile lives. Back then, more meetings than time seemed like a crisis worthy of a retreat. They had left on good terms with the Abbot, a fellow lover of Shakespeare. Stewart thought he would still be welcome there, at least for a few days, while he figured his next steps. The Abbott had said the Retreat's library was in bad need of organizing. It probably still was, and Stewart was the man to organize it. He could divert himself with a project like that.

He lit his oil lamp and set it in the corner with the flame adjusted high for good light. A little luxury but no reason to conserve fuel now since he wouldn't carry the lamp or fuel with him. The lamp was bulky and fragile and the fuel heavy. Whatever was to come, he would need to be nimble.

He spread his army blanket on the ground and emptied the contents of his backpack onto one side of it. That pile was made up of his walking-around necessities and the items he couldn't risk being stolen from his tent. In the heap were his pain relievers, glucose pills, allergy tablets and eye drops, his prescription stomach medicine, his hand sanitizer, wet wipes and antibacterial cream. There was also a plastic water bottle–the kind that campers used to filter germs– a rain slick, and a ski-cap, the cap so his head wouldn't get cold and invite a migraine. A nine by twelve manila envelope held the minimal paperwork necessary for his new life: his store ID card, his still valid driver's license with a photo just three years old but now unrecognizable, his library card, a copy of his birth certificate that he had for some reason carried with him all this time. He turned the backpack upside down and shook it to make sure he had everything. His SPF ChapStick fell out along with salt and pepper packs, artificial sweeteners, and a wet wipe.

Toad was singing now. A painful, off-key rendition of one of Scrap-Iron's old blues songs. *Cause no...no...nobody knows you when you're down and out.* Toad tried to imitate everything Scrap-Iron did, and the big man favored the blues above all other music. He said it was for all the wisdom imparted.

Stewart took his three cardboard boxes and emptied them onto the other side of the blanket. Mostly clothes in that pile, his socks and underwear, hooded sweatshirts, spare jeans, and his store uniform pants and shirt. Gallon Ziploc bags held his toiletries: toothbrush and paste, deodorant, mouthwash, shampoo and conditioner.

Everything he owned was in those two heaps. He squatted and stared at what lay before him. If the philosophers were right and wealth consisted not in having great possessions but in having few wants, then he was at least halfway to being a wealthy man. He had these pitiful possessions and wasn't sure what he wanted.

He would decide what he would carry and what had to be sacrificed. The things that he couldn't live without would go into his backpack. The backpack would never leave his sight. He'd call in sick for work tomorrow, after he was at the retreat, far away and safe. That way he wouldn't be fired for at least a few days. Another lesson learned the hard way–you burned your bridges at the last possible moment. Even the poorest, ricketiest bridge was harder to build than burn.

The tent would have to be left behind, sacrificed both for mobility and deception. His lamp and stove were better than Slink's, and Stewart wanted him to inherit them. Toad would probably big-ass Slink out of both, but that was unavoidable. He'd leave the shampoo, conditioner, and mouthwash behind too. They were heavy and easily replaceable. Wherever he ended up, he hoped he wouldn't need a tent or a stove. He might be a wanderer at heart, but he missed his comforts. To be a true wanderer, you probably had to start young.

His books were a special case–too valuable to leave behind and too heavy to carry. He packed them in a plastic garbage bag. He'd carry them as far as the train station where he could store them in a locker for future retrieval. He thought of the books as a promise to himself, a treasure he'd retrieve when his life was better.

He was of one mind now, no second-guessing and no hesitancy. This was cut and dried. He had no hope that Scrap-Iron could be reasoned with. For some twisted reason, Scrap-Iron was determined to make him a killer. Mix that with the big man's taste for violence and cruelty and a potential victim as unpredictable as Ramon, and what did you have? A sure recipe for a life-destroying tragedy.

What would Scrap-Iron do when he heard he was gone? Would he be furious, or would he say good riddance and that it just proved the Professor was a pussy? Scrap-Iron would be furious. He wouldn't like losing a toy, especially one he was just learning to enjoy. That's why staying local was out of the question. Stewart needed to take the train west and put all this behind him. He peeked through the flap. Toad had stopped singing but was still awake and still drinking.

He pulled off his sneakers and lay in his sleeping bag. A dog's barking came from far away. Despite his medicine, his stomach hurt. Maybe after he was his own man, living without physical and psychological terrors, his stomach would stop revolting. A man at odds with himself can't have a good stomach.

He'd try and sleep a little. Tomorrow he would need his strength.

32

A loud scratching noise roused him. He wiped his eyes and stared at the tent's top.

It was still dark out. That was a relief. His alarm clock read 4:23. He had slept but not overslept. He could hear Toad snoring. Sunrise was 5:52. He would be on the tracks and to the train station before full daylight.

The scratching at the tent's flap continued. He knew who had come calling. A cat's hunger was not subject to the clock or the sun or the desperate plans of humans. He'd give his special guest ten minutes.

He had never wanted to get attached to the big tomcat with the smudge on his face and the forlorn look in his eyes. That's why he'd never named him—to name him would have made things too personal. But it was too late for detachment. He worried who would feed the cat? Who would give him his dental treats to prevent tartar buildup, and who would do the now expected head scratching? He suddenly felt weepy about all that. He and the cat were two endangered species brought together by circumstance and lucky to have crossed paths. Now they'd have a last meal together, marinated morsels of chicken for the tomcat and an energy bar for Stewart. Today he was going to need all the energy he could muster.

He opened the flap, and the cat entered but stopped suddenly and stared at the backpack and satchel. He came up and sniffed both. He didn't trust new things or old things in new places. He didn't trust change. There was much to learn from feral cats. They were wise in the ways of the world. They had to be, or they died young. They lived by that simple equation. Stewart slowly peeled the lid off the cat food can to avoid the popping noise. His visitor didn't like the popping noise. With the smell of the chicken released, the cat circled him, whining, food the one thing that could compete with his natural suspicion.

He spooned the cat food onto a doubled paper towel and wiped the can clean and filled it with fresh water. As they ate, he talked to the cat in a half whisper. He said he would miss him. He implored him to be careful, as if careful wasn't his *modus operandi*. The cat looked up and stared at him, wide-eyed, a drop of water hanging from his furry chin. Out of hope, he offered the cat his lap. But this wasn't a lap cat. Among felines, that kind of thing had to be learned young or not at all. Stewart didn't promise to come back, and he didn't promise they would meet again. Promises were meant to be kept.

He stepped to the front of the tent, and the cat crouched in a defensive posture. The cat didn't like having anyone between himself and the open flap to freedom. When Stewart stepped to the side, the cat ran out. Stewart knew he would never see him again. He'd leave the two remaining cans of food for Slinky, hoping he would take up the big tom and his feeding. It would be good for both of those lonely souls.

Everything else packed, he dressed in his black pants and long-sleeved white shirt. He rolled up his sleeping bag and pillow and stuffed them into his satchel. He couldn't be sure where he would spend the night, so he needed to take the sleeping bag and pillow along. The satchel was so full he had to kneel on it to get the zipper closed.

Toad's drunken snoring sounded like industrial machinery at work. Stewart slung his backpack over his shoulders, picked up the satchel in one hand and the bag full of books in the other. He stepped out of the tent and stood up straight while keeping an eye on Toad. He took one step toward the path out of camp. Then he froze.

Sitting there, on two water buckets strategically set between him and the path, was Scrap-Iron. Despite the morning coolness, the big man wore just a T-shirt under his overalls and seemed relaxed, with his hands intertwined behind his head. His gap-toothed smile was visible in the lingering moonlight.

"Howdy, partner," Scrap-Iron said.

Stewart didn't answer.

"I didn't know you were such an early riser," Scrap-Iron said.

Stewart's legs weakened.

"Look at that shit," Scrap-Iron said and pointed to Toad. "You didn't think that I would leave something as important as you to that simpleton?"

Toad sat slumped against the railroad tie, his head on his chest, his eyes closed, and his mouth hanging open, seven empty beer cans scattered at his side.

"I'm leaving," Stewart said with feigned composure. He couldn't deny he was running, standing there outside his empty tent before sunrise with his bags packed. "You have no right to stop me."

"You know," Scrap-Iron said, "for a professor, you're a slow learner."

"Toad," Scrap-Iron yelled.

When that failed to rouse Toad, Scrap-Iron stepped over to him and gave him a kick in his thigh that spun him half-around.

Toad jumped up, rubbing his eyes. "I was just resting," he said. He looked to Stewart. "You was right, Scrap. He's trying to run. You're always right, Scrap."

"Put your shit back in the tent," Scrap-Iron said to Stewart.

Stewart started to walk away. Maybe if he just acted boldly, something good would happen.

Scrap-Iron looked to Toad and then to Stewart. Toad took the signal and ran behind Stewart and grabbed him by his backpack, using that leverage to pull him backward and to the ground. Stewart dropped the satchel and books and looked like an upturned turtle, unable to do anything other than make half a circle propelled by a comical kicking.

"What's going on?" said Slinky, awake now and out of his tent.

"The Professor tried to go rabbit," Scrap-Iron said. "Like I knew he would. I know his kind."

Slinky looked at Stewart and then leaned to him and offered his hand. Stewart refused it and, by getting his knee underneath him, got the leverage to stand. He wiggled out of his backpack and stood, exposed and trapped again.

"Listen," Stewart said, "this whole thing is crazy. You kill Ramon, no matter who does it, you all end up in jail for the rest of your lives. You can't get away with something like that."

"You're just chicken," Toad said.

"Scrap-Iron's using you," Stewart said. "He's manipulating you."

"Is that right?" Scrap-Iron said, in his best mocking tone. "I'm manipulating him?"

"No one manipmates me," Toad said.

"You can't kill Ramon," Stewart said. "Scare him, threaten him, beat him up even, but you can't kill him."

"Judgment has been passed," Scrap-Iron said.

"You guys would wake the dead," Herc said, stepping out of the woods. "I could hear you from way back at my place."

"We caught the Professor running," Toad said. "He's a rabbit."

"And you're surprised?" Herc said.

"Listen," Stewart said. "You're all about to make a big mistake. It'll cost you all. I want you to think about it."

"We've been through all that," Herc said. "It's got to be done."

"Not by me," Stewart said. "I'm not going to do it."

"You're not?" Scrap-Iron said.

"I'm not," Stewart said. "I don't care what you do." He said it like a man with nothing to lose.

A yawning Bandito joined the group. "What's up?" he asked. Everybody ignored him.

"So you're telling us again what you're not gonna do?" Scrap-Iron said to Stewart, shaking his head in mock disbelief.

The big man looked calm, more like a disappointed parent than an angry giant. But before Stewart could say another thing, Scrap-Iron took him by the throat and with that one-handed purchase lifted him over his head and held him in the air like a child's rag doll.

Stewart fought for breath. Scrap-Iron's hand encircled his whole neck, his powerful grip squeezing as if he were wringing a sponge. In an unthinking panic, Stewart kicked his feet, aiming for some vulnerable spot on Scrap-Iron. His kicks just bounced off.

"Let me know when you've changed your mind about participating," Scrap-Iron said. "You can just wave your arm."

The big man's face showed no effort from holding Stewart aloft, and he talked to his captive eye to eye, calmly and conversationally, as if he were a ventriloquist and Stewart his dummy.

Within seconds Stewart was flailing both arms. His lungs burned from lack of air; his neck felt like one of Scrap-Iron's iron vises had closed on it. Without lowering him, Scrap-Iron let go, and Stewart landed hard and rolled to the ground in a heap. He lay there gasping for breath, both hands to his throat, trying to reposition his Adam's apple, which he was sure had been either crushed or dislocated.

"You're gonna go, and you're gonna do it," Scrap-Iron said. He leaned toward Stewart and put his face in his. "I'll kick your ass all the way if I have to, but you're gonna go, and you're gonna do it."

Scrap-Iron pulled Stewart to his feet. Slinky came and stood next to Stewart. It was Slinky who was crying.

33

"I see the look of a predator in your eyes," Scrap-Iron said as he led Stewart out of camp. "If it's in your nature, you can't hide it."

Stewart said nothing.

"Your ingratitude surprises me," Scrap-Iron said. "It's the ultimate power, to be a taker of life, and I'm yielding it to you."

***

They went through the woods, and when they reached the tracks, the first hint of red was in the eastern sky. Scrap-Iron walked fast. The gravel crunched under his heavy steps, and his thick thighs made a rubbing sound. His strides made two of Stewart's. He shoved Stewart forward as needed, almost knocking him over once, but keeping him a half-step ahead where he could watch him.

Stewart stretched his legs for all he was worth. His throat ached as if Scrap-Iron's hand was still there and squeezing. He breathed heavily, and even his inhalations hurt. Running away was not an option. If he ran, Scrap-Iron would catch him, and his aching throat wouldn't be his only pain.

What would happen when they got there? If Ramon was drugged out, he would make easy prey. Would Scrap-Iron actually make him stick Ramon with a deadly needle? Did Scrap-Iron even bring a needle, or was all his talk of killing Ramon a ruse just to torment his new boy? If Ramon was awake, there would be a struggle. If it came to a struggle, would Scrap-Iron snap Ramon's neck, the way Herc said he would?

Every Thanksgiving, Stewart's father used to buy a precooked turkey. After he carved it, he'd set the wishbone on the kitchen windowsill, and after it had dried out sufficiently, he and Stewart would play tug-of-war until the bone snapped. The one holding the larger piece was granted a special wish. When the young Stewart won, he always wished for a mother. When he got older, the game seemed foolish, but he still recalled the sharp, snapping noise of the wishbone. The recollection made him shiver.

***

"Just down that sidetrack and past those trees," Scrap-Iron said and pointed ahead and to the right. He was puffing more than Stewart now. His physique wasn't suited to aerobics.

"Quiet," Scrap-Iron said, when they started down the sidetrack.

Stewart wasn't sure his throat would allow him to make a sound, even if he wanted to.

When they cleared the copse of trees, the railroad car came into view. They were within a hundred yards of it. There was no sign of life. In the dim light, the railcar was a dull, weather-beaten red. As they got closer, faded letters could be made out on the side. *Morristown & Erie.*

"Professor," Scrap-Iron said, "get ready for the thrill of your life. What could be more thrilling than correcting one of God's mistakes?"

The big man was genuinely excited at the prospect of murder. Stewart asked himself again, what kind of man was this? A sadist who could torture someone like Slinky for amusement and then comfort him with a gentle hug; a gifted mechanic who entertained himself by sabotaging the work of others; a man with a love of learning who quoted the classics and the Bible but who pornographically humiliated the one person who could nurture his intellectual curiosity. All of his earlier nightmares were nothing compared to coming under the control of this vile enigma.

Scrap-Iron stopped ten feet from the railroad car and its sliding door, which was open about two feet. He stepped closer and looked in. He motioned for Stewart to come closer, by his side.

"I don't see him," Scrap-Iron whispered.

Stewart prayed that Ramon wasn't there. If he had one wish coming, one leftover from those old wishbone games, make it that Ramon wasn't there.

The inside of the car was in deep shadow. Scrap-Iron pulled a small flashlight from the top pocket of his overalls. He reached into the car with it and spread the light left to right. He repeated that motion and then held still.

"He's here," the big man said. "In the corner."

Stewart's chest tightened. So much for wishes. "Wish in one hand…"

Scrap-Iron could never fit through the narrow opening, so he braced himself and gave the door a powerful push. Reluctantly, with a loud grating noise, as if it hadn't been open wider in a long, long time, the heavy door slid along its rails. It stopped after about six feet.

Still no sound or movement from inside the car. From where he stood, Stewart couldn't see a thing.

Scrap-Iron pulled Stewart closer and in one motion put his hands on his waist and lifted him up and set him in a sitting position on the freight car's floor. He did it with as little effort as if he were putting a baby into a highchair.

His heart pounding hard now, Stewart stood. The car smelled of sweat and urine and sickness. Scrap-Iron shone the light on Ramon who lay curled in the far corner. He was on an old mattress, in a fetal position and dead still, his head on his left arm, his knees angled toward the door.

Scrap-Iron had more trouble lifting his own weight. He braced himself on the edge of the railcar and heaved himself up and rolled inside. Ramon still didn't stir. Stewart wondered if he was alive. He wished that he wasn't. In this situation, any wish was justified.

As if he wanted him to wake, Scrap-Iron shone the light in Ramon's face. Ramon still didn't move. Flies circled around his head.

"He's all fucked up," Scrap-Iron said. He motioned for Stewart to come closer.

Ramon looked as if he were in a coma. Saliva ran down his chin and onto his brown and yellow stained pillow. He was just as Scrap-Iron predicted, comatose and completely vulnerable.

"Maybe he's dead already?" Stewart said.

Scrap-Iron stood and bent closer to Ramon and studied him. Ramon was breathing, his diaphragm moving up and down with each breath.

"He's not dead yet," Scrap-Iron said. "You still got your reaper's work to do."

Scrap-Iron reached into the bib pocket of his overalls. He pulled out a plastic case and snapped it open. A hypodermic needle inside. He held it up and shone the light directly on it, so Stewart could see its liquid-filled barrel.

"There's enough shit in here to kill a horse," Scrap-Iron said. "A stick and a plunge and it's over. Just a few seconds and a better end than he deserves."

He handed the needle to Stewart. Stewart took it between his thumb and index finger, holding it at arm's length from his body, as if it could bite him.

Scrap-Iron knelt next to Ramon and pushed him on his back. Ramon didn't wake, just muttered something unintelligible.

"Don't tell me you don't know how," Scrap-Iron said. "As smart as you are. You just jab it in. Hard because you're gonna hit muscle. Then you push the plunger." He grinned. "You don't have to worry about air bubbles."

Stewart looked away. He felt faint and nauseous. A bitter bile reached his throat and burned it. He knew Scrap-Iron could sense the fear coming off him, and he knew Scrap-Iron liked it.

"You're gonna poke him, just like you poked Betty."

"Come on, Scrap," Stewart said, using that nickname for the first time, hoping for some intimacy.

His cracked and raspy tone adding to his pleading, he said, "We can't do this. This should be for God, and I know you believe in God."

"You think," Scrap-Iron said, "that he believes in me?"

"Look," Stewart said and showed Scrap-Iron his hands. They were trembling.

"You don't jab him," Scrap-Iron said, "I do him and save some for you. It'll look like two freaks were partying."

Scrap-Iron folded Ramon's arms to his side. Ramon looked like a corpse on a slab. A new and sour wave of stink came off him. When Scrap-Iron pinned his forearms to the mattress Ramon finally stirred, unconsciously fighting the confinement.

"You ready," Scrap-Iron asked Stewart.

Nothing to lose now, Stewart said, "If it's such a great thing, why don't you do it yourself?"

Scrap-Iron grabbed Stewart and jerked him to his knees. "Get closer," he said. "Someone as weak as you is gonna need leverage."

Stewart got closer.

"I am weak," Stewart said. "And you're strong. So you do it. You deserve the thrill."

"Get a better grip on that needle," Scrap-Iron said. "Grab it like you would an icepick."

Stewart thought of refusing, but he didn't want Scrap-Iron to hurt him again. He bent forward and held the needle above Ramon's arm. There were needle tracks along Ramon's forearm. Against his brown skin, they looked like little white circles with scabs in the middle. Scrap-Iron pressed harder on Ramon's left arm and angled the swelling triceps toward Stewart.

"Go ahead," Scrap-Iron said, excitement in his voice. "One good stab and you're done."

"Scrap," Stewart said. "Please."

"It's him or you," Scrap-Iron said. "Easy choice. Even you can't complicate it."

Stewart held his breath, closed his eyes and then opened them. He raised his arm, and, flashing-back to the newspaper box and how his first punch wasn't strong enough, he started his fist down with all his strength. Instead of coming down straight, the needle angled toward Scrap-Iron, and that's where Stewart plunged it, directly into the big man's bulging arm and deep into the triceps muscle. He felt the needle penetrate, and he pushed the plunger all the way down.

Scrap-Iron let go of Ramon and rolled to a sitting position. Ramon's arms rose in a reflexive action, but he didn't wake. Stewart fell back and, crablike, scuttled sideways until he banged into the railcar's door.

The needle hung from Scrap-Iron's arm, and he made no effort to pull it out. He just closed his eyes and tilted his head back.

"You kilt me," Scrap-Iron finally said.

"No," Stewart said.

"Oh yes," Scrap-Iron said. His voice weak, he got one last thing out. "Killer."

Stewart moved closer to the open door. He was shaking.

Scrap-Iron began to cough and fight for his breath. Then he passed out.

34

Stewart jumped out of the railcar. He wanted to run but stopped himself.

"Slow down. Slow down and think."

It was his father's voice, the same voice that had scolded him as he labored over algebra problems. His father was right. He had to get control of himself. Stop shaking and slow down and think. What he did in the next hour would determine his whole future.

So what to do?

He walked down the sidetrack to get away from the railcar. He stopped after about one-hundred feet. Nobody was around. He was lost and alone. A crazy thought—what would Scrap-Iron do in his place? Scrap-Iron would employ his core principle: "The strong take away from the weak, but the smart take away from the strong." He couldn't hope to have Scrap-Iron's level of street smarts and cunning, but he could try and imitate what the ruthless manipulator would do.

Self-preservation must rule. That meant leaving and right away. The police would suspect him, and the boys would all turn on him. But leaving might not be easy. The only thing for sure was that there would be chaos and confusion. Make chaos and confusion his friend. What he needed was time to gather his things and get away. He could go back to camp and tell the boys Scrap-Iron needed their help to get into the railcar—that Ramon was awake and bracing the door closed and insulting Scrap. That Scrap was mad and had changed his mind and wanted to do the backstabbing bastard by himself and with a vengeance. The boys wouldn't question that; they would just respond to Scrap-Iron's command. That would buy him time to get his stuff and get to the train station.

He liked that and started down the tracks again, but soon he had second thoughts.

He couldn't leave. Even if he got away, his running would make him a fugitive, and was there ever a soul more ill-equipped to be a fugitive? If he ran, he would be more than a suspect; he would be guilty by assumption. To live looking over his shoulder constantly, never having a secure and settled moment—for him that would be punishment cruel and unusual beyond any means the law could apply.

He stopped and squatted there on the tracks with his head in his hands, indecision torturing him. He could concoct a good story and go to the police with it. He could tell the truth right up until he couldn't, right up until Scrap-Iron's death. He would say things didn't go as Scrap-Iron planned, that Ramon had woken and Scrap-Iron and Ramon had fought. Finding a man like Scrap-Iron dead in the den of a man like Ramon, the authorities would assume violence. When the immediate cause of Scrap-Iron's death wasn't obvious, no physical signs or wounds, the police would assume heart attack from exertion. Ramon wouldn't know what happened. He'd be so spaced out that anything he said would be dismissed.

He felt a quick flare of elation thinking how that story could work. He stood, prepared to head straight for the police station. But there was a problem. The needle still hung from Scrap-Iron's arm.

"Shit!"

He had to go back to the railcar. No choice. He had to do it.

He walked back to the car and looked in. Enough of dawn now that he could see Scrap-Iron through the open door. He looked like a man who was taking a nap. He looked satisfied to leave this world. But it wasn't like that. That was no nap. The man was dead, and he had killed him. How could such a thing happen? He was a proponent of the sanctity of life, and now he had killed.

He lifted himself into the car. The smell seemed worse. He took a step toward Scrap-Iron. Like in some B-grade horror film, he imagined the big man defying death and sitting up and grabbing him by his throat. Staying as far as possible from the body, he reached and pulled the needle out and stepped back. The syringe was empty. He had injected the whole dose into Scrap-Iron. Enough to kill a horse. He found the plastic case, put the syringe back in it, and put the case in his pocket.

He could hear Ramon's labored, phlegmatic breathing. Amazingly, he still showed no signs of waking. Would Ramon ever wake up? To make his fight story more believable, he kicked Ramon's stack of girlie magazines around. The car was messy enough, but a struggle between two such men would have upset things more. He thought of repositioning Scrap-Iron, who looked too tranquil for a violent ending. But moving the big man's body was beyond his strength. He thought of hitting Scrap-Iron in the face to leave some mark of a struggle. He couldn't do that. Too ghastly. Scrap-Iron in death had already taken on a new standing. The dead deserved respect. Besides, the authorities had ways of knowing whether a wound or bruising occurred before or after death.

Satisfied with the scene, he jumped back out of the railcar and started down the tracks. He threw the syringe case into the weeds next to the copse of trees. But before he reached the main line, despair struck him. It was all too complicated. Wouldn't Ramon need to show signs of a struggle? Wouldn't the police run a tox screen on Scrap-Iron? What other obvious flaws was he missing? When you started to lie, there were too many things that could go wrong. There was always some mistake in a liar's story, and when found and worked at, like the loose end in a knot, it caused everything else to unravel.

He couldn't do this Scrap-Iron's way. He knew what he had to do. He would do what his wife would advise him to do. He would go to the police and tell the truth and the whole truth and end this madness. He was innocent. And if justice failed him he would face the consequences, whatever they might be. Nothing could be as bad as continuing to descend through the circles of his current hell.

Suddenly, it was all clear. He would have called the police right then, but he had no phone. He thought of Scrap-Iron's phone, but the big man never carried it with him. He would walk straight to the police station. Then it would be the truth and nothing but the truth. There was something empowering and invigorating in the simple clarity of that.

The main tracks ran straight into town and within a block of the police station. On his way, he started to rehearse his story but stopped. No need for that.

The truth would set him free.

35

For the first time in this nightmare, he felt the end might be near. The sun was rising, and he was walking toward the light. But even as a truth-telling innocent, the police would judge him, and his initial appearance would be important. He should be sufficiently shaken but able to relate the key facts.

Would the police hold him? If so, they would give him one phone call. Who would he call? It was a measure of his life's sparsity that there was only one person he could call.

What would his wife make of such a call? If it came to posting bail, would she do that? He dreaded spending any time in jail. If he needed a lawyer, would she help with that? Was there a smoldering ember or two left from their previous love? Or would she say, "you made your bed and now sleep in it?" If she did, she would be justified.

***

Just past a switch point, he stopped to catch his breath. A bird lay along the tracks. A red-tailed hawk. A beautiful bird. He was afraid to touch it with his hands, so he gently nudged it with his foot. The hawk didn't look like a victim of sickness. Its eyes were open and alert, as if it were still alive. Its muscular chest was white, its upper parts speckled brown, its tail rust-colored. The bird must have been shot. Death was on the prowl. He picked it up and gently moved it off the tracks. He didn't want a train running over it.

He stepped up his pace as he approached the woods and the trail to Scrapville. To be safe, he moved off the tracks and walked along the right side of the embankment, so no one could see him from the woods.

The mall and its back lot came into view. He had a terrible thirst, but he would have to ignore it—there was too much risk in diverting and stopping at Burger-Land, and what would the cops think of a man who, on his way to report a violent death, stopped for a drink of soda? Innocent or not, little things like that made a difference.

Shouldn't he feel more? Shouldn't he be awash in guilt and regret? He knew that, in the whole history of his life, this was the day that would define him. He should hate himself. That he didn't, didn't fool him. He knew himself too well for that. Guilt would come to him the way it always did—slow burning but never extinguished. He dreaded his coming dreams.

Safely past Scrapville, he returned to the tracks. It was easier to walk there. He could see Harristown in the distance, the church spire, the two towers of the Headquarters Plaza office building, the thick overhead wires of the train depot. The police station was a block from the train depot.

He was almost to the path that led to the mall's back lot when it happened. The Bandito and Toad popped up from that path and stopped dead, right in front of him. They were square in his face, not twenty feet away. They looked as surprised as he did. Toad had a large, grease-stained Burger-Land bag in his left hand.

There was no hiding and no retreating.

"Where's Scrap?" The Bandito asked.

"Something happened," Stewart said.

He tried to take on the appearance of someone who just witnessed a shocking tragedy. He wasn't much of an actor but he had one advantage–he had just witnessed a shocking tragedy. He didn't have to fake his weak and trembling voice.

"What happened?" The Bandito asked.

Stewart chose a tale most likely to move the boys to immediate, reflexive action.

"An accident," he said. An odd choice of words, accident, but that's what came out.

"Accident?" The Bandito said. "What do you mean?"

The Bandito and Toad came closer. Stewart felt corralled.

"Ramon woke up when we got there," he said. "We thought we could take him by surprise, but we didn't. He woke up when Scrap-Iron pushed the door open. The door made a lot of noise."

"So?" The Bandito asked.

"Scrap climbed into the car, and then he and Ramon started arguing. Scrap told him what a backstabbing bastard he was. Ramon kept saying to get out. Scrap was going to punch him."

"Yeah?" The Bandito asked.

"Then something happened."

"What happened?"

"Scrap grabbed his chest and went down. He had some kind of attack."

It took a moment for what Stewart said to sink in. Even then, disbelief reigned in both The Bandito's and Toad's eyes. The image of Scrap-Iron down and vulnerable to Ramon or anyone else was hard to accept.

"What do you mean?" The Bandito asked. "You saying Scrap fell down or passed out or what?"

"He slumped," Stewart said. "He grabbed his chest, and then he sort of sat down. He didn't fall down."

"He got back up though?" The Bandito asked.

"No," Stewart said. "He stayed down. He was all red and couldn't get his breath."

"Where was you?"

"Scrap-Iron told me to stay out of the car until he got control of Ramon. He said I'd be in his way."

"What did Ramon do when Scrap fell down?"

"He kicked at Scrap and kept saying to get out of his place."

"And you didn't do nothing?" Toad asked.

"What could I do?" Stewart said.

"How about help Scrap?" The Bandito said.

"Yeah," Toad said. "Maybe do artificial something."

"Ramon was crazy," Stewart said. "He wouldn't let me get in the car."

"So you just left?" The Bandito said.

"I had to get you guys. I had to hurry. I ran the whole way."

"How come you went right past camp then?" The Bandito asked.

"I saw you and Toad. I saw you coming through the mall's back lot, and I kept coming so I could get to you faster."

"Shit!" The Bandito said.

"What we gonna do?" Toad asked.

"You go get Herc," The Bandito said. "Tell him Scrap's hurt, and we got to get over there right away. We'll wait on the tracks for you."

"Maybe you guys can help," Stewart said.

"Go!" The Bandito said to Toad.

Toad started down the tracks. He still had the Burger-Land bag in his hand.

"Move it!" The Bandito shouted after him.

Toad broke into a run.

"You better hope Scrap's okay," The Bandito said to Stewart. "If he ain't, you're gonna wish he was."

The Bandito spat on the ground and then turned Stewart and pushed him forward, back down the tracks.

36

Herc and Toad came from the woods at a run. Herc bounded onto the tracks and went right for Stewart and grabbed him by his shoulders and shook him. It made Stewart's throat hurt more.

"Was Scrap breathing or what?" Herc said.

"He was breathing," Stewart said. "I tried to help, but Ramon was crazy."

"Did Scrap say anything?"

"I don't think so."

"Let's go," Herc said and started down the tracks. The Bandito and Toad followed him and then, to Stewart's surprise, Slinky came from the woods, coming toward them with urgency, forcing himself to half-run.

Stewart tried standing still, as if he were waiting for Slinky.

"Hey," Herc said, over his shoulder. "Get your ass moving, Professor. You're coming too."

"Should we get help?" Stewart asked. "The cops or an ambulance? I could do that."

"No help," Herc said. "I'm gonna check this out before we get anyone involved, and you better be telling the truth."

37

The boys meant business. They marched along the tracks at double-time and without their usual banter and horseplay. They looked like a posse in hot pursuit. Herc was in the best shape and the fastest. He kept checking over his shoulder to see that Stewart didn't lag too far behind. A case of nightmarish *déjà vu* for Stewart, being forced to go down this same route again, reliving his horrific morning.

Stewart worried for Ramon now. The boys' reaction to Scrap-Iron, lying there in Ramon's place, dead, would be emotional and violent. He didn't want to be responsible for another death. But he didn't dare tell the truth. He didn't want to be responsible for his own death.

***

The railcar looked the same. The door was still in the half-open position. Herc stopped about ten feet away. He had picked up a piece of steel pipe from along the tracks, and he held it at his side and ready. He looked as if he knew how to use it.

Stewart stayed back. He knew what was inside the car and didn't want to see it again.

"Scrap!" Herc yelled.

No answer.

"Scrap!" Herc yelled again. He moved closer and stood on his tiptoes, trying to see deeper into the railcar.

"What you want, mother-fucker?"

It was Ramon, suddenly appearing at the door, naked except for his undershorts, standing there and challenging Herc, like an aggressive dog at the edge of its yard.

"Where's Scrap?" Herc said.

"How should I know?" Ramon answered. He looked perplexed by the question and by the angry group at his door. He kept blinking in the morning light, trying to get focused.

Herc stepped closer and moved side to side, still trying to see inside the car. Ramon moved side to side too, mirroring Herc's movements like a mime, blocking his view.

"You ain't getting any of my shit," Ramon said. "I ain't owing you nothing."

"I don't want any of your nasty shit," Herc said. "I wanna know where Scrap is."

"You crazy man," Ramon said. "How would I know where he at?"

The Bandito and Toad stayed a safe two steps behind Herc. Stewart stayed behind them.

"Where was Scrap?" Herc asked Stewart. "Which end?"

Stewart pointed to the right side of the car.

"I told you," Ramon said. "There ain't nobody. Now get the fuck out of here."

"I ain't going till I look inside," Herc said.

"Hell no, fool," Ramon said. "This is mine. You ain't coming in; you ain't looking in, and you ain't taking nothing. You a crazy mother-fucker anyways. Always was."

Standing above them all, with the leverage that position gave him, Ramon, despite being hungover or still stoned, made a formidable barrier.

Herc looked to The Bandito as if to say, what now?

"What you do to Scrap?" The Bandito shouted at Ramon.

"I told you assholes," Ramon said, "he ain't here. I ain't even seen him in a long while. Now, get outta here."

Without warning, Ramon bent over and vomited out the door.

"Shit!" Herc said and jumped back, bouncing into The Bandito.

"I told you; I ain't good," Ramon said. "Now get your shithead selves moving."

Ramon wiped at his mouth and kicked something toward the boys, a stone or mud or maybe a piece of what he had vomited.

"I'm gonna try and get him to come down," Herc whispered to The Bandito. "If I get him down here, we can take him."

Slinky had finally caught up and was kneeling in the short weeds alongside the tracks. He looked as if he were about to faint. He held his soft sun hat in his hands, wringing it as if it were a wet washcloth.

The Bandito's cell phone erupted. He used Godzilla's roar as his ringtone.

Confusion among the group. The Bandito the most bewildered. Only one person ever called him. Only one person had his number. He dug the phone out of his pants, flipped it open, stared at the screen and froze.

Godzilla roared again.

"Answer the fuckin' thing," Herc said.

The Bandito swiped at his phone and raised it to his ear. He looked too spooked to talk but finally said, "Hello?"

"Where are you?"

It was Scrap-Iron's voice.

"Jesus," The Bandito said. "It's you Scrap?"

"Who'd you think it was?" Scrap-Iron said. "Godzilla?"

"But Scrap?" The Bandito said.

Herc grabbed the phone out of The Bandito's hands. "Scrap?" he said.

"Where are you?" Scrap-Iron said.

"We're...Scrap, we thought you was hurt or something. We thought..."

"Where are you?"

"At Ramon's. At his railcar. It's what he told us, Scrap."

"What who told you?"

"The Professor. He said you were at Ramon's and had an attack and you was down and needed us. I come running right over."

"The Professor told you that?"

"Yeah, Scrap."

"Where'd you see him?"

"On the tracks. He was on the tracks but without you."

"Where is he now?"

"He's here with us, Scrap."

"He is?" Scrap-Iron's voice rose. He was skeptical of miracles.

"Yeah, Scrap," Herc said. He turned and looked at Stewart. "He's right here."

"That's good!" Scrap-Iron said. "That's better than I hoped for. I figured he'd be gone."

There was one major weakness in Scrap-Iron's otherwise perfect plan. After breaking the Fifth, Stewart would run. Scrap-Iron knew that. And that meant he might only enjoy the man's ensuing and lifelong psychological misery vicariously. He had given himself credit for having the maturity to accept that limitation. No plan was perfect. But it would be so much more fun to witness the misery firsthand.

"So Scrap," Herc asked, "it's good? I mean that he's here with us?"

"It's better than good. It's perfect."

"I stopped him," Herc said. "I made him come, too. That was my idea. I was thinking right away this shit ain't right."

"Good thinking," Scrap-Iron said.

"Thanks," Herc said.

"Listen," Scrap-Iron said. "Tell the boys that I'm here sitting in my shop and having to run for my own beer."

"That's great news," Herc said. "I mean you being okay, not about the beer. Scrap, I'm so happy. But what happened?"

"I'll tell you later," Scrap-Iron said. "What I want you to do now is take charge there."

"You got it, Scrap," Herc said. "What should I do?"

"You keep the Professor close. He'll try and run again."

"He's right here," Herc said and looked again to Stewart, as if in this crazy time he had to make double sure.

"Make sure he stays with you," Scrap-Iron said. "Don't let him out of your sight."

"Don't worry, Scrap," Herc said. "The ass-wiper ain't going nowhere." Malevolence in his voice and eyes as he stared at Stewart. He didn't know how, but he knew Stewart had done Scrap a bad wrong. "How about Ramon? How about him?"

"Forget about Ramon."

"But Scrap, he'll talk."

"Forget that. I took care of all that. What I want is all of you back in camp. I want you to put the Professor in your fort and keep him there. Don't put him in a tent. I want you all here with him at the garage at sunset. I'm counting on you. You're my man."

"You got it, Scrap," Herc said. "We'll be there and the Professor too, dead or alive and with a ribbon on him if you want."

"I want him alive," Scrap-Iron said. "Tonight we're gonna have some real fun with him."

V

38

Herc's fort was dark and musty with a smell like degrading dog shit. But there was no escaping. The thick railroad-tie walls were impenetrable except for cracks of light where the mud insulation had fallen out. Prisoner Stewart put one eye to a crack but couldn't see anything but tree trunks.

All that was missing from a medieval torture chamber was for Stewart to be fettered in chains and hung from a wall. Chains weren't necessary because the boys sat right outside the door. He could hear them, speculating on what Scrap-Iron had in mind for him.

"You think he'll kill him?"

"He's got the right. The bastard tried to kill him."

"Fair's fair, ain't it?"

"Eye for eye."

"How's he gonna do it?"

"Scrap's got ways we can't even think of."

"I think he's just gonna hurt him bad. Teach him a good lesson."

"Before Scrap's done, maybe the Professor will want him to kill him."

***

Stewart decided not to lie on Herc's bunk. Who knew what life it harbored? He didn't want to sleep. He was afraid that if he slept, he would dream of a normal life, and when he woke to this horrific reality he would not be able to bear it.

In the stillness, his body ached. He had trouble swallowing. He sat on a plastic cooler and massaged his throat and Adam's apple. It was as if all the parts wouldn't mesh. He was sure Scrap-Iron had done permanent damage.

Was Scrap-Iron really alive? Yes, he was. Herc and The Bandito didn't have the cunning or acting skills to play out such an elaborate deception.

So he wasn't a killer. He should feel great relief at that. He didn't. Scrap-Iron had gone to a lot of trouble with his elaborate plan and wasn't done yet. What came next wouldn't be good. This night would surely be full of further pain and humiliation. What would satisfy Scrap-Iron? Would it require he beg for mercy? Or was mercy not on Scrap-Iron's agenda?

Suddenly the Pennsylvania retreat, now out of his reach, seemed like a paradise lost. He recalled the big dining hall with its great wooden beams and natural stone walls and simple wooden tables and two-sided fireplace. He recalled the intimacy of the small and Spartan room he and his wife shared, with its two small iron-framed beds that they pushed together, and its little writing desk and simple dresser, and the plain wooden crucifix above the bed. His wife had said it was a nice change for a weekend but not for any longer. She needed more than that simple life. But he would be happy there, where not every stranger posed a lethal threat. He now longed to read and sleep under the protection of a simple wooden crucifix. Knowing the devil firsthand made God's existence more plausible.

***

Before sundown, he pushed the fort's crude wooden door open and stepped out to relieve himself. He was immediately intercepted by Herc and Toad.

"Where you goin'?" Toad said.

"None of your business," Stewart said.

"I'm watching you," Toad said.

Stewart walked into the woods. Toad stayed right behind him like a guard walking a prisoner. He even followed Stewart behind his chosen tree.

"Do you mind?" Stewart asked.

Instead of his usual mix of repulsion and sympathy, he now felt nothing but contempt for Toad—his infantile reverence for Scrap-Iron, his jealousy over the sarcastic praise the big man lavished on Stewart, how Toad was so stupid he didn't even understand Scrap-Iron was being sarcastic.

"You want to watch me piss, Toad-Boy?" he said. "That's a good job for you. Maybe you could be my piss-boy, too."

Slinky had told the story about the time, when everybody was around to watch, that Scrap-Iron had ordered Toad to bring a bucket to him out in the junkyard. Scrap-Iron had to piss, and instead of doing it against some junk car as he usually did, he made Toad hold the bucket while he pissed in it. For the rest of the day, Scrap-Iron referred to Toad as his *piss boy*.

"Herc knows I'll watch you good," Toad said.

As he urinated, Stewart had the urge to swing himself around and piss on Toad's sneakers. He wanted to do to Toad what the whole world kept doing to him.

39

Just before sunset, Herc came for him. Stewart followed resignedly, his will to resist lost in a weary fatalism. He was exhausted in both body and soul, all but shut down by physical and mental whiplash. Just this morning Scrap-Iron was dead, and now he wasn't. Just this morning he was a killer, and now he wasn't. Just this morning he was about to escape and come clean, and now he was trapped worse than ever.

***

The garage's doors were closed but a booming bass beat came from Scrap-Iron's jukebox. Loud music was no sure indicator of the big man's mood; he could be happy and celebrating, or he could be in one of his dark places and trying to escape.

Stewart tried to gather himself. He was a man afraid of change and uncertainty put into a horrific tumble cycle of both. How was that for a personal hell?

Herc opened the garage's side door. The jukebox was playing a scratchy old song. Scrap-Iron was in his chair with his eyes half-closed and his head swaying back and forth with the music.

Now the doctor's gonna do all he can,
But what your gonna need is an undertaker man

Herc reached back and grabbed Stewart by the arm and pulled him into the garage with a flourish. His job done and done well, his ward delivered.

Scrap-Iron shut off the music but stayed in his chair, leaning forward to accept the boys' grateful hugs. When the boys finished, he turned to Stewart and said, "What, no hug?"

What do you say to a man who, just hours ago, you stuck with a needle and killed? Stewart said nothing. Instead he looked in Scrap-Iron's eyes, expecting to see distilled hate. He didn't see hate, but what he did see scared him more. Scrap-Iron's eyes lacked their usual sharp focus. He had the look of deep intoxication that Stewart often saw on street people, a look that marked them as a breed apart. He had never seen that in Scrap-Iron before. It terrified him. He didn't want to be near a man of such strength and cruelty when whatever inhibitions he might harbor were obliterated by drink.

"Fancy meeting me again, huh, Professor?"

"I don't know what's going on," Stewart said and stared at the floor. He had tears in his eyes.

"I've arisen," Scrap-Iron said. "And I didn't wait two days." He raised both arms in the air and sang, "Hallelujah!"

A slur to the big man's speech. He must have been drinking all day and with a purpose. Stewart had seen him drink prodigious amounts of beer in a couple hours and show no effect.

"So you don't know what's going on?" Mockery in Scrap-Iron's voice. "You didn't expect what, another meeting tonight?"

"You know what I mean," Stewart said.

"Everybody sit," Scrap-Iron said.

The Bandito and Herc sat. Toad looked at the bucket seat, lowered his eyes, and stepped toward the sofa.

"Where you going, Toad-Boy?" Scrap-Iron asked.

Toad shrugged his shoulders.

"Take your proper seat," Scrap-Iron said, and nodded toward the bucket seat.

Toad grinned and sat in his seat but first went out of his way to bump Stewart with his shoulder. Stewart took a seat at the end of the sofa.

From the side pocket of his chair, Scrap-Iron brought out a Bible. Its black leather cover was well-worn. A red ribbon marked his place.

"I'm sure," Scrap-Iron said, "you all know Matthew 5:28?"

He looked to the boys. They didn't know Matthew.

"How about you, Professor?" Scrap-Iron asked. "You know your Bible, don't you?"

"Not like you," Stewart said.

Scrap-Iron stared at him a long moment, as if deciding whether Stewart meant to be sarcastic. He decided he didn't, or if he did, it wasn't worth getting sidetracked over.

Scrap-Iron pulled the ribbon and opened the Bible to his selected chapter and verse, and, as if suddenly sobered by the sanctity of the occasion, read it in the deep profound voice of a prophet, speaking with a slow, forced clarity.

But I say unto you, that whosoever looketh on a woman to lust after her hath committed adultery with her already in his heart.

The boys confused at that. Stewart too.

"You familiar with the sentiment, Professor?"

"I've heard it," Stewart said.

"Then let me," Scrap-Iron said, "paraphrase my good friend Matt: 'I say to you that whosoever plunges a needle into a man with murderous intent has already broken the Fifth Commandment in his heart.'"

Stewart no longer confused. He knew enough of this strange man to know where this was heading.

Scrap-Iron turned to the boys.

"Today I set out to determine something," he said, "something very important. I wanted to know was there anyone among us who was truly capable of breaking the Fifth and doing it the old-fashioned way. I don't mean from a distance, the way the politicians and generals do. I mean up close and personal, staring right in your victim's eyes and watching the life drain out of them. Was there one among us with a heart black enough for that? You gotta have a black, black heart for something like that." He looked to Toad and Herc and The Bandito. "I didn't think any of you did."

Both Herc and The Bandito looked as if they wanted to object. They didn't. It wasn't the time to argue qualifications.

"But it turns out," Scrap-Iron said, and looked to Stewart, "that there is such a one among us."

The boys looked at Stewart too. Stewart rubbed the side of his head. A hot tingling there, the warning of shooting pains about to come.

"The first time I met our new man," Scrap-Iron said, "I detected something in him. You know what that was?"

The boys didn't try and answer that. They had learned to recognize a rhetorical question when they heard one.

"Darkness," Scrap-Iron said. "That's what." He nodded his head for emphasis. "Was it a darkness sufficient to break the most important Commandment of all? Could he do that? I didn't know. Who could know that for sure about any man? So, I needed to test him."

Stewart involuntarily flinched at a short but sharp stab behind his right ear.

"To test him properly," Scrap-Iron said, "I had to deceive you boys. See, the story I told, about Ramon and the cops, that story wasn't true. It was for the greater cause. Now don't misunderstand. Ramon is a backstabber. But he could never sufficiently communicate our accomplishments to law enforcement. He doesn't have the proper vision to see or the proper voice to tell. I ask you, who would choose Ramon as their advocate?"

The boys' faces answered for them; nobody would.

"So my story was a false witnessing. I get credit for breaking number Eight."

The boys good with all that. As Scrap-Iron himself once said, if he told his boys a mosquito could pull a plow, they'd hitch it up.

"So I tested our new man. Was he a killer? Would he kill? Would he break the Fifth?" Scrap-Iron let the question hang until he finally said. "The answer is this. He would, and he did. He passed the test."

"What he do that was so good?" Toad asked.

"He broke the Fifth!" Scrap-Iron said. *"Thou - shall - not - kill."*

"Who'd he kill?" Toad asked.

"That's the greatest thing of all," Scrap-Iron said. "He killed me. He killed his lord and savior and protector. That makes him Judas and Pilate and the executioner with his hammer, all in one."

"Listen," Stewart said.

Scrap-Iron silenced him with a look.

"He killed you, Scrap?" a more-confused Toad asked.

Scrap-Iron told the whole story, dramatizing Stewart injecting him by re-enacting the stabbing with an imaginary syringe, holding up his big thumb with its black blood-blistered thumbnail and dramatizing the pushing down of the plunger before faking his death again by dropping his head to his chest and letting out a long, final breath.

"Right here," Scrap-Iron said and held his right arm out for all to see, twisting it so the triceps bulged. There was a red mark and a swelling there.

"If that needle was filled with skag, like our dark-hearted assassin here believed it was, I wouldn't be here with you now. I'd be dead. Stone cold dead at the hands of a stone cold killer."

"What a bastard," The Bandito said. His was a genuine astonishment at the level of Stewart's bastardy.

"So," Scrap-Iron said, "the man did it, and now he takes his place in a celebrated line of killers starting with Cain. I can't take any credit for it. Because that kind of darkness you can't teach. No one can learn that. That has to be deep in your soul."

Stewart was sure that his end was near.

The boys anxious now for knowing the Professor's just punishment. Whatever his up and comings might be, the show would be fun to watch. If they were lucky, they might get to participate.

They were surprised at what came next.

"What we're here for now," Scrap-Iron said, "is to celebrate. Yes, to celebrate the deed and more importantly the man who did it."

Scrap-Iron clapped his hand hard on his thigh. It made a great popping noise that caused Stewart to jump.

"This man," Scrap-Iron said and looked to Stewart, "stands singular among us now. He walked the walk. He made the plunge." The big man raised his eyebrows and grinned at his unintentional play on words. "See," he went on, "he actually stuck the needle in. That commands your respect. The only one among you to break all Ten Commandments."

"I would've done it," Toad said.

"You'd have killed me?" Scrap-Iron asked.

"No, Scrap, I wouldn't kill you. Never, for nothing or nobody. I would've killed someone else though."

"See Toad," Scrap-Iron said, "you're like a lot of people. A talker, a faker, a pretender. A fraud, a phony, an imposter. A cheater, a slicker, a shammer. A dreamer but not a doer. A bullshit artist." Spittle came out with *bullshit*.

Toad slumped deeper into the bucket seat's soft cushion.

"But you know what?" a suddenly subdued Scrap-Iron said. "Maybe you could say all that about me too." He closed his eyes and lowered his head for a long moment before coming back to life. "I've never broken the Fifth. I can't claim kinship with Cain and his disciples. So maybe I'm a bullshitting bullshitter too."

Even Toad had the sense not to touch that.

"There's to be no skimping here," Scrap-Iron said. "The celebration must match the achievement. In celebrating this killer's heart, we can help the man see who he really is. It's important he embraces his true nature, as dark as it may be."

"What we gonna do?" Toad asked.

"What do we always do for big achievements?" Scrap-Iron asked. "What did we do when Herc stole that heavy-ass generator right from that warehouse lot and rolled it back here down three miles of streets under the noses of all the simple citizens?"

"Fireworks!" Toad said.

Scrap-Iron smiled.

"We don't have to wait until Saturday?" Toad asked.

Fireworks were traditionally a Saturday night show.

"No, we don't, Toady-Boy," Scrap-Iron said. "This is so special that we're gonna celebrate tonight. Right now."

"It's gonna be a big one?" Toad asked.

"Real big," Scrap-Iron said. "The biggest."

"We're gonna blow some shit up!" Toad said.

"That we are," Scrap-Iron said.

40

Celebration, especially some violent form, was the boys' favorite outdoor sport.

The big man's pyrotechnics never disappointed. With his stash of black powder, he could build bombs and firecrackers far more powerful than the law allowed. Before his big shows, he would warn his cop friends of what was to come, so they wouldn't be caught off guard. Once, on another summer night, he had set off such a display that a frantic citizen had called the police and reported someone was bombing Harristown.

Scrap-Iron featured his explosives in exciting ways. He once stacked three refrigerators on top of each other, two big ones and one small one, with enough black powder sealed between them that when he ignited it, the top refrigerator flew sixty feet in the air. Refrigerators over Harristown–a sight to remember. Another time he launched a small rocket topped with his own specially designed capsule holding a live field mouse. He conducted the launch while delivering an impromptu lecture on the history of the space race and the imperative to return passengers alive. The mouse did return alive, but when released it ran in circles until Toad stepped on it, earning him a slap upside his head that left him partially deaf in his right ear.

***

"Are you ready to celebrate?" Scrap-Iron asked the boys.

"We was born to celebrate," The Bandito said.

Launching the fireworks required a level surface, and Scrap-Iron always launched from the flat roof of his bunker. From there, the yard's night-light allowed him to see what he was doing.

Herc and The Bandito carried the steamer trunk filled with the implements of mayhem from the garage to the roof, so Scrap-Iron could dip in and out of it as he pleased. Lawn chairs were set up for everyone except the big man. He had his recliner moved there. No plastic lawn chair could hold him.

The drink was plentiful and handy. Scrap-Iron's long-necked PBRs and the boys' canned Budweisers chilled in a fifty-gallon trash container half-filled with ice. No limit on the boys' drinking, as long as they didn't pull out a PBR. Just your regular old family, out to celebrate personal achievement the American way— with some backyard fun under an August moon.

Scrap-Iron started the show with the aerial spinners. Small explosives with wings that after ignited spun on the roof then rose into the air and combusted with a burst of color and a bang. He lit them with his ancient Zippo lighter, a relic of his smoking days. The lighter had a short flame, and in his drunken condition he had trouble closing the distance between the flame and the wicks. The bottle rockets he launched from one of the empty beer bottles. They made a loud whistling sound upon launch and left a tail of bright sparks. Upon reaching maximum height, they burst with a bang into a show of colorful stars. Toad whooped at each new burst, like a kid at the county fair.

Next came the aerial tube devices. These ejected shells into the air that burst at a high altitude into a large multicolored spectacle accompanied by whistling and comet tails and crackers that exploded in the air. Scrap-Iron's specially altered shells rose over 300 feet. Oohs and aahs from the boys.

Only the one being celebrated couldn't enjoy the show. At every pause, Stewart hoped the end was near, and he could retreat to his tent for the night. Could a celebration of his willingness to kill be enough to satisfy the big man? Or was it preparation for something more? How do you second-guess a maniac?

Scrap-Iron took a long pause, tilted his head back, and closed his eyes. It was a muggy night, and thick smoke hung over the yard. The howling and barking of unsettled dogs came from all directions. It might have been the aftermath of some apocalyptic battle.

Scrap-Iron was less than satisfied. There were no lectures on the history of gunpowder and fireworks. Not that night. He wasn't in the mood. Instead he guzzled more beer and took deep breaths, inhaling and savoring the smell of burnt gunpowder.

"Toad-Boy," Scrap-Iron said, when he finally came back to the present. "You think your old man was a jerk. He probably was. But don't think you're the only one. Not just because you got some scars on your ass."

A hint of self-pity in Scrap-Iron's voice. Stewart had never heard that before. The others didn't seem surprised. Maybe they didn't notice. Maybe they had heard it before.

"My old man," Scrap-Iron said. "He…Oh, fuck it. And fuck him too." He nodded his head in the affirmative, agreeing with his own assessment. His face and forehead were beaded with sweat.

"You think," Scrap-Iron asked while staring at the half-moon, "that there are fathers that really love their sons?"

Dead quiet.

"Even Betty," Scrap-Iron said. "Even her."

A patch of lingering smoke drifted over the roof.

"You know something?" Scrap-Iron said. "She burns my ass. It was like she was in heat."

A cloud of smoke blocked out the moon.

"You know what else burns my ass?"

"What, Scrap?" The Bandito asked.

Scrap-Iron held his hand out, to indicate a height of about four feet. "A flame this high," he said.

Everybody laughed at that. Exaggerated laughs for the relief of it. Stewart made a point of laughing. He felt he'd better. The big man teetered on the brink of deeper self-pity or some explosion of his own.

"Something else burns my ass," Scrap-Iron said.

"What's that, Scrap?" The Bandito dutifully asked.

"You fucking guys. How you need me for everything. Like I'm your daddy." Scrap-Iron shook his head in disgust. "You know what you guys need?"

More quiet. The boys letting things blow over. It seemed like the quiet might last forever if Scrap-Iron didn't break it. He did.

"You need someone to light a fire under your asses."

He leaned over and dug into the steamer trunk until he pulled out a thick red firecracker with a double-twisted wick about two inches long. He lit the firecracker and held it until the wick had burned perilously low. Then he tossed it toward the boys, so it went skittering under The Bandito and Herc's chairs.

Boom!

An ear-piercing blast. The Bandito flipped backward and out of his chair. Herc jumped up and then off the two-foot-high roof. The Bandito checked between his legs, as if something might be missing. Slinky and Toad both cowered with their hands over their ears. After the blast, Stewart's ears were ringing. He thought he might be concussed.

"There," Scrap-Iron said. "Maybe that'll pucker your assholes." He hadn't been that far from the blast himself, but he never flinched.

Without rising, Scrap-Iron gave his almost empty beer bottle a heave. It flew in a great arc all the way to the garage, beer trailing out of it like a comet's tail, until it shattered against the cinder block.

"I just ain't got good manners," Scrap-Iron said and laughed. Then, sounding more sincere, "I was raised up like an animal."

He reached back into the steamer trunk. After scrounging there with growing impatience, he came out with a German Luger pistol. He slid the fully loaded eight-round magazine out, inspected it, and shoved it back into the pistol's handle where it snapped home.

"Look at this nasty bastard," he said and held the gun up for all to see. With its black grip and sleek design, it did look nasty.

"Where'd you get it, Scrap?" Toad asked.

The Bandito was still on the roof but kept sneaking closer to the edge as if he wanted to join Herc, who was still standing in the yard.

"My old man took it off a Nazi," Scrap-Iron said. "Then he stuck it up the Kraut's ass and blew him a new one."

Stewart doubted the story. Scrap-Iron probably got the gun from some unsavory character and in exchange for doing something illegal. But the gun's provenance was meaningless. What was important was what this drunk and dangerous man was going to do with it.

"Toad-Boy," Scrap-Iron said, "get over here."

Toad leery of the command.

"Get your ass over here," Scrap-Iron demanded. He stood, lumbered forward half a step, and waved the gun for Toad to come forward.

Toad got out of his chair and came.

Scrap-Iron pointed the gun toward the driveway. Toad stepped off the roof. He was barefoot, and he walked gingerly over the gravel driveway. He kept looking over his shoulder at Scrap-Iron, suspicious of what was coming next.

"I wanna see you dance," Scrap-Iron said. He pointed the Luger toward Toad and made a shooting motion including an imaginary recoil, as if he were shooting at Toad's feet. Toad tried to dance, but halfheartedly.

"Remember," Scrap-Iron said, "those old cowboy movies where they made some simpleton dance by shooting at his feet? When I was a kid I liked that shit." He looked back to the moon. "When I was a kid," he said again. He spit over the roof and onto the driveway and said, "I never was a kid."

Scrap-Iron lowered the gun against his leg. Stewart thought he might shoot himself in the foot. That would be a break. That would end this night.

"Yeah, Scrap," The Bandito said. "Those old movies were cool."

"How 'bout," Scrap-Iron said, "that other one, that mafia movie where that guy, what's his name, he plays a great mafia guy—remember he was making the kid dance then shot him in the foot? That was funny shit."

Scrap-Iron started laughing uncontrollably at that memory until tears ran down his cheeks.

It struck Stewart as incredible to see tears on Scrap-Iron's face, no matter the emotion. It scared him too. He knew enough of men and their tears to know those tears weren't from laughter.

"It was Joe Pesci," The Bandito said. "The movie was *Goodfellas*."

"I knew that, shithead," Scrap-Iron said. "I know my movies. I'm not a dumb bastard."

"I didn't mean that, Scrap," The Bandito said.

Bam!

Without notice, Scrap-Iron shot the gun in the direction of The Bandito, but high.

"Shit!" The Bandito screamed and jumped off the roof.

The sudden bang of the gun, not as loud as the firecrackers but with a menace all its own, made Stewart flinch. He needed to stay quiet and out of the big man's focus. This night would likely end in tragedy and probably death—but it didn't have to be his death.

Bam!

Scrap-Iron spun around and shot again. Stewart saw the muzzle flash this time, and the bullet ricocheted off the gravel about a yard wide of Toad's feet. Toad jumped and hurt his foot landing on the stones. He started hopping around, his foot in and out of his hand.

"I blew one of his piggies off," Scrap-Iron said. "But I ain't calling no ambulance. You know why?"

"We don't want the cops, right?" Herc said. "We got to be careful, Scrap. Shooting might bring the cops. We don't want the cops."

"Fuck the cops," Scrap-Iron said. "I won't call an ambulance because what we need is a toe truck."

Scrap-Iron waited, but nobody laughed.

"Okay," he said, "who else among you humorless ass-lickers wants to dance?"

He looked to Stewart. Stewart's chair slid backward. An involuntary action. His legs with a mind of their own. Scrap-Iron turned to Slinky.

"Slink," he said, "how about you? You dancing should be good stuff. You do some funny shit on your feet without even trying."

He waved the gun toward Slinky and then toward the driveway.

Slinky got up and started that way. He couldn't manage the big step down from the flat roof. He had to sit on the edge first and then lower himself. Toad sensed his opportunity and made his limping escape toward Herc and The Bandito.

"Better hope I don't miss," Scrap-Iron said. "Slink's fucked-up enough already."

Bam!

Slinky hadn't turned to face the roof yet, and the shot was well wide of him. It kicked up a stone, and either the stone or the ricochet hit the side of a junk car with a flat, dull report. When Slinky turned, he was trembling.

Bam!

The next shot landed closer to Slinky.

Stewart fought the urge to leave the roof. That would draw Scrap-Iron's attention.

Herc moved behind Toad, trying to make himself a smaller target.

Scrap-Iron turned to Stewart. Stewart was sure that this was it.

Without warning, Scrap-Iron tossed the gun to him. Stewart caught it out of reflex but almost dropped it. It was heavier than he anticipated, and the barrel was hot.

"You make Slink dance," Scrap-Iron said. "Even if you miss and get him, so what, you're already a murdering bastard. But don't expect extra credit. Once you've broke the Fifth, you've broke it. You don't get nothing more for doing it twice. You greedy fuck."

Stewart had never fired a gun. He had never held a gun. He didn't know what to do with it. He was afraid of it. He gripped it by its handle, kept his finger away from the trigger, and pointed it down toward the flat roof.

"You don't make him dance," Scrap-Iron said, "then you're gonna dance. And I'm pretty drunk and I could miss and that would be an accidental. It would be a inadvertent, incidental, accidental."

Scrap-Iron staggered some more. He looked like a great tower, swaying in the throes of some natural disaster.

"Shoot!" Scrap-Iron commanded.

Stewart aimed wide of Slinky and pulled the trigger. The Luger jumped in his hand, its kickback

271

unexpected. The shot hit about ten feet away from Slinky. That was closer than he intended.

"Professor, my ass," Scrap-Iron said. "You're like the rest of them. Useless." He lurched forward and took Stewart's right hand in his hand, covering gun and all. He pointed Stewart in Slinky's direction.

Bam!

By luck or God's hand, the shot appeared to go between Slinky's legs, and it hit the driveway just a foot behind him.

Slinky was crying now.

"You think you're a hotshot," Scrap-Iron said to Stewart. "You think you're smarter than me and a hotter shot too." He grabbed Stewart's hand again, harder than before. "This time," he said, "you'll shoot the poor, crippled bastard and put him out of his misery. Even animals put each other out of their misery."

Scrap-Iron staggered backward. His great weight spun Stewart toward him.

Bam!

Scrap-Iron released Stewart's hand and staggered backward. Stewart dropped the gun.

Scrap-Iron put his hand to his chest. Blood ran between his fingers. He looked at it, as if he were just curious, then he looked at Stewart, and, in what seemed like complete control, fell slowly to his knees.

After the fireworks and gunshots, the sudden quiet seemed unreal. It was Scrap-Iron who broke the silence.

"Okay," he said. Then he sat back on his haunches. He moved his hand and inspected his chest again and the unstaunched bleeding.

Stewart and the boys stood frozen in place.

Scrap-Iron made a gurgling sound. Stewart's first instinct was to try and help him, but he was afraid to get close to him.

"You really did it this time," Scrap-Iron said.

"I didn't," Stewart said.

"You really did," Scrap-Iron said. He blinked his eyes and held up his bloodstained hands. There was no fear in his eyes.

"You know," Scrap-Iron said, "I really wanted to talk poetry with you some time."

Then he fell forward, face-first, onto the roof. He made no attempt to break his fall. His legs jerked for a moment, and then he stopped moving. His eyes were still open. Blood ran out from under him and began to collect in a great pool. Stewart didn't know that much blood could come from one man.

41

Herc was the first to reach Scrap-Iron. He jumped onto the roof and bent over the big man. "Shit!" was all he said. It was a declaration of no hope, a declaration of death.

Stewart knew Herc was coming for him. He tried to brace himself, but Herc grabbed him by his shirt and then knocked him backward onto the roof and straddled him.

"You kilt him!" Herc screamed. His face was red with rage and just an inch from Stewart's.

"I didn't do it," Stewart said.

He wasn't sure what he had or hadn't done. The gun just went off. Scrap-Iron had squeezed his hand so hard that he had lost feeling in it. Maybe Scrap-Iron pulled the trigger. Maybe the gun went off by itself. Maybe guns did that.

"You lousy…" Herc said.

Herc pulled Stewart halfway up and shook him.

The Bandito and Toad were back on the roof. The Bandito came to Scrap-Iron's side and stared down at him, as if he were waiting for the big man to arise and instruct him. Toad jumped up and down and in a circle, as if his shock needed some physical release.

Herc let go of Stewart's shirt and stood up. The Bandito stepped over and kicked Stewart in his ribs.

Stewart slid sideways and toward the edge of the roof. Toad moved to cut him off and attempted his own glancing kick.

"Stop it!" Slinky said. He had managed his way onto the roof.

The Bandito kicked Stewart again. "You're a dead man," he yelled.

Slinky stepped behind The Bandito and slipped the phone from his back pocket. The Bandito was busy aiming another kick Stewart's way.

Slinky turned away and called 911 and with surprising calmness and efficiency relayed his emergency and the location. "A man is shot at the junkyard on Murdock Road. He needs help. You better get here fast."

"Who'd you call?" Herc asked.

"An ambulance," Slinky said.

"That means the cops," Herc said. "We don't want the cops."

"Scrap needs help," Slinky said.

"Scrap's dead," Herc said. "And that asshole," he looked to Stewart who was rolled into a defensive ball, trying to protect himself, "he did it."

"It was an accident," Slinky said.

"Accident my ass," Herc said. "He tried it before. With the needle. He wanted Scrap dead."

"We don't want this with the cops," The Bandito said. "We want it right here." He directed another kick at Stewart.

"The cops are coming," Slinky said. "I called 911."

He held up The Bandito's phone as further proof.

"Give me that," The Bandito said and grabbed the phone.

Herc bent over Stewart and pulled him up to a standing position. Stewart's shirt ripped.

Herc put a chokehold on Stewart, who went slack from the futility of resisting.

"I'm gonna snap his scrawny neck," Herc said.

"Stop," Slinky said. He had picked the gun up from beside Scrap-Iron and had it pointed in the direction of Herc and The Bandito. His gun hand was shaking.

"He didn't do it," Slinky said.

"He did it," Herc said. "Like Scrap said, he's a black-hearted son-of-a-bitch."

Slinky shook the gun at Herc.

"You ain't got the balls," Herc said.

"He won't do it," The Bandito added but moved away from Herc.

"I'll do it," Slinky said. "I don't care any more. I'll do it."

Bam!

Slinky's shot went high over Herc's head. Slinky was sobbing now, and the way his hand shook, he might do it by intent or accident.

"Why you taking his side?" Toad asked.

"I ain't taking nobody's side," Slinky said. "I'm doing what Scrap would want."

"Scrap would want the asshole dead," Herc said. He pulled Stewart closer to his chest. He could snap his neck in half-a-heartbeat.

A faint siren in the distance. Probably the ambulance coming to them. Stewart's life came down to Slinky's skills as an interlocutor.

"The fucker deserves to die," Herc said. "He did it. Look at the shit he tried before."

"Do it," The Bandito said. He gestured to Herc, with a motion as if he were breaking a twig in two. "Go ahead and do it."

"You kill him," Slinky said, "and you're the one who's fucked. You kill him, and we're all fucked.

"We should be smart," Slinky said. "Like Scrap would."

He was holding the gun steadier now, aiming it between Herc and The Bandito and still aware of Toad, ready to go in any direction necessary.

"And how's that?" Herc asked. "How would Scrap do it?"

"We got to look out for each other," Slinky said. "Like Scrap always says we should."

"What's that supposed to mean?" Herc asked.

"It means," Slinky said, "that we keep the cops out of our shit. We say that Scrap's shooting was an accident. We say he was playing with the gun, and he was drunk. We all stick to that. But if you kill The Professor, the cops are in our shit, and big time."

Everyone was quiet, listening.

"Stewart keeps his mouth shut, too," Slinky said. "If he tells the cops anything about us or even Scrap, we'll all testify against him, tell about the needle and that he shot Scrap in cold murder. He knows we mean it."

"You know that?" Herc asked Stewart, talking to the top of his head and tightening his grip as he asked.

"Yes," Stewart said. It barely came out. He thought Herc might asphyxiate him.

The siren was louder and closer now.

"We can't trust the asshole," The Bandito said.

"He knows," Slinky said, "that if he talks, we talk. It's four against one. He plays it smart. We play it smart. That's the only way we all get away. Like Scrap always says, if we stick together there's no way anyone can beat us. But if we got two dead bodies, we're all fucked. Two is too many. You all know that."

Slinky said no more. There was nothing more to say. He just waited.

Stewart waited too. Herc lightened his grip, and Stewart felt a strange comfort in the tight but not too tight grasp. Maybe it was shock. Maybe he had just had too much. If Herc snapped his neck, it would be a quick way to go. It would be just like a hanging. If that was his fate, so be it.

The siren changed to short, piercing, punctuated blasts that echoed off the garage. A cop car had beaten the ambulance, and with its flashing lights it entered the yard.

"Okay," Herc said. "We do it that way. We do it Scrap's way. We keep the cops out of our shit."

He let Stewart go, but only after he changed his chokehold into a full nelson and applied a short, powerful squeeze to let Stewart know what almost happened and what still could.

42

The patrol car's light bar was flashing red, white, and blue. Two cops were in the car. They left the headlights on and shining toward the strange menagerie gathered on Scrap-Iron's roof. Even idling, the car's big engine made a heavy rumbling sound.

"Get in a straight line," Herc said. "Face the cops. Keep your hands out of your pockets. I'll do the talking."

Herc knew cops, and he knew when they were responding to gunshots, you didn't want to pose any threat.

The engine quit, and both cops got out of the car. One was middle-aged; the other one looked like a teenager playing at police. The younger cop kept tugging at his belt.

The older cop took charge. He approached cautiously but without drawing his gun. "Don't move," he said. "Stay right where you are." He scanned the area, his eyes sweeping the whole roof. He stopped and took one look at Scrap-Iron and knew he was gone.

Slinky had set the gun on the far side of the body. With a pen through the trigger guard, the older cop picked the Luger up and secured it in an evidence bag. He took a quick look into the steamer trunk. The younger cop stood in front of the boys, waiting for his superior's direction.

"What happened?" the older cop asked.

"He shot his self," Herc said.

"You boys got any weapons on you?" the older cop asked.

They said they didn't, but he checked them all anyway.

The younger cop kept glancing at the dead Scrap-Iron. The senior cop got his attention and told him to sit the boys along the edge of the roof and keep them quiet. Stewart ended up sitting between Slinky and Herc. He hugged himself in an effort to ease his aching ribs.

An ambulance turned into the yard. It parked next to the cop car and turned its lights off. The senior cop signaled for the EMT crew to come over, and a man and a woman hurried onto the roof with a four-wheeled aluminum stretcher. After one look at the lake of blood there, they slowed down. They did the obligatory checks for vitals and by way of conclusion just shook their heads.

"Frankie might want this," the older cop said to the younger one. "He knows the dead guy." He stepped to the side of the roof and made a call with his cell phone.

"You good?" Slinky asked Stewart in a half whisper.

"I don't know what I am," Stewart said. "I don't know if I'm good or bad."

Stewart pulled his shirt out of his pants to get a look at his side. Even in the confused light, he could see it was already a nasty shade of red. The way it hurt, he thought he had broken ribs.

"Don't tell the cops about that," Herc said.

"I just want to get out of here," Stewart said.

"Don't tell them anything," Herc said, "and you might."

***

A second patrol car was there in just a few minutes, and it was closely trailed by an unmarked car. The driveway was crowded now. The yard a kaleidoscope of flashing lights. A uniformed cop got out of the patrol car and walked to the unmarked car. He talked through the open window to the lone detective inside. Then the uniformed cop got back in his car and that car left.

The detective got out of the unmarked car, and the senior cop came from the roof and talked to him for a moment. From that point on, everyone deferred to the detective.

The detective stepped onto the roof and put on latex gloves. The EMT duo gave him room. The detective squatted next to Scrap-Iron and tried to roll the body, so he could get a look at his wound. He needed the help of the EMT guy.

This time there was no doubt. Scrap-Iron was dead. He lay there on his back like a fallen statue, his huge chest accentuated. Stewart's mind went to a faintly remembered image of Goliath, champion of the Philistines struck dead by the heroic David. Scrap-Iron a credible Goliath, but Stewart couldn't see himself as David.

The detective stood up and looked into the steamer trunk. He pushed some things around in there and shook his head and walked to where the boys sat.

After staring at them all for a long moment, the detective spoke to Herc. "Step over by my car," he said.

As Herc got up, he looked to Slinky and Stewart. Determination and challenge in his look.

"What happened?" the detective asked Herc, after he had moved him to the far side of his car.

"Like I told the cop," Herc said, "he shot his self."

"That's it?" the detective asked.

"He was drunk," Herc said. "Doing fireworks and screwing around with the gun."

"I know about his fireworks," the detective said.

"Then," Herc said, "you know how he does."

"How did the gun come into it?"

"He just started playing with it."

"Does he usually play with guns?"

"No."

"Where'd he get the gun?"

"He pulled it out of his box of stuff." Herc looked to the steamer trunk. "He's got a lot of shit in there."

"I noticed," the detective said. "Then what?"

"I didn't see," Herc said. He pursed his lips, as if to say there wouldn't be much more coming out of them.

"You saw nothing?" the detective asked.

"I was watching the fireworks," Herc said.

"How many shots were there?"

"I don't know. The firecrackers were louder than the gun."

"So you think it was an accident?"

"Nobody was near him."

"You think he shot himself?" the detective asked.

Herc just hunched his shoulders. What else could have happened?

The detective didn't have a pad or pen out. He just listened carefully.

"Where were you? When the gun went off."

"I didn't hear the gun go off," Herc said. When it came to cops, Herc was quick on the uptake, and he knew this one was trying to trick him.

"Okay," the detective said. "Where were you when you first knew he was shot?"

"I was over there." Herc pointed to the ground alongside the back of the roof.

"You weren't on the roof?"

"No."

"Why not?"

"I guess I'm afraid of fireworks."

"You guess, or you are?"

"I am," Herc said. "I'm sensitive to that kind of shit."

"You afraid of guns too?"

"Scrap had the gun," Herc said. "Not me."

"Why did he start firing it?"

"I don't know. I think he was celebrating."

"Celebrating what?"

"I don't know. Scrap celebrates a lot. He likes to celebrate. Maybe he got laid."

"You mean," the detective said, "he *liked* to celebrate."

"That's what I said."

"You said he *likes* to celebrate," the detective said. "He doesn't like anything any more. He's shot dead."

Herc just made a face at that, like he would at anyone trying to crack wise.

"Where was everybody else?" the detective asked.

"Toad and The Bandito," Herc said, and pointed those two out where they sat on the roof under the yard light and with the police car's flashing lights striping their faces. "They was standing by me."

"Why weren't they on the roof?"

"The smoke? The firecrackers? I don't know. Maybe they like each other. You'd better ask them."

"How about that other guy?" The detective pointed to Stewart. "Where was he?"

"He was on the roof with Scrap."

"Smoke doesn't bother him?"

"Scrap wanted him to help with stuff. Scrap thought he was smart."

"Smart?" the detective said.

"Yeah," Herc said. "You should talk to him. He's real smart."

"What you're telling me," the detective said, "is that he's gonna tell me the same thing you're telling me."

"He'd have to," Herc said.

"Why's that?"

"Because that's how this shit went down. I mean you can talk to all of them. But I don't think it's gonna do you any good."

"Why's that?"

"Because, first of all, Toad-Boy there," Herc nodded toward Toad, "he's a little retarded."

"You know," the detective said with a grin, "you're not supposed to use that word."

"Even when it fits good?"

"How about that one?" The detective pointed to The Bandito.

"He ain't a whole lot smarter," Herc said.

"But the other guy, he's smart?"

"Yeah," Herc said.

"And him?" The detective pointed to Slinky.

"He's all emotional," Herc said. "He loved Scrap."

"How about you?" the detective asked. "Did you love Scrap?"

"I liked him," Herc said. "Most of the time. As much as I can like anyone."

The detective looked up at the moon as if to say this was some kind of a major circle-jerk.

"I could ask you if there was trouble among you all," he said. "But that's like asking if geese shit because I know there's always something with you guys, and you ain't gonna say so."

"Yeah," Herc said. "Why can't we just all get along?"

"Okay," the detective said. "Make sure you give the patrolman your name and where we can reach you."

The detective walked Herc back to the rest of the boys. Studying that crew made him shake his head, and, seemingly accepting Herc's assessment of their intellects, he motioned for Stewart to get up and walk to his car. As Stewart stood, Slinky tapped him on the arm in support.

The detective and Stewart walked to the unmarked car. The EMT crew wheeled Scrap-Iron's body by them. The crew had trouble moving the cart and its great load over the gravel driveway, and Stewart diverted his eyes, afraid the decedent might come sliding off.

The detective positioned Stewart behind his car and with his back to the boys.

"You new here?"

"Yes," Stewart said. He had warned himself to say as little as possible. He had watched enough crime shows to know that.

"What happened tonight?"

"I'm not sure. It could have been a ricochet."

"You weren't here?"

"I was here. But it was confusing."

"Confusing?"

"There was a lot going on."

"Tell me."

"Well Scrap-Iron had the fireworks going. He was blowing a lot of them off."

"Why was he doing fireworks?"

"Just for fun," Stewart said. "The boys like fireworks."

"You one of his boys?"

"I was just staying a little while. To get back on my feet."

"You're not wanted for anything?" the detective asked. "Running from anything?"

"No. I've never been in trouble. I've never even had a ticket."

"Okay," the detective said. "So he's doing fireworks, and then he just pulls out a gun and shoots himself?"

"He was showing it off. The gun."

"But he fired it?"

"Yes."

"How many times?"

"Five times, maybe six."

"That's a lot of showing off."

"He was real drunk."

"What did he fire at?"

"Just in the air and at the driveway. Maybe at one of the junk cars."

"Then he got shot?"

"Yes. Somehow."

"How do you think?"

"I'm not sure?"

"You're not sure?" Disbelief in the question. "You were right there? You were on the roof. You were his helper. Because you're the smart one. Isn't that true?"

"No."

"How far away from him were you?"

"Maybe ten feet."

"But you don't know how he got shot?"

"I didn't see it. I just heard it. I thought it was another firecracker. Then he was down kneeling on the roof."

"Where was everybody else?

"They were standing in the driveway."

"Why were they in the driveway?"

"To get a better look at the fireworks."

"They couldn't see them better from the roof?"

"It was smoky up there."

"Smoke doesn't bother you?"

Stewart didn't answer that. He didn't like any of this. He thought about asking for a lawyer or challenging the cop to either arrest him or let him alone, but in these circumstances, that seemed the wrong thing to do. Just tell the truth as much as possible as long as it didn't implicate him.

"Okay," the detective said. "So you had the best view of what happened when the gun went off?"

"But I wasn't looking that way."

"So Scrap-Iron is shooting this gun. God knows why or at what, but he shoots it a lot and with shots going off like that all-around you, you're not even looking at him?"

"It wasn't like that."

"What was it like?"

"He was blowing off fireworks and shooting the gun a couple times in-between the fireworks. It was like the gun was part of the fireworks. So I didn't know what was coming next. Then he was down on his knees."

"So you just think he just pointed the gun at himself and pulled the trigger or what?"

"I don't know. He was very drunk."

"You keep saying that."

"It's true."

"We'll check that. You sure the blood test is gonna show that?"

"It has to."

"Did you guys talk about this before we got here? Did these other guys tell you what to say?"

"No," Stewart said.

"Are you afraid of these other guys?"

"No," Stewart said. He had been making every effort not to show the pain he was in every time he breathed, the pain from his ribs superseding the pain from his throat.

"Give all your personal information to the patrolman," the detective said. "Name. Where you lived before. Where we can contact you."

Stewart started to walk away.

"One other thing," the detective said.

"Yes?"

"What did you think of Scrap-Iron?"

"I'm not sure what you mean?"

"Did you like him? Love him? Hate him?"

"I liked him."

"You did?"

"I did."

"Those marks on your neck," the detective said. "Where'd you get those?"

"Oh," Stewart said and touched his neck. "That was from playing around. You know, wrestling with the boys."

"You wrestle with these guys?"

"Yes."

The detective made a sour face. "You don't look like a wrestler to me," he said. "And it looks like you get the worst of any wrestling."

The detective took the front of Stewart's shirt between his thumb and forefinger and rubbed it as if testing the quality of the fabric.

"Your shirt's torn too," he said.

"You're right," Stewart said. "I'm not much of a wrestler."

"Was Scrap-Iron a good wrestler?"

"I never wrestled with him. I've only been here a couple weeks. I only met him twice, maybe three times."

"He say anything tonight that indicated he might be in a bad mood or something like that?"

"Scrap-Iron?" Stewart said.

"Yeah," the detective said. "Scrap-Iron."

"Not that I heard," Stewart said,

"You sure?" the detective asked.

The way he asked it made Stewart think he knew something, maybe something Herc had said.

"Well," Stewart said, "he did seem kind of down."

"How so?"

"Nothing specific. Just the way he was acting and talking."

"How was he talking?"

"Saying things like his father didn't raise him right. His father didn't love him."

"He said that his father didn't love him?"

"Yes," Stewart said.

"So he got drunk and shot himself?"

"That," Stewart said, "could be it."

The detective shook his head.

"He was a nice guy though?" the detective asked. "A gentle sort? Never nasty or anything? He didn't have a bad temper?"

Stewart ignored that.

"You know," the detective said, "some people would say that he was a no good son-of-a-bitch that specialized in corrupting and hurting people and that I should wrap this thing up pro forma like and get back to protecting and serving honest, taxpaying citizens?"

Stewart astonished by that.

"Is that," the detective asked, "what a smart guy like you would say?"

"All I know," Stewart said, "is that he let me stay here."

VI

43

Herc chose Friday for the ceremony. No reason specified and nobody in the mood to argue. It was a cool morning, a hint of fall and a hint of change in the air. Leaves from the yard's ash trees, the early abdicators, already littered the junkyard's driveway. Scrap-Iron had been dead for only four days, but the yard already felt totally different. It was no longer charged with his peculiar magnetism.

Slinky had made it a point to arrive early. He wanted to set Scrap-Iron's flag at half-mast in preparation for the day. And he wanted to do it alone. The boys wouldn't know how to respect the moment. It wasn't that they wouldn't want to, they just wouldn't know how. He thought of inviting Stewart to add some class and maybe the right words. But that was too tricky. Scrap couldn't expect Stewart's sympathies, not after all Scrap had done to Stew.

Slinky was still prideful that there had been something special between Scrap and him. Scrap may have had a funny way of showing it, even a cruel way, but when someone saves your life and when someone cares enough to be your protector, that was something special.

***

Getting to the flag was a problem, the way it hung from the old truck. Even if the truck still had an engine and a working wench, Slinky wouldn't have known how to lower its boom. The only way to get to the flag was to climb along the boom's horizontal support braces. The climb would be a challenge even for an agile man. But Slink wanted that flag at half-mast, so he made his precarious way.

At first he felt okay, but the support braces narrowed in width as he went higher, and about halfway up his fear started getting the better of him and he was afraid of getting stuck and not being able to go up or down. The boys would love that. They'd probably leave him there all night. But he willed himself to the top and cut the flag free with his pocketknife.

He made his way back down to the halfway point and tied the flag there. Tomorrow he would come back for it and, making sure it never touched the ground, fold the flag into a neat square. He wouldn't fold it into a tight triangle, the way he had seen honor guards do it, because he didn't know how, but he'd save the flag in his shoebox with his history medal and other special stuff.

44

"Get back," Herc screamed.

He ran from the doorway of Scrap-Iron's bunker with his hands over his ears and joined the others in the garage. Everybody stood just inside the overhead door, careful to keep some of the cinder-block sidewall between them and what was coming.

Ten seconds later, a muffled but powerful explosion shook the ground and rattled all the garage's hanging tools. The boys watched in wonder as the roof of Scrap-Iron's bunker rose and rippled like a wake crossing a smooth pond before collapsing in on itself and filling the yard with a dense cloud of smoke and dust.

After a moment of stunned silence, Herc said, "I told you I knew what I was doing."

"I guess you did," a wide-eyed Bandito said.

"Scrap got his wish," Slinky said, not taking his eyes from the dust cloud. "He's buried deep and in his proper place, just like Big John."

He meant *Big John* from the old Jimmy Dean song of that name. Scrap-Iron liked that song, and in his more maudlin moods, he often expressed his burial wishes. He said that when he died, he wanted to be laid out with the middle finger of his right hand stuck straight up and don't bury him in any cemetery, just put him in his bunker and blow it up so he had a ton of dirt over him like *Big John*.

"I taped the dynamite right to the beams," Herc said. "That's what Scrap would've did. It's all about knowing the weakest spot."

"At the bottom of that mine," Slinky said, by way of a eulogy, "lies a big, big, man."

Everyone bowed their heads, even Stewart. To himself, he said, *earth to earth, ashes to ashes, dust to dust*.

45

That Stewart was still in camp and allowed to witness Scrap-Iron committed to the ground was a marker of the new and grudgingly given respect Herc had for him. It was the way Stewart pitched in after the big man's death that had swayed Herc.

The boys knew Scrap-Iron deserved their best. They didn't know how to provide it. There had been death among them before. Just last winter one of their own expired in his tent. He was an older man named Gavin. But Gavin wasn't Scrap-Iron, and his passing didn't require much of a ceremony.

Gavin's passing wasn't a surprise. Death had shadowed him for as long as the boys knew him. His skin and eyes were a perpetual jaundiced yellow. "Mellow Yellow" was what they called him. Herc had diagnosed cirrhosis of the liver. That based not only on the man's sallow pallor, but also on the way he easily bruised and his perpetually swollen ankles. It was a good guess and supported by the fact that the deceased had been an alcoholic for forty years, since he was fourteen years old. The boys found Gavin in his tent, not cold yet, but dead. They wanted nothing to do with the authorities. After dark, they found an unlocked BMW in a nearby office parking lot. Using his sleeping bag as a body bag, they transported Gavin and laid him in the backseat, as if he had gone to sleep there. It was a nice leather seat, and laying there, he looked comfortable. Herc said about the car owner's coming ghoulish surprise that, "Nothing good ever comes from working too much overtime." That night, at the stroke of midnight, everybody toasted the departed by finishing the six-pack they found in his tent. His last six-pack was all the man bequeathed the world.

Scrap-Iron required much more. The boys wanted to bury the big man in his bunker, per his wishes. The authorities wouldn't allow that. It was as if they thought the big man's decaying remains would contaminate the town. In the decision-making vacuum that followed, Slinky suggested they look to the Professor, and it was Stewart's idea to cremate the body and then bury the ashes in Scrap-Iron's place. Herc added the explosive twist. Stewart coordinated the cremation process, even negotiating with nearby funeral homes to get the best price. He enjoyed showing the boys his competent side; even in their world there was a time and a place where he could be useful.

***

There was another problem that required some business sense.

Customers still came to the yard. It was only right that they be informed of the tragedy. The yard had been a neighborhood fixture for three generations. Something like that deserved a formal end. So Slinky sat at the front gate all week, in his lawn chair, wearing his sun hat and sipping on a bottle of water, informing customers of the tragedy. All expressed shock that the big man was gone and from an accident. He seemed too big for that; his death was meant to be tied to something more cataclysmic. It was Stewart's idea to post a formal notice of Scrap-Iron's death and, with some help from Herc, to combine it with a chance for profit.

Herc said it was a shame for Scrap's professional array of tools to go to waste. But what to do with them? The boys weren't about to become master mechanics. Stewart suggested gathering all of Scrap-Iron's belongings into the garage—the fancy audio and video stuff, along with all his tools and legal toys. They could have a sale that would benefit the boys. Weren't a man's boys his rightful heirs?

Instant and unanimous agreement at that. It was just what Scrap would have wanted. The sooner the better. The weekend would be best. Take advantage of the confusion before any blood-sucking government officials got their hooks in. As Scrap always said: "Get your bread in the gravy while it's still hot."

The Bandito painted a sign to place on the yard's front gate. His first attempt read:

Scrap is dead
Everything must go

After careful consultation so as not to wound The Bandito's pride of authorship, the sign got changed to:

Owner Deceased
Tool & Equipment Sale
Cash Only

Saturday & Sunday

***

The proceeds exceeded expectations. The boys were surprised by the aggressive mob of buyers who gathered two hours early, before they were ready for them. Some were from miles away. Who knew that the news of a posthumous bargain traveled so fast?

The high-end welding equipment went first, the buyers pulling and tugging and fighting over it. Stewart and Slinky managed the financial transactions; The Bandito and Toad did the carrying and loading, and Herc the security. A sign of his new standing, Herc decided Stewart would divvy up the proceeds. Slinky lobbied for Stewart to get an equal share. The boys agreed on his getting a half share—seniority had to have some privilege.

46

"Stew?"

It was Slinky calling.

Stewart didn't want a tearful good-bye. He had hoped to walk out of camp without ceremony. His plan was to just disappear. Just as he had disappeared from his finance job with a few handshakes but no good-bye lunch or even a cake.

"You awake, Stew?"

"Yeah, Slink. But I'm a little busy."

He was still in his sleeping bag, but he was busy thinking about the coming day. He never expected it to be this way—that he could pack and leave at his leisure. It had been a week since the garage sale, and with his portion he put a security deposit on a room back at his old boarding house. The room had been vacated and repainted, and he could move in tonight.

"You've got a guest," Slinky said.

A *guest*?

Stewart didn't know what was more absurd, someone actually being there to visit him, or Slinky announcing it as if he were a doorman and Stewart's tent a Newport mansion.

"Who is it?" Stewart asked. The only possibility that ran through his mind was his boss or one of the boss's underlings. Could the store be that desperate for Saturday morning help?

"It's a lady," Slinky said. "I'm going now."

Slinky was inordinately nervous around ladies, especially classy, pretty ones.

"Stew?" a new, softer voice said.

It was a familiar voice. Stewart stopped breathing. It was as if by being perfectly quiet, he could hide.

"Stew?"

Was he still asleep and dreaming? No. He knew where he was, in his tent and in Scrapville. His senses were working. He could smell the dewy woods and hear the sounds of the highway. He didn't know what else to do, so he pinched himself. It hurt.

"Marian?" he said, tentatively and not knowing for sure if he wanted to be right or wrong.

"Yes, Stew. It's me."

His first reaction was fear and that was followed by an urge to get away. He didn't want her to see him in this place and in this condition. With escape impossible, he found his handheld mirror and tried to make himself presentable.

Presentable wasn't going to be easy. He hadn't shaved yet. His hair, as short as he now kept it, wouldn't obey. His neck was still a rainbow of sickly colors, even sicklier now that they had faded some. His eyes were red and gunky from ragweed season and had dark bags under them. All of that made him look like a survivor of some atrocity. He was a different man from the one his wife had last seen. He could only imagine how he smelled.

"Stew, I want to see you."

"Okay. Just a minute."

Why was she here? How did she find him? He considered crawling under the back of the tent and running. This time there wouldn't be anybody standing guard to stop him.

He put on his best clothes, his black pants and his remaining, untorn white shirt. He wet his fingers and tried to tamp down his hair. He stopped and stood there, stooped over in the tent's cramped quarters. He was ashamed of himself.

Marian fiddled with the tent's flap.

"I'm coming," he said.

He made his way out of the tent and when he cleared it and stood straight, Marian took a step backward.

"Stew," she said.

It sounded like a question. He started to reply *honey* but changed it to, "Marian."

She stepped closer to him, and he lowered his eyes and tried to hide within himself. Instead of hugging him, she reached out and took his hand in hers. A gesture of pity. His hand was shaking.

"I'm sorry," he said.

"I'm so glad I found you," she said.

"You sure?" he said.

"I'm sure."

He made brief eye contact with her.

"First," she said, "let me know you're all right. You look so thin."

"I'm all right."

"What happened to your neck?"

"It's nothing," he said but put his hand to his neck to hide the color. "It's better now," he said.

Uncomfortable silence until Marian said, "Is there somewhere we can sit and talk?"

He wanted to get her away from Scrapville as soon as possible. He was lucky Toad or one of the other boys hadn't appeared yet. That would add to his humiliation.

"I'm parked over by that junkyard," Marian said. She pointed in the direction of Scrap-Iron's place. "That was the address I had. That young man was there. He was just sitting there, and I told him who I was looking for, and he was nice enough to bring me to you. He said my car was good there."

"That's Slinky, the guy who brought you," Stewart said. He felt a new affection for Slink.

Marian looked around in continuing amazement at the semicircle of tents and the fire pit and the flagpole that made up Scrapville. Stewart could imagine her shock at her morning's journey—parking in Scrap-Iron's yard, meeting Slinky and walking the tracks with him, coming through the woods and finding Scrapville.

"There must be some other place where we can talk," Marian said.

"If you want," Stewart said, "there's a diner that's not far away."

He couldn't risk Burger-Land. He wanted to go someplace they wouldn't be seen or interrupted.

"Let's do that," Marian said. "Let's walk back and get my car. We really need to talk."

47

Other than simple directions, the ride to the diner was silent. There was too much to say, and it was all bunched together like a logjam that would take one of Herc's deftly placed charges to release.

It felt strange for Stewart to be in her car again, the interior neat and immaculate as always, the seat soft and with the leather smell he always liked. The car eight years old now but still looking and smelling new. That was her meticulous way. He kept his face to the passenger window and adjusted the vent so the air blew directly at him and away from her. He was sitting next to the woman he had spent so many intimate years with, but he was as nervous as if on a first date.

***

The diner was chilled with air conditioning. He was glad for that; it would help dry up the sweat he felt all over his face and body.

His wife looked beautiful, fresh, and young. Standing there with her and waiting to be seated, he felt conspicuous. A man like him with a woman like her. People would think she was a social worker and he her client.

The hostess led them to a small two-person table near the front, but Marian asked if they could have a booth in back. She had always been more forthright than he. She always knew what she wanted.

As soon as they sat down, a young Spanish man brought them water. Stewart took a long drink.

"I know," he said, "that I don't look like much."

"Don't worry about that," Marian said. "Right now, I'm just relieved you're okay. I imagined the worst."

He didn't answer.

"I hope you're okay?"

"I'm okay," he said.

"You know," she said, "I haven't seen you in two years. It's been ten months since I even heard from you."

Accusation in that, and justifiable.

"I'm sorry," he said. "I know I've been derelict. I just, I don't know, I just slipped into something bad."

She gave a slight nod.

"How did you find me?"

"That's a story," she said.

"Okay?"

"I got something in the mail from a guy who said he was your landlord."

"Something in the mail?" he said.

"Yes."

"What was it?"

"Well, it wasn't nice. I'm sure it was meant to upset me. And it did."

"What was it?"

"It was a DVD. It was a movie that you were in. It was a sex thing."

Stewart's face heated, and his chest tightened. Scrap-Iron had reached out from the dead and once again grabbed him by the throat.

"That movie," he said. "I was forced."

"I thought I could see that," his wife said. "It looked like that. It looked like something wasn't right. At least at the beginning. I mean all the time, but, you know, at the end, it looked different."

His stomach ignited.

The waitress came. A smiling young woman asking if they were ready. Marian got coffee and a hard roll. Stewart just a decaf tea. He wouldn't dare anything else on his stomach right then.

"I don't know how you got into all this," Marian said. "I wouldn't have believed it."

"It's a crazy story," Stewart said. "Especially that movie."

"I don't mean the movie," Marian said. "I mean your choices. I never could understand your whole fascination with, I don't even know what to call it, maybe, I guess, a different life."

"The whole time," Stewart said, "I mean the past two years, it's just been crazy."

"I'm sure," Marian said. "But here's what I could never figure out–you wanted it this way. Is that not true? Is it unfair to say that you wanted this?"

"Maybe I did," Stewart said. "I guess I did. But I don't think I really did."

"Remember," Marian said, "that quote of Thoreau's that you always liked?"

"Which one?"

"Men hit what they aim at."

He winced at that.

306

"But I've learned some things," he said. "I've been through a lot, and I've learned a lot about myself."

"I've been through a lot too, Stewart."

He didn't try and answer that. When she called him *Stewart*, it was time to just listen.

They sat silent for a while. The waitress came and poured Marian more coffee. Stewart declined more hot water.

"Now what?" Marian asked, after a long look out the diner's plate glass window. "What do you plan from here on? I mean you can't go on like this forever. Don't you agree?"

"Yes."

"What's that mean?"

"It means I can appreciate things better. Including what we had. Especially what we had."

He felt more comfortable. This was his territory, telling his story the right way and shedding the proper light on it. A lot depended on how a story was told. He started to formulate what he wanted out of this miraculous meeting. Another chance is what he wanted. The short ride to the diner with her had solidified his thinking. He wanted to go back and live with Marian. He could satisfy his, what to call it now—how about intellectual wanderlust? —with books. He would read about the dangerous life while in his comfortable bed with his wife sleeping next to him under a hypoallergenic quilt with an amber-tinted reading lamp—never on a backlit device so as not to have blue light interfere with his circadian rhythms and sensitive sleep mechanism. Maybe he was still a man out of touch with the times, but these times had their benefits.

"I've missed you," he said.

"I've missed you," Marian said.

"How's the house?"

"It's okay."

"The lawn, did it get that brown fungus this summer?"

"Listen, Stewart. I don't want to talk about the lawn. I've got people who take care of the lawn. The past two years have been tough on you. I can see that. They've been tough on me too. The first year especially. You can't imagine. But then I decided something."

"What's that?" Stewart asked, not sure he wanted an answer.

"You've spent a lot of time trying to figure out who you are. Now I know we all have to figure out who we are. I know who I am now. At least better than I did."

Stewart saw tears wetting his wife's eyes. He couldn't stand the thought that he was the cause of them. She dabbed them away with her napkin.

"I don't need to dwell on that anymore," Marian said. "I just want to do the best I can and live a good life and be happy doing it. Be happy, at least most of the time. So that's what I've done. I've gone on with my life. If I can tell you one thing, it's that it's important for you to do that too."

"I understand," Stewart said. He was buying time and furiously recalculating.

"I'm not sure you do," Marian said. "See, I've made a new life. It doesn't mean I lost my feelings for you. I still care about you. You don't spend all those years together and then stop caring for someone. At least I can't. That's why I found you and why I came here. If I didn't care for you, I wouldn't have done that.

But, I'm not going backward. I've figured that out and made the changes that allow me to live a good life. But, and I mean this with love and not anger, it's time we finalize things."

Shock must have showed in his face because she looked surprised that he was surprised.

"I mean," she said, "this can't be much of a surprise to you."

He was stunned and disappointed. Maybe that was a measure of his cluelessness. Even after the grinding decline of the last two years and the frightening abuse of the past few weeks, he had still held some naïve belief that things would always work out for him, as if he were a chosen one.

They were silent for a moment. When the air conditioning kicked back on, Stewart shivered. He knew his wife well enough to know her words were final. Maybe she had someone else. That didn't seem important now. Later it probably would. What was important now was that destiny's bill had come due and in total, and now he owned his myth, the one he had chosen to explain his self to himself. Now he knew the price of that, and he was paying it in full.

Nothing is for free.

"Listen," Marian said, with a change of voice that signaled she had said what she wanted to say and was switching to practical things. "There's been a small windfall. There's two-thousand dollars from an unclaimed insurance policy. The policy belonged to both of us. I don't even remember taking it out. Maybe you did. I think it was at the time we thought I might be pregnant. Believe it or not, someone saw our names in the paper in a list of unclaimed funds and told me about it. I figured it was a scam, but it wasn't. I have a check here for you. You should use it. Use it however you want."

He didn't know if the story were true or not. Maybe the money was pure charity. He didn't pick the envelope up when she put in on the table. He didn't refuse it either.

"I should be going," she said. "Let me give you a ride back."

Part of him wanted to stay with her as long as possible and another part wanted to get away as soon as possible, from her and his shame.

"I'll walk back," he said.

"You sure? I'd be glad to give you a ride."

"I need a walk," he said. He couldn't bear another ride in her car.

"Even when it's all done," Marian said, "we should stay in touch."

"Yes," Stewart said. "We should."

He knew they were both telling the lubricating lies necessary to smooth their painful parting. He felt as if he and Marian were now strangers. He slid the envelope off the table and put it in his pocket without looking at it. They walked out of the diner and into the parking lot.

Marian hugged him before she got in her car. She was crying.

He saved his crying for later.

48

Four Months Later

"Merry Christmas," Stewart said to the waitress.

The waitress's name tag said Gabriel, and he had heard the other women call her Gabby. He wanted to call her that but thought it too soon for that intimacy.

"Merry Christmas, Sir," she said.

Stewart was now one of the diner's regulars, and the waitress liked him. She appreciated his politeness. Politeness could be hard to find these days, even on Christmas.

"You have to work today?" Stewart said. "That's too bad with your kids at home."

"They're good," the waitress said. "They're with my mom and dad, and they spoil them."

"That's good," Stewart said. "Grandparents should do that."

"You want your usual, Sir?"

He did. Eggs over easy, bacon crisp, dry wheat toast.

The waitress had brought his pot of hot water and his ceramic cup and two decaffeinated tea bags. Stewart had had breakfast at the diner every Sunday for the last three months. He was always alone and always sat in the same corner booth, even if he had to wait.

Something different today. He had a companion. The waitress turned to that companion and said, "And for you, Sir?"

Shy Slinky lowered his eyes at the waitress's smile.

The meal was Stewart's Christmas gift to Slinky, and Stewart insisted he go big. Slinky went big. He ordered the Super Breakfast–pancakes, eggs over easy, sausages, and toast. Despite his slight frame, Slinky could really eat. Where he put it all and why it never stuck to him, Stewart didn't know.

Stewart could make breakfast in his room, where he had a little refrigerator, a hot plate, and electric teapot. He did that on Saturdays, when he had the time. On Sunday mornings, he preferred the conviviality of the diner and its morning crowd. Breakfast at the diner was also a marker of his modest renewal.

Using Marian's check from the mysterious insurance policy—it was for the full $2,000—he had invested in himself. He had seen a doctor and a dentist and bought some decent clothes. Sometimes you need a little luck, and he had had some. Slinky knew a woman at a local charity who had helped him get the special shoes that he now wore to compensate for his mismatched legs. Slinky told her about Stewart, how smart he was, what a range of experience he had. The woman had a friend who ran another charity and had an opening requiring Stewart's skills—a manager's position overseeing volunteers on behalf of abused and neglected children. Stewart did well in the interview. The job required a comprehensive background check that involved many of the Ten Commandments. Without as much as a traffic ticket on his record, Stewart came out clean and got the job. The job suited him, and he developed a passion for the work and proved valuable beyond his modest salary. He liked his employers, and they liked him. In his sixty-day review, his supervisor said his only flaw was taking his cases too personally.

He had had all kinds of fantasies about how he would quit his store job. But he left with class, telling his boss that he had a better opportunity. A *management opportunity* is what he said, and he did enjoy the stupefied look on his former boss's face.

"I don't know where you put all that food," Stewart said.

Not interrupting his breakfast, Slinky just smiled. His new glasses looked better. They didn't magnify his eyes to freakish size and weighed half as much and stayed mostly straight.

Stewart enjoyed seeing Slinky healthier and happier. He had seen to it that Slinky got his fair share from the garage sale, plus a little extra to compensate for the boys' previous advantage-taking. He helped Slinky manage that money and his monthly disability check, now electronically deposited each month at the credit union. And they were neighbors again. Slink had moved into a room at the boarding house. A small room, where Scrap-Iron's old recliner with the permanent indentation of his great bulk molded into the seat took up half of the living space but served double duty as lounger and bed.

Stewart and Slinky had catching up to do.

"You've gained some weight," Stewart said. "I can see it in your face."

"Seven pounds," Slinky said.

Stewart had gained eighteen. Soon he would have to watch his weight.

"What do you hear from the boys?" Stewart asked.

"I saw Herc in Burger-Land, about two weeks ago," Slinky said.

"What he say?"

"He's still living in his fort. He bought a battery-powered television set and DVD player, and now he's got his own entertainment center."

Stewart lined up the salt and pepper shakers so they stood parallel to his paper placemat. His compulsions still lurked because a lot of bad things still lurked.

"What's going on with the junkyard?"

"It's up for sale," Slinky said. "Herc said Scrap had some kind of cousin in Arizona. The cousin doesn't want any part of the yard, so it's for sale. It's pretty complicated. It's probably gonna take a while."

"I'm sure," Stewart said.

"How about Toad and The Bandito?"

"Herc said Toad's still a pain in his ass. With what's left of his new money, he keeps buying porno movies and wants Herc to show them all the time. Herc said he gets tired of them. Imagine Herc tired of porno?"

"How about The Bandito?"

"He's in Massachusetts."

"Massachusetts?"

"Yeah. Herc said they got some program up there where The Bandito gets a room and money every month for food and stuff. They even sent him a bus ticket to get there."

"That sounds a too good to be true," Stewart said. "But leave it to The Bandito to find something like that."

A young man refilled their water glasses. Slinky gazed out the window at the Christmas lights on the diner's railing. His look turned pensive.

"You know," Slinky said, "as bad as Scrap could be, he looked out for me and that made him the closest thing I ever had to a father or at least a big brother. Does that seem weird to you?"

"Yes," Stewart said. "I got to say it does seem a little weird. Being that he almost shot you."

"Yeah," Slinky said. "There's that."

The waitress asked if they were good. They were.

"I ever tell you," Slinky said, "about the guy from the car wash who said he was gonna dip me in the hot wax barrel and straighten me out. That guy hated me. I don't know why because I never did a thing to him."

"What happened?"

"Scrap made a special trip to the car wash."

"What he do?"

"I don't know, but that guy didn't bother me again."

Tears in Slinky's eyes now.

"Anyone bothers you now," Stewart said, "I want you to tell me."

"I will," Slinky said.

"I mean it," Stewart said.

"I know you do," Slinky said.

The diner was filling up. That was okay. They were isolated in their booth.

"You know," Slinky said, "it was nice of you to help the boys with everything. I mean the cremation and sale and all that. After everything that happened to you, that was good of you."

"It wasn't that much," Stewart said.

"To bury his ashes there, that worked just the way Scrap wanted."

"It was better," Stewart said, "than having him laid out with his middle finger in the air."

They both laughed at that.

"I've got something for you," Slinky said.

Stewart hoped Slink hadn't spent any of his meager funds on a gift for him.

Slinky reached in his pocket and pulled out his new cell phone. He played with it a moment and then handed it to Stewart.

What Stewart saw caught his heart. It was a picture of the big tomcat with the smudge on his face. He was sitting on top of the railroad switch in front of the woods. He looked healthy and regal against the snow-covered background.

"I just took it a couple days ago," Slinky said. "I'm going to have a print made for you."

"That's so nice of you," Stewart said. He couldn't take his eyes off the cat and only reluctantly gave Slinky his phone back.

"You'll never guess who I saw over at the mall," Slinky said.

"Who's that?"

"Guess."

"How would I know?" Stewart said. He hated it when Slinky played this game.

"Okay," Slinky said. "I'll tell you. But you're gonna be surprised."

"Who?" Stewart said.

"Betty," Slinky said.

"Betty?" Stewart's insides tightened.

"Yeah. You know. Boxcar Betty."

Stewart knew who he meant.

"She said it was too bad about Scrap," Slinky said. "She said something else that surprised me."

"What's that?"

"She said she was surprised someone hadn't shot Scrap sooner."

Stewart didn't want to probe. He didn't want Slinky getting back into the whole Betty thing. But he couldn't help it.

"She ask about me?"

"No," Slinky said. "She just talked about Scrap. I mean she asked me how I was and all that but nothing about anybody else."

Stewart felt disappointment at that. He tried to hide it from Slinky.

"You hate Scrap?" Slinky asked, while staring into his water glass.

Stewart moved his head back and forth, yes and no.

"You probably should," Slinky said.

"He put me through a lot," Stewart said. "But I guess I'm just too worn out to hate anybody."

"He was a different kind of guy," Slinky said.

"You got that right," Stewart said.

"The junkyard's gonna get cleaned up," Slinky said.

"I bet," Stewart said.

"I'd buy it if I had the money," Slinky said, "but you won't believe how much they say it's gonna go for."

"How much?"

"Guess."

"I don't want to guess," Stewart said.

"Over five-hundred-thousand dollars. Just for the land."

"No."

"Yep. That's Jersey. They say they can get four lots out of it. They're gonna put a street there."

"Hard to believe," Stewart said.

"I visit it a lot," Slinky said. "I want to remember it as it was. Pretty soon it'll look like every place else."

Stewart nodded to that.

"I'm gonna have dessert," Slinky said.

"You're gonna have dessert with breakfast?"

"Yeah. That way it fuels you the whole day."

"Okay," Stewart said. "You get dessert. I'm just gonna have some more tea."

Slinky ordered rice pudding. Brown sugar and whipped cream on top.

"Why do you think," Slinky asked, "that the cops quit so easy on Scrap's case? I thought they'd dig a lot more."

"I've thought about that a lot," Stewart said.

"So, what do you think?"

"I don't know," Stewart said. "But it could be that with Scrap-Iron having no relatives around here or anyone else to push things, he just wasn't a priority."

"I thought," Slinky said, "that the cops would push it, you know, being some of them were Scrap's buddies."

"I thought about that too," Stewart said. "I think maybe that's where Herc might have been on to something."

"What's that?"

"Herc predicted they wouldn't push it. He said Scrap-Iron was into so much stuff that he shouldn't be, with so many other people that shouldn't be, not only with the cops but inspectors and all that, that nobody wanted to dig too deep."

Slinky's rice pudding came, and the way he looked at it made him look like a little boy.

"So you think that's it?" Slinky asked. "Scrap was into too much stuff with too many people?"

"Maybe," Stewart said. "With a man like that, who knows?"

***

That night, Stewart lay in bed staring at his ceiling fan. His physical hurts had healed, neck and throat and ribs, and his stomach medicine worked better now that every day wasn't filled with life and death anxiety. A good night's sleep still evaded him.

He thought of how Slinky was right, that Scrap-Iron's place would soon be like every other place—probably a cul-de-sac filled with five-thousand-square-foot houses with manicured lawns and flower beds and four-car garages and not a trace of the cinder-block garage and its multicolored roof or the self-dug bunker or the junkyard with its tall boom and desirable detritus. Crazy as he knew it was after all that had happened, the thought of that depressed him.

When his mind went where he had forbidden it to go, to what Scrap-Iron had said about his black heart and then to thoughts of his lost wife and lost years, he picked up his bedside book. Reading would help him find sleep.

The book was *Thus Spoke Zarathustra*. It opened to the Third Part, Chapter 45, The Wanderer.

I am a wanderer and mountain-climber, said he to his heart, I love not the plains, and it seemeth I cannot long sit still…

And whatever may still overtake me as fate and experience—a wandering will be therein, and a mountain-climbing: in the end one experienceth only oneself…

Thus spake Zarathustra, and laughed thereby a second time. Then, however, he thought of his abandoned friends—and as if he had done them a wrong with his thoughts, he upbraided himself because of his thoughts. And forthwith it came to pass that the laugher wept—with anger and longing wept Zarathustra bitterly.

The End

About the Author

James Ward's award-winning short stories have appeared in literary journals throughout the United States, in Canada, and most recently China and Africa. *Safe to Say*, his first novel, was published in 2012. After a long and varied career, he is delighted to be writing full time. He lives in New Jersey with his wife Barbara.

Photo by Douglas Miller.